*Christmas in
Peppercorn Street*

Christmas in Peppercorn Street

ANNA JACOBS

Allison & Busby Limited
11 Wardour Mews
London W1F 8AN
allisonandbusby.com

First published in Great Britain by Allison & Busby in 2019.

A CIP catalogue record for this book is available from
the British Library.

First Edition

ISBN 978-0-7490-2463-5

Typeset in 11/16 pt Sabon LT Pro by
Allison & Busby Ltd

The paper used for this Allison & Busby publication
has been produced from trees that have been legally sourced
from well-managed and credibly certified forests.

Printed and bound by
CPI Group (UK) Ltd, Croydon, CR0 4YY

Chapter One

December

Heavy rain blurred the windscreen in spite of the wipers, as Luke Morgan drove slowly along the twisting country road. It wasn't yet four o'clock but it was already almost dark. Well, it was the first of December, heading towards the shortest day. He couldn't help yawning. He'd got up at five o'clock this morning to drive to Birmingham and give a talk at a conference and had just driven back to Wiltshire, so he was feeling exhausted.

He'd have stayed overnight at a friend's house, only nowadays he had to get back to his daughter. OK, Dee was sixteen, but he didn't want to leave her alone in the house.

His ex had been avoiding him ever since she'd brought Dee to live with him a few weeks ago, turning up out of the blue with a tear-stained daughter and all her possessions. The only explanation Angie had given was she could no longer cope with Dee, who kept upsetting her new partner.

Angie had taken off for Spain with that partner the day afterwards and wasn't responding to his emails or attempts to phone her. He was worried sick about poor Dee, who was clearly upset but was refusing to talk about it.

He was glad to be off the motorway and driving along these quieter country roads. Seeing the sign for the village of Bartons End, he slowed down, looking forward to getting home and—

Suddenly a large golden dog bounded onto the road in front of him and as he slammed on the brakes, a woman chasing after it ran right into the path of his car.

He pumped the brakes hard and everything seemed to happen in slow motion as he skidded towards her. 'Jump back!' he yelled, as if she could hear him.

By the time the woman became aware of the car, it was too late. She opened her mouth in an involuntary scream and turned just as the front wing of the car sent her flying sideways like a human skittle. The dog vanished through a hedge and the car squealed to a halt a few yards past where she was lying.

Sick to his stomach, Luke wrenched open the car door and rushed back to where she was sprawled like a broken doll by the side of the road. She wasn't moving.

Oh, hell, she wasn't moving!

He knelt beside her, half dazzled by the headlights of another car which had also stopped. Willing her not to be dead, he reached out and groaned in relief as his fingers found a pulse beating in her throat. For a moment, he couldn't think, couldn't move, only kneel there with relief shuddering through him that she was alive.

Then he realised there was blood on her forehead and

she needed medical help, so jerked to his feet and turned towards his car.

A man immediately blocked his path. 'You're not going anywhere.'

'My phone's in the car. I need to call an ambulance.'

The man gestured to the other vehicle. 'My wife's already phoning for one.'

'Thank goodness! Do you know anything about first aid?'

'Sorry, nothing at all.' The man walked back to his car.

Only then did Luke realise that rain was beating down on them all. Dragging off his leather jacket, he flung it over the woman and knelt again. If he remembered correctly, you weren't supposed to move an unconscious person who'd been injured.

'Use this.' The man was back, thrusting an open umbrella into Luke's hands.

He tried to hold it over her face. Wind howled around them and the umbrella nearly turned inside out, so his companion muttered something and took over holding it, protecting it from the wind with his body.

How long would the ambulance take to get here?

When the woman stirred and moaned, Luke bent closer. 'Lie still! You've been in an accident.'

She blinked and tried to focus her eyes. He leant closer to hear what she was saying.

Claire squinted up at the man bending over her, his head haloed by light so that she couldn't see his face properly. Everything seemed slightly out of focus and she was cold, so cold it hurt. Or was the pain from something else? Where was she? What had happened to her?

She closed her eyes for a moment then tried to move, letting out an involuntary 'Ahh!' as pain jabbed her shoulder.

'Lie still! You've been in an accident.'

'How?' Why couldn't she remember?

That same deep voice said, 'You were chasing a dog and ran into the road right in front of my car. I couldn't avoid hitting you. We've sent for an ambulance. What's your name?'

'Claire P— Small.' She corrected herself in time.

She realised she was lying on the ground beside the road and rain was pattering down on an umbrella someone was holding over her. She shivered, still unable to bring the scene into proper focus. To have an accident now, of all times! Fear trickled through her, even sharper than the physical pain.

Her shoulder hurt a lot if she made the slightest attempt to move it. Was something broken? Oh, please, no! She'd be so helpless.

'The ambulance will be here soon. Lie still, Mrs Small.'

How could she lie there? Gabby would be waiting for her. Once again she tried to move but the pain was too bad and she had trouble co-ordinating her body. 'My daughter – I need to pick her up from school. And my dog . . . can you see her?'

'It was a dog which caused this accident and it ran away afterwards. A golden Labrador. If it was yours, you should keep it under better control.'

She couldn't hold back the tears, felt them spill from her closed eyes and make lukewarm trails on her chilled cheeks.

A warm hand clasped hers. 'Sorry. I didn't mean to shout at you. I've never had an accident before and I'm a bit shaken up myself.'

She was glad the stranger had continued to hold her cold hand between his. She clung to that warmth, shivering uncontrollably. 'I try to – keep Helly in – but the landlord won't – mend the fence.' She looked up at his face, so close to hers under the umbrella. 'I'm sorry! Is your car badly damaged?'

'Who cares? It's you I'm worried about, not my car.'

Without thinking she moved her arm and pain jabbed through her again, so sharply that a cry escaped her control.

For a moment her companion's face came into better focus. Good-looking in a rugged way with dark, rain-slicked hair. But then the image blurred again and she gave in to a sudden need to close her eyes.

She was desperately afraid she'd be incapacitated, unable to look after Gabby. Then how would they keep safe?

The stranger's hands were still there, large and warm around hers. Comforting. She couldn't bear to let go of them as she made an effort to speak.

'My daughter. Gabby. She'll be waiting at the primary school. She's only eight. Have to pick her up. And get the dog back.'

Luke stared down at the woman's hands, slender and shapely but as damp and cold as the rest of her. She looked vulnerable and was clearly in pain, yet her concern had been for her child, not herself. And for her dog.

It suddenly occurred to him that there was something he could do to make up for knocking her down.

'Look, I'll pick your daughter up from school myself just as soon as the ambulance comes and we'll find the dog.

Tell me her name and where to find her, and I'll bring her to you at the hospital.'

'She's called Gabby P—' The woman groaned in her throat, then said, '*Small*. Gabby Small.'

That was the second time she'd started to say P and corrected it to Small. She must have changed her name recently – divorced, perhaps? 'Bartons End Primary?'

'Yes. It's not far from here.' Her voice was a mere thread. 'And the dog. Could you catch Helly and tie her up. *Please!* I don't want them putting her in the pound. She's a good watchdog and Gabby would be lost without her.'

'I'll see to everything. I know the school. We used to live nearby and my daughter went there when she was little.'

'Thank you.' With a soft sigh, she closed her eyes.

He wasn't sure whether she'd slipped into unconsciousness again or was just resting. Either way, he didn't want to disturb her, so stayed where he was, not trying to talk.

But the other man said, 'You can't pick up a strange child from school. They won't let you.'

'Someone has to. And she agreed to it.'

'She isn't thinking straight, probably concussed.'

A car drove past, slowed down and stopped. The window went down and a voice called, 'Need any help?'

'No, thanks. We're just waiting for the ambulance to arrive.'

'Good luck, then.'

It drove on and silence reigned again. The man from the other car was no talker, that was sure, but at least he was still holding the umbrella over them. His wife hadn't even set foot out of their vehicle.

Luke stared along the road. 'Where's that ambulance?'

'They told my wife it'd take fifteen minutes. That's about eight more minutes.'

It was the longest eight minutes of Luke's life. What if Claire was bleeding internally? What if she never recovered consciousness again?

He stayed where he was, crouching at the roadside, still holding her hands to try to share some of his warmth. The rain had eased off a little, thank goodness.

His thoughts kept wandering all over the place, but he kept his eyes on the woman. With that long hair she looked like one of the water fairies in the books he'd read to his daughter when she was little. No doubt the books would now have been thrown away by his ex, together with everything else from their life together. That'd be a pity. He'd enjoyed reading them because the illustrations were so beautiful.

What stupid things came into your mind after an accident!

His daughter had been a hell of a lot easier to deal with when she was little, pretty and feminine in those days. Now, Dee wore nothing but black, had her nose and one eyebrow pierced and seemed to hate the whole world, him included. Their latest row had been about her desire for a tattoo.

What the hell was he going to do about her? His ex had washed her hands of Dee, saying the girl was impossible and since she took after her father, he could bloody well look after her from now on.

As if you could wash your hands of your own child, whatever she did!

He groaned in relief as he heard the faint wailing

of a siren in the distance. It grew rapidly louder and an ambulance appeared, stopping beside them. Its blue light was still flashing, but the noise stopped, thank goodness.

A paramedic jumped out and came to kneel beside him, feeling for the woman's pulse as he asked, 'What happened?'

'She was chasing a dog and ran out in front of my car. I couldn't stop in time and she was flung sideways.'

'Right. Thank you, sir. If you'll just move back a little.'

The other driver thrust the umbrella at him. 'You can hold this now. I'm frozen.' He walked back to his car, shoulders hunched.

'Sir, could you please try to keep the umbrella over her face? Good. That's better. Just hold it for a little longer till we can get her in the ambulance. Terrible weather, isn't it?'

'Yes.' Luke stayed there, shivering, his shirt soaked and clinging to him, water trickling down his neck. The rain was only falling lightly now, thank goodness.

Within minutes, the woman was in a neck brace and was being wheeled away on a stretcher. She was still only semi-conscious and Luke hoped she'd stay like that until they got her to hospital. He'd broken an ankle once and it had been damned painful at first.

He turned to find a police car drawing up.

An officer got out and came to stand beside him. 'Sir, are you the driver of this vehicle? Oh, it's you, Luke.'

'Yes. Look, Ted, I have to go and pick up the injured woman's daughter from school. Can I make a formal statement tomorrow?'

'Sorry, but there are some things we have to do now.' He whipped out a breathalyser.

'I haven't had anything to drink. Oh, very well!' Luke

blew into the mouthpiece impatiently and wasn't surprised when Ted nodded and said it was fine.

As if he'd drink and drive! He wasn't stupid.

Luckily the other couple who'd stopped could corroborate his description of how the accident had happened and he had his driving licence with him, showing an unblemished record.

He looked at his watch. 'I promised her I'd pick up her child and take her to the hospital.'

The female officer shook her head. 'Do you know them?'

'No.'

'Then I can't let you pick up a strange child from school.'

'I've known him for years. He's OK,' Ted protested.

'Doesn't matter. We'll have to pick her up, not him.'

'The mother's worried about the dog, as well,' Luke said.

Ted grinned at him. 'You go and look for it. We'll go to the school and collect the daughter. Meet you at the hospital.'

'I'll follow you to the school first. The daughter may know where I can find their dog.'

'OK. See you there.'

Luke ran to his car. He knew he couldn't have avoided the accident but he still felt guilty. Well, at least he could find her dog for her. That'd be something.

Some Christmas music jangled away on his radio and he switched it off impatiently. He was sick of hearing Christmas songs and it was only early December. He hadn't figured out how to celebrate Christmas in a way that would cheer Dee up. She'd just shrugged when he asked her.

* * *

When Luke arrived at the school, the police car was standing in front of the entrance and he could see the two officers inside, together with a woman and a child. The little girl was wearing a bright yellow rain cape with the hood thrown back and jigging up and down, peering outside then looking up to say something. The resemblance to the injured woman spoke for who she was.

He joined them inside. There were Christmas decorations all round the reception area. He should at least put some up at home, whatever Dee said.

Ted introduced Luke to the woman. 'It was Mr Moran's car that Mrs Small ran in front of. Unfortunately he couldn't stop in time.'

When the teacher looked at him suspiciously, Luke said, 'Miss Roberts, isn't it? You taught my daughter Dee a few years ago.'

'Oh, yes. A very bright child. She left the school rather suddenly.'

'My wife and I split up.' Angie had left with Dee while he was away on a job. He'd come home to an empty house and most of the furniture gone with her. He'd missed his daughter dreadfully, but not Angie. By that time they were barely polite to one another.

He watched as the female officer bent to talk directly to the child. 'Your mother's been hurt in an accident, Gabby.'

The child's smile vanished instantly.

'It's all right. She's not badly hurt but she's been taken to hospital to be checked up, so we've come to take you to her.'

Luke stepped forward. 'And I promised your mother I'd go and find your dog.'

Ted's phone rang just then. He moved a few steps away and answered it. 'Oh, hell! Just a minute.'

He turned to the teacher. 'Is there any chance you can take Gabby to the hospital to join her mother, Miss Roberts? There's been a big pile-up a couple of miles away and we're the closest unit.'

She sighed but nodded. 'Very well.'

Luke intervened. 'Do you know where the dog is likely to be, Gabby?'

'Yes. In Fountains Park. She always goes there when she gets out.'

'Fountains Park. I know it.' He looked at Ted. 'I'll take the dog to the hospital and find out what the woman wants to do about it.'

Ted nodded. 'Thanks. We have to get off now.'

Miss Roberts didn't look happy and she was scowling at Luke as if he'd caused the accident on purpose.

The two officers ran back to the police car and while the teacher locked up, Luke went out to his own car.

As the teacher and Gabby reached him, the child stopped. 'If you bring Helly to the hospital, Mr Morgan, I'll look after her while I wait for Mum. We can't afford to pay the fine if the council officer takes her away, you see.'

He saw the tears in her eyes and promised, 'I won't let the council officer take her away.'

Her face cleared immediately. 'Thank you.' Only then did she let herself be pulled away by the teacher.

Luke started his car, shivering. He could have done without that icy wind on a damp shirt. Which reminded him that his leather jacket had gone off to hospital in the ambulance.

They must have thought it belonged to their patient. He'd have had to go there to get it back, anyway, even without taking the dog there.

He found the stupid animal trotting round the edge of a pond and grabbed a couple of biscuits from his emergency supplies before getting out. He bent down and called her. 'Good dog. Here you are, Helly.'

She edged a little closer, tail wagging tentatively and studying him, as if working out whether to trust him or not. He remained still, praying she'd not run away.

After another sniff at the biscuit he was holding out, she took it from him and as she swallowed it, he was able to grab her collar. Speaking soothingly, he walked her slowly towards his car and she came with him.

He groaned aloud. That dog was very wet indeed, not to mention muddy, and he definitely didn't want to let her into his car, which was only two months old. Unfortunately, there was no choice. When he opened the nearest rear door and gave her a push, she leapt inside and he shut it quickly. What that would do to the leather upholstery, he didn't like to think.

He drove off, praying the dog wouldn't jump about and make it difficult for him to drive safely, but she settled down as if used to being in cars.

The hospital was on the outskirts of the nearby town of Sexton Bassett and it took him twenty minutes to drive there at a modest pace and find a place to park.

He left the animal sitting in the car with the window slightly open. There was an overpowering smell of damp dog already and muddy water all over the pale grey leather of his almost new Mercedes.

He ran through the rain to the casualty department and found Gabby inside standing next to her teacher at the reception desk. She turned to look anxiously at him as he joined them.

'I got Helly. I left her in my car.'

'Oh, thank goodness!'

The woman behind the counter consulted a list on a clipboard. 'Mrs Small is being attended to now. Are you a relative?'

'I'm Gabby's teacher.'

Luke moved forward to join them. 'And I've got her dog in my car, so I need to see her too.'

Miss Roberts looked up at the clock and then told the woman behind the counter, 'I can't stay. I have to go and pick up my elderly mother. Can Gabby wait for her mother here?'

The woman frowned. 'Isn't there someone else who can pick up your mother? The child's a bit young to leave on her own.'

'No. My mother has dementia and she's at the day care place. She wouldn't go with anyone else but she still recognises me.'

'I'll sit with Gabby,' Luke volunteered. 'And the people can see her from here, so she'll be safe. I can't leave till I've asked her mother about the dog.'

'Very well.' The teacher turned and walked away.

Another shiver reminded him to ask the receptionist about his jacket. 'I used it to keep Mrs Small warm and I need it myself now.'

She looked as if she was going to refuse to look into that, so he said, 'Please! I'm really cold.'

'Could you describe it, please, sir?'

Impatiently he did so, enumerating the contents of the pockets as well.

She beckoned to an orderly, who went off to look for it.

When he looked round, there was no sign of the teacher.

Gabby looked up at him. 'Miss Roberts said I was to stay in reception and not go off with you in your car.'

'Fair enough.'

'Here you are, sir.' A man held out the jacket.

Luke took it back with relief. It was a bit creased but not damp on the inside, so he shrugged into it, glad of the extra warmth.

He phoned Dee to tell her he'd be late, was about to explain why, when she said OK and broke the connection. With a sigh he put the phone away.

An unconscious man was brought in just then and people came rushing with a crash cart.

'Please wait over there, Mr Morgan, I'll call you when the doctor's finished with Mrs Small.'

He gestured to some seats and the child sat down next to him.

'Where's Helly?' she asked.

'In my car.'

'Did she come to you?'

'Yes. But I had a biscuit.'

'She doesn't usually go to people, only the ones she thinks are all right. Mum says she has good instincts. I feel safe with you anyway. You have a nice smile.'

'Thank you.'

There was something about the child that touched him. He'd definitely stay with her till they'd finished with the mother, wanted to make sure she was all right. The A&E people were all very busy. Who knew how long Gabby would have to wait for them to finish with her mother?

Anyway, there was still the dog to think about. He hated to think what she was doing to his car.

Chapter Two

After yet another glance at the clock on the wall, Luke noticed Gabby looking longingly at a machine dispensing drinks. He was about to offer to buy her something when a nurse came through a door to one side of the reception desk, checking it to make sure it was locked behind her.

When the receptionist pointed to them, the nurse walked across. 'They're just X-raying your wife's shoulder and arm now, Mr Small. The doctor doesn't think anything is broken, but her shoulder's been dislocated and we have to be certain there isn't a hairline fracture. I'll fetch you when that's been done and the shoulder strapped up, but she'll be at least an hour, probably longer. They're really busy in X-ray today.' She smiled down at the child. 'Goodness, you do look like your mother!'

She turned and started walking briskly away before he could correct her mistake about him being Claire's husband.

Another shiver made him gesture to the drink dispenser. 'Would you like something warm to drink, Gabby?'

The child's face lit up. 'Could I have some drinking chocolate, please? It's much nicer than tea or coffee.' From the look on her face, she was hungry as well, so he bought them a packet of crisps each.

'Mum and I can't afford to buy crisps now,' she confided, licking her lips. 'I haven't had any for ages.'

She looked at the small, shabby Christmas tree next to the vending machine. 'Isn't it pretty? We have one at school, but Mum can't afford one for home this year.'

She ate half of his crisps as well as her own, then sat quietly beside him, swinging her feet to and fro, watching everything that was going on around them with great interest.

'Do you have any relatives we could contact, Gabby?'

The open expression immediately vanished. 'No. And we don't want any. There's just us and Helly, and that's a nice little family.'

'Yes, but – well, you don't know me and – maybe you'd be better with someone you do know.'

'You mean like *stranger danger*. That was why my teacher brought me here, not you, wasn't it?' She looked up at him. 'You don't look dangerous to me and the policeman told my teacher he knew you.'

Another long gaze at him, then, 'You'd better dry your hair, though. It's still soaking wet and it's dripping all over your shoulders.'

'Your fringe is dripping too.'

She grinned and swiped at her forehead. 'It's nice and warm in here, isn't it?'

'Yes.' He found himself smiling back, enjoying the company of this child, who was treating him like a favourite uncle and telling him all sorts of things about how she and her mother managed without much money, things which would embarrass the injured woman big time, he was sure.

Gabby was a great kid. She reminded him of what his own daughter had been like a few years ago.

He was beginning to suspect that this child and her mother were on the run from the father, but in that case, why had they lumbered themselves with the dog? It didn't make sense.

By the time another nurse came looking for them, he'd bought them each a second cup of hot chocolate and found the ladies' restroom for his companion.

'Mr Small?'

He shook his head.

Gabby giggled. 'This is Mr Morgan. I'm Gabby Small, though. He's a friend and he brought me here to see my mum.'

The nurse smiled down at her. 'Well, you'd better come with me, then, Gabby. She's asking for you.'

Luke stood up. 'All right if I come, too? I need to find out what she wants me to do with the child, and with her dog.'

'Yes. But be warned. Mrs Small's very groggy. She may not make much sense.'

He was taken first to see a doctor, who spoke rapidly, with one eye on the clock. 'The good news is that your wife's arm isn't fractured; she'd only dislocated her shoulder, which has now been put back in place. That area of her body will be very sore for a while, though, and she should use the arm as little as possible for the next few days. She's been given strong painkillers so she'll not be very coherent.'

Luke was greatly relieved the injuries weren't worse, because he still felt guilty about the accident.

'Mrs Small ought to stay in here overnight but she's insisting on going home, and I must admit we're short of beds. But it'll be best if she stays a little longer, so we can keep an eye on her recovery. If there are any problems after you take her home, don't hesitate to bring her straight back. The nurse will give you some more of the painkillers for her.'

As the doctor walked away, Gabby tugged Luke forward and they followed the nurse along a line of cubicles, all with other patients in them.

The injured woman lay flattened against the pillows of the high, narrow bed, eyes closed. She looked like a limp rag doll. He felt sorry for her after talking to the child and realising how hard their life was.

He glanced sideways and saw that Gabby's lips were quivering and she looked as if she was fighting back tears. Before he knew it, he'd held out his hand and she was clutching it again.

She leant closer to whisper, 'Mum looks so pale. And why is she still asleep? Will she be all right?'

'Of course she'll be all right. She's just resting.'

When he looked down at their joined hands, a strange feeling shivered through him, as if it was right to hold her. He hadn't been able to hold his own daughter's hand for several years; Dee was too old for that now.

Angie had been openly hostile to him when they broke

up, as if it was all his fault, when she was the one who had initiated it to 'find herself'. She'd only let him have Dee for a day here and there since then. What made him furious was how she seemed to have poisoned Dee's mind against him – or was it against all men? And how cunning Angie had been about changing the arrangements for him to see Dee at the last minute.

He'd tried lawyers' letters but she always had an excuse for cancelling.

And then after years of rubbing it in his face that *she* had custody, Angie had dumped the girl on him without warning. Not that he'd have refused to have Dee, of course he wouldn't, but he'd have appreciated a bit of notice. He'd only just moved into a new house and hadn't even had a spare bed that first night, had had to sleep on the sofa.

He realised the nurse was talking to Gabby and got annoyed with himself for not paying better attention.

'Your mother's a bit sleepy from the anaesthetic and painkillers, dear, but she'll be all right.'

As if she'd sensed her daughter's presence, Mrs Small opened her eyes and looked sideways. 'Gabby.' Her voice was a croak and her cheeks were colourless, but her loving smile lit up her whole face. 'You all right, love?'

Gabby let go of him and went to clutch her mother's hand, leaning on the bed beside her. 'I was worried about you, Mum, but my teacher brought me here and Mr Morgan found Helly. He's been looking after me and bought a drink of hot chocolate. No, two drinks.'

Claire stared at Luke. 'Who on earth are you?'

'I'm the guy who knocked you down.'

'Ah. Yes. I remember now. You held my hand. But the

accident was my fault, not yours. I didn't look where I was going. We don't need to call in the police, do we?'

'They've already attended the scene of the accident. They breathalysed me and took statements from witnesses. I don't know whether they'll want to speak to you, too, but I don't think there will be any charges or need to follow things up. And my car doesn't seem to be damaged, maybe a scrape or two on the paint, which can easily be fixed.' Though not cheaply, but he could easily afford it and she couldn't.

'Thank goodness.'

Gabby tugged her mother's hand to get her attention. 'Helly's outside now, waiting in Mr Morgan's car.'

'Thank you. That's such a . . . relief.'

Luke watched as Claire tried desperately to stay awake. Her eyes closed slowly, then snapped open again, but she looked as if she was having trouble focusing properly.

He went to the end of the cubicle and beckoned to the A&E nurse, who came across and checked the patient. 'Is she all right? She keeps falling asleep in the middle of saying something.'

'She's fine, Mr Morgan, but she'll be in and out of consciousness for a while as she recovers from the anaesthetic, and the painkillers make you dopey too.' Someone called and she yelled, 'Coming. You can wait with her here, if you like, as long as you don't make a noise. These curtains aren't soundproof.' She indicated the blue curtains surrounding the cubicle as she hurried away.

So they sat there for a few minutes, then a sudden scream nearby made Claire jerk awake again and stare at him as if she didn't know where she was.

'You're in hospital,' he reminded her. 'You've got concussion. You need to rest.'

'Oh, yes. Sorry. Thank you for looking after Gabby, Mr . . .' Her voice trailed away and her eyelids began to droop. 'Just give me a little time to recover, darling, and then we'll go home.'

The nurse had just come back and overheard that. 'You really ought to stay in hospital overnight, Mrs Small.'

'No! No, I *can't*!'

Luke frowned. That was definitely fear on Mrs Small's face and panic in her voice. The child was looking anxious too. What the hell were they afraid of? He knew Bartons End – the worst things you usually met there were problems with parking, and a few drunks in the evening, who were usually fairly cheerful about the world. He'd enjoyed living in a village, had only moved away when Angie left him and they'd had to sell the house as part of their divorce settlement.

'I can't stay here. I have to look after Gabby. Have to . . .' Claire's eyes closed and she sighed into sudden sleep again.

'I can sit here next to the bed till Mum's more awake,' Gabby volunteered. 'I won't be any trouble.' Then her face fell. 'Oh, but what about Helly? She's still shut up in your car.'

'Hospitals don't usually let people sleep in their chairs, especially children on their own. Maybe you have some friends you could go and stay with tonight? I could drive you there.' Oh, no. He'd better not. The police hadn't wanted him to do that.

'We've only just come to live in Bartons End. We don't

know anybody in the village. That's why we went there.'

What a strange thing to say! His guess must be right and they were running away from someone. 'Where does your mother work, then?' Though wherever it was would probably be closed by now.

'At home. On her computer.'

'Oh.'

The nurse exchanged glances with him. 'We'd better call social services to help with the child.'

'*No!*' Claire exclaimed.

She must have heard the last bit. He watched her struggle in vain to sit up.

'Please don't try to call anyone. Give me an hour to rest and I'll be all right, then my daughter and I will go home. We can get a taxi. I'm feeling much better already. Really I am!'

'If you have no other adult at home, you'll definitely need to stay in overnight, Mrs Small,' the nurse insisted. 'You need someone to watch you. It's important.'

'I *can't* stay here.'

Luke looked from mother to child and saw that both had the same expression on their face. Fear. Definitely fear. He tried to tell himself not to get involved, but he couldn't help feeling that he had a responsibility to look after them, because he was the one who'd knocked Claire down. Though he had more than enough on his plate at the moment with his daughter and the new house, without taking on anything extra.

The trouble was, he *wanted* to protect and comfort them both, because he hated hearing fear in a child's voice, especially a delightful little girl like Gabby, who was looking at him now as if she trusted him to solve the problem.

If the mother was with them, no one could complain of him giving the child a lift in a car. Besides, there was one large wet dog waiting outside as well.

A tear trickled down Claire's face, silver on white. That tear tipped the scales.

'Look, there's no problem, nurse. They can come both home with me. I'm a friend of the family and my daughter lives with me, so she'll help as well.' Well, he was a friend now, he hoped. And surely Dee would lend a hand.

The woman in the bed looked at him in puzzlement, but without fear, at least.

The nurse was shaking her head, so he dealt with her first. 'I've done a first aid course, so I have some idea of what to look for after concussion.'

'Well . . .'

He turned back to Claire. 'Is that all right with you?'

'We're not your responsibility.'

'He's kind. I like him.' The child beamed at him and that warm feeling ran through Luke again.

'I have a large house and you won't be any trouble,' he said. They would cause him some extra work, of course, but not much. Well, he hoped not much. 'And my garden is fenced in properly, so the dog won't be able to get out.'

On second thoughts, he wasn't sure he placed much reliance on that, though he didn't say so. Helly looked intelligent and he'd bet she came from a long line of escapologists. But hey, that was a minor consideration. Christmas was coming. Peace and love and all that jazz.

He glanced at his watch. Damn, he was very late. Not that Dee would be worrying where he was now he'd phoned her. She'd have her headphones on and be listening to something weird and loud. He and his daughter definitely did not share the same taste in music. Or in anything else, it seemed. He sometimes felt as if she'd built a fence around herself, a fence he was desperate to knock down.

'Look,' he said to the nurse, 'leave us to talk it over for a few minutes, will you? You're obviously busy. We'll work something out, then I'll come and find you.'

The nurse looked at the patient for confirmation, received a nod and left.

Claire didn't beat about the bush. 'Why are you offering to help?'

He shrugged. 'Because I feel guilty.'

'You needn't. As I've already admitted, the accident was my own fault. And Helly's.'

'Mr Morgan's a kind person, Mum. Helly likes him and so do I.' The child lifted her mother's hand, pressing it against her cheek for a moment. 'I think we should go and stay with him. We'd be safe there.'

It was ridiculous how touched Luke was by the child's simple, tender gesture with her mother's hand. And by the expression of love in the woman's eyes as she turned to look at her daughter.

'I don't know – can't seem to think straight.' She moved her head restlessly and winced again.

He intervened. 'Then stop trying to think and leave everything to Gabby and me.'

She closed her eyes. 'I shouldn't. But just for tonight, if it's not too much trouble.'

He waited a couple of minutes, but she didn't open her eyes again, so he put one finger to his lips and gestured to the child to come away from the bed. This part of A&E consisted of a line of beds in curtained-off spaces, and the staff looked to be very busy. What a wonderful job these people did!

'We'll let your mother sleep for an hour or so, Gabby, to give her time to recover properly, then we'll come back and get her. We'll see if we can find something to eat while we wait and I'll phone my daughter again to let her know I'll be even later than I thought.'

They spoke to the nurse, then went back into reception. The man who was now behind the counter said there were a few shops just across the car park where they could get something to eat.

Luke went to the entrance and stared outside. The small row of shops was only about a hundred yards away. Two or three of them had their lights on and were clearly still open. He was starving hungry and one of the shops was so brightly lit he could read the sign. 'Do you like pizza, Gabby?'

'I love pizzas. Mum makes them for us sometimes.'

'Are you hungry?'

'Yes. But I can manage if you can't afford to buy one. The best way when you're hungry is to think of something else.'

What sort of life had she led? 'You don't need to manage without. I can definitely afford pizza and I'm ravenous. We'll share one. Come on. I think the rain has stopped for the moment.' Again, he held out one hand without thinking and she took it immediately.

No one called after them to stop. No one here cared. And he knew he'd never hurt a child.

They went inside the shop and found another scrubby little Christmas tree winking at them from a corner and some elderly and rather dusty tinsel draped across the inside of the window.

Gabby stopped, head on one side. 'I'll save a piece of my pizza for Helly, if you don't mind, Mr Morgan. She'll be hungry, too.'

Damned if that didn't bring a lump into his throat as well. 'We'll get enough to give her a share, don't worry. And call me Luke. What toppings do you like?'

'Anything. We can't afford to be fussy.'

The dog wasn't fussy, either. She gulped down a couple of pieces of pizza, obligingly peed on the grass when told to 'be a good girl', lapped up some water from a rainwater puddle then got back into his car.

He hoped Gabby hadn't seen him wince as Helly scrabbled her paws on his leather upholstery, but he had nowhere else to keep the creature. Perhaps she wouldn't have actually scratched the leather, just dirtied it.

He'd have the car detailed once this had been sorted out. Definitely. Damp dog was not his favourite perfume and there was mud scattered around too.

When Claire opened her eyes again, she was alone in a hospital bed. Terror rose in her as she looked round. Where was Gabby? Had they taken her away? She saw a bell and rang it, then rang it again impatiently.

The nurse came into the cubicle, took her pulse, examined her eyes and said dubiously, 'Your colour's a little better now, but you really ought to stay in here overnight.'

'Where's my daughter?'

'She went out into the waiting room with your husband. He's very good with her, isn't he?'

'Um – yes.' She'd better not reveal how little she knew about him, Claire decided, or they might call social services after all. If he could get her out of here, she'd persuade him to take her home to get some clean clothes, then refuse to go anywhere else. He didn't look like a violent man, though, had been really nice with Gabby.

She and her daughter would manage till the shoulder got better. They always did. Yes, that would be her best plan. Get him to take her home, then thank him and send him on his way.

The nurse came back with a plastic cup of water. 'Time for another painkiller.'

Claire hesitated, but the shoulder did hurt, so she swallowed it.

Her daughter came back a short time later with her usual breathless rush, but it was the stranger Claire watched as she listened to the tale of the pizza and how he'd bought an extra-large one so as to have some left for Helly, who had wolfed her share down and then been a good girl again on the hospital lawn.

'You've been very kind,' she told him when there was a break in Gabby's recital.

He shrugged. 'Least I could do.'

'We'll be all right now, though.' She struggled to sit up in bed and it was harder than she'd expected because her shoulder hurt when she tried to put any weight on that arm. The next few days were going to be – challenging.

'You're definitely going to need help for a while, Mrs Small. Look, I'm not offering you the earth, just a bed for the night.' He studied her face and amended that to, 'Maybe even for two nights. Just think how virtuous that'll make me feel!'

She shook her head in a gesture of blind panic. 'I can't pay you back and – we don't know you – and—'

'Helly likes him a lot,' Gabby said. 'She licked his nose. You always say she's a good judge of people.'

Luke grinned. 'I wouldn't set a lot of store by that. I'd just fed her a big chunk of pizza.'

'I'm surprised she took food from you.'

'Most dogs like pizza – given half a chance.'

'Helly doesn't usually like men, though,' Gabby said and before Claire could stop her, she'd added, 'My dad used to kick her, you see.'

'Ah. Well she must have realised that I'm not the sort of person who kicks dogs, or anything else, for that matter.'

Claire could tell that he was putting the pieces together to form a picture of their life. Well, she didn't want his pity, thank you very much. She could manage. She *would* manage. When her head stopped thumping and she could see clearly. She just had to get home.

Her shoulder was throbbing. She wished this painkiller would kick in.

What a mess this was!

Luke waited and when the injured woman didn't seem to know what to say or do, he spoke gently. 'I can understand why you're dubious about accepting my hospitality, Mrs Small. You're worried that I might have ulterior motives – and might use violence to enforce my, er, wishes?'

He watched her hesitate then nod. Her face still had no

colour in it at all, but her hair did. Some of it was dry now, showing a lovely reddish gold, and it was long enough to hang down her back, with tendrils curling round her gaunt face. In fact she'd have fitted well in an art nouveau painting, wearing a long robe and reaching out towards a handsome knight.

He tried to think how to reassure her. 'Actually, you won't be alone with me. My daughter will be there as well. Dee's sixteen.'

He watched Mrs Small rub her temple with those long, elegant fingers. Was she going to faint on him? Or was she thinking it over?

If you couldn't help someone in trouble, you weren't worth much, were you, especially so near to Christmas. He made a last attempt. 'I don't think you have much choice, actually. It's either let the hospital take care of you and social services find somewhere for Gabby, or else allow me and my daughter to do it. Dee's sixteen. She'll make a good chaperone.'

After a long silence and more study of his face, she said, 'Thank you, then. Gabby and I will accept your kind offer. But we'll need to go to my home first to pick up some clothes and dog food.'

'Now you're being sensible. I'll call the nurse in and she can help you get ready to leave.'

'Your husband's a nice guy,' the young nurse said as she helped Claire to the bathroom.

They all kept assuming Luke was her husband. She couldn't be bothered to explain yet again who he was. She was feeling so weary.

'Good-looking for his age, too.'

For his age? He didn't look all that old to Claire. She was thirty-four, and he was probably few years older. Well, he must be if he had a daughter of sixteen. But that still wasn't *old*.

And he was kind. No question about that. He'd looked after Gabby, let their muddy dog sit in his car and bought them a pizza. Yes, the nurse was right. He was a nice man. As far as anyone could tell, she added mentally. You could never be totally certain.

She felt bad that she was planning to cheat him and stay in her own home. But she was desperate to get out of here before anyone started asking awkward questions or asking for her ID, which would leave a trail for someone to follow. She'd told them her purse had been left behind and given them a wrong date of birth, saying she'd phone her details through.

Luckily there had been several other people brought in with urgent problems and they hadn't had time to pursue the matter.

Luke was her best chance to escape, her only chance probably.

She yawned and lay quietly, trying to make plans. As they left the hospital she mustn't do anything that drew attention to them and made people remember them. She and Gabby seemed to have got away from her ex this time. It had been several months without hearing from him.

She didn't think she could face another of those sudden midnight moves – or afford one, either. It'd have to be a women's refuge if he caught up with them again, and she hated the thought of that.

After Gabby had been born, Martin had become more and more difficult to live with. That child was the only good thing to come of her marriage, so she'd tried to make it work. Tried too hard. She should have left him years ago. When he started thumping her, however, that had been the final straw.

She wasn't getting together with him again, whatever he said about a child needing two parents, whatever his mother said. They were divorced and were staying divorced.

She yawned, feeling suddenly so sleepy it was hard to keep her eyes open let alone answer any more questions.

Chapter Three

The nurse in charge of Claire's discharge insisted on an orderly taking her out to Luke's car in a wheelchair.

When they reached it, Luke held open a door for Gabby to join the dog in the back. He couldn't help grimacing as he looked at the mess the hairy monster had already made.

Claire let him help her out of the wheelchair and into the front seat, lying back with that limp, boneless air people get when they've pushed themselves to their uttermost limit.

She didn't attempt to fasten her seat belt so he did it for her. Her eyes were closed and he wasn't sure whether she was awake or asleep. Should she have stayed in hospital overnight? Who knew? But he'd keep a careful eye on her, make sure she recovered properly, and he'd call for help if there were the slightest worry about her condition.

He set off, trying to drive as smoothly as possible. Claire hadn't opened her eyes since they left, well, not that he'd seen, and he'd glanced at her a few times at traffic lights and junctions, so it was Gabby who directed him to her home once they reached Bartons End. The house was a bungalow on the opposite side of the village from where he'd once lived, in the scruffy area near some workshops and small businesses. It was rather isolated now because all the other houses nearby had been pulled down and new ones were being built on the cleared space.

When he stopped, he studied Mrs Small. Her eyes were still closed and as far as he could tell, she hadn't moved since she got into the car.

He looked at the house again. It was a seedy little bungalow with a roof which was sagging in parts. The whole place looked ready to fall down in the first strong wind. Some of the nearby row of industrial units looked to be deserted. Perhaps they were going to be pulled down too. The nearest one had a faded sign saying 'Electrical Repairs'. There were no lights showing in any of them except for what seemed to be security lights.

Only half of the front fence of the house was still standing and there was a makeshift fence across the side of it, consisting of a piece of rusty corrugated iron propped up by a pile of bricks. It more or less connected with a side fence which wasn't in much better condition. The landlord should be ashamed of letting the place get into this state.

There was a modest car parked on some gravel in front of the house, a bit of a rust bucket but the model was known for lasting many years. He was surprised this one had got through its last MOT test in that condition, though.

He came to a decision and put one finger on his lips, signalling to Gabby to be quiet before he let her and the dog out of the back of the car. Mrs Small muttered something in her sleep as the cooler air wafted in but she still didn't come fully awake.

'I think it'd be better for your mother to carry on sleeping, Gabby. Do you have a key to the house?'

'Yes.' She fished at her neck and pulled out a chain with a key attached.

'Can you help me pack some clothes for you both?' he said in a low voice as they stood in the narrow hall.

'Yes. I'm—'

'Shh! Don't wake your mum.'

She nodded and lowered her voice. 'I'm good at packing in a hurry. We've practised doing it. Shall I pack all our clothes in case anyone breaks in again, or just a few?'

'You've had a break-in?'

'Yes. But Mum had the new computer in the car because she was bringing it home that day, and they didn't take the old one, only pushed it onto the floor.' She wrinkled her neat little nose. 'They took some of our food, though, and they made a terrible mess with the rest. Mum cried after I'd gone to bed. I heard her.'

Dear heaven, how the other half live! he thought. It might do Dee good to take note of this child's cheerful acceptance of adversity.

'Better pack all your clothes if you can, Gabby. They'll be safer and I've plenty of room at my place.'

He walked round inside the house. Everything was clean but painfully bare, with only the basic furniture needed, the sort of stuff you picked up free from charity shops or from street verges. In the office there was a state-of-the-art computer and printer sitting on an old wooden table and another old garden table holding some papers and folders.

There were no Christmas decorations anywhere, except for a child's drawing on the fridge door and one piece of tinsel on Gabby's bedroom door.

He frowned as he looked at the computer. They couldn't leave that here. Someone might steal it. You'd only have to bump against that flimsy front door to push it in. There wasn't even a decent bolt on the inside.

As he scanned the rest of the room, he saw the boxes in which the computer had been delivered piled neatly in a corner and nodded in satisfaction. It'd be a close fit, but his car had a large boot.

He went to find the child. 'I'll pack all the computer stuff in the boxes while you pack your things, Gabby, toys as well as clothes.' Something told him she wouldn't have a lot of toys. 'Then start on your mother's clothes. I'll check that the drawers and cupboards are clear afterwards.' She nodded.

He went to the front door which he'd left open, in spite of the cold, to peep out at Claire, but she was still fast asleep, so he went back inside and set to work to disconnect the computer.

The dog sat and watched him, wagging her tail every time he looked her way.

'It's all your fault, Helly!' he said, trying to be severe. But who can stay severe when a furry hound is grinning at you and coming across occasionally to lick your hand and thump her tail against your leg. He certainly couldn't.

Gabby reappeared. 'I've packed my stuff and put Mum's things out on the bed, but her suitcase zip broke last time we moved so what do I put them in?'

She hadn't been exaggerating when she said she could

pack quickly. 'Just let me put the printer in this box.'

The zip of the suitcase was beyond repair, but he could perhaps tie it shut. He felt like a voyeur as he inspected Claire's collection of clothes. Faded cotton, most of them. Clean, neatly folded but well worn. 'Nightdress? Toilet things?'

She giggled. 'Oops! I forgot! The nightdress is under the pillow – here you are. I've emptied all the drawers. I'll get the toothpaste and other things from the bathroom next. I can put them in the waste paper basket. That's what we did when we moved last time.'

He stared at the pitifully small piles of clothes on the bed. Surely there were other garments? No. The wardrobe was empty. His ex-wife's clothes had taken up three-quarters of their huge walk-in wardrobe and overflowed into a spare room. These wouldn't even fill a small wardrobe. 'I'll just check to make sure you haven't forgotten anything.'

'Mum does that when I help her pack. But I don't forget. I know if I leave anything behind, I can't come back for it.'

'Right.' He laid the clothes in the suitcase and tied some string round it to keep the lid more or less closed, then carried it awkwardly out to the car.

On the way back in he picked up a letter he'd noticed lying behind the front door to add to the pile of papers from the office. He couldn't help seeing the name on it. 'Who is this for?'

'It's for us. Mum said we should call ourselves Small this time because it's easy to remember, but we were using her maiden name before, Porter.'

This time? What had been happening to them? He

didn't ask what her father's surname was, but he'd bet it was different again.

It had taken less than an hour to pack all their possessions and Claire hadn't woken. When they set off again, they left only the cruddy furniture behind and a few pieces of chipped crockery.

And still Claire slept. The painkillers must be very strong.

By the time they got to Sexton Bassett and turned in to Peppercorn Street, Gabby was asleep like her mother, with the dog's head on her lap. Luke drove slowly past the small blocks of flats at the bottom end of the street, weaving in and out of the many parked cars. The road was clearer near the modest houses in the middle stretch with only a couple of cars parked in the street at the top end.

When he stopped outside Number 4, which was one of a row of five big, detached houses, he smiled, as he always did, admiring the exterior. He loved his new home. It was too big for just him, really, even with the recent addition of Dee, but it was a magnificent example of late Edwardian residential style and he'd fallen in love with it on sight earlier in the year. Inside it had rather a quirky layout and varying levels, because the ground was lower at the back.

Restoring it as it deserved would be an interesting project, and he'd find room somewhere for a workshop because he enjoyed woodwork and intended to do as much of the renovating as he could himself.

He turned in to the drive, pressed the remote and waited for the big, old-fashioned roller door to jerk and rattle its way up and allow him to drive into the garage. This had been added later in a haphazard way and was between the front level and the lower area at the rear that had once been the servants' quarters. It wasn't nearly as elegant as the rest of the house and needed attention, or knocking down and something more tasteful put in its place.

In the rear-view mirror he saw Helly raise her head briefly to look round then lay it down again on Gabby's lap. He closed the garage door before he got out, so that the dog couldn't go gallivanting off, as his grandmother would have said.

Leaving Claire, Gabby and Helly in the car with the doors open, he hurried into the house and took the half-flight of stairs to the main living area two at a time. Dee was messing about with her computer in the small downstairs room he'd insisted she keep it in, instead of her bedroom. They'd had a big fight over that, but he wasn't having her staying awake till all hours fiddling online. Even her phone had to stay on the kitchen table.

She didn't even turn her head when he went in, though she must have heard him coming.

Only then did he remember that they'd had yet another row yesterday evening about tattoos and he'd left for Birmingham before she got up this morning. Clearly she was still in a huff. If tattoos weren't permanent he'd have agreed to one, but they were, and he'd seen how awful they could look on older, sagging flesh, and how out of date they became.

Goodness, how long ago and unimportant that quarrel seemed now!

He stopped by the door and rapped on it to get Dee's attention. 'We've got guests.'

She didn't turn, just shrugged her shoulders. 'You mean, *you* have guests.'

'No, *we* have guests and I need your help.'

She half turned her head. 'Why should you need *my* help with them?'

'The woman – her name's Claire Small – has been hurt in a road accident. Well, I was involved, actually. My car hit her but it wasn't my fault. She ran out into the road chasing her dog and I didn't have time to stop. She's got a daughter, Gabby, who's eight. They both fell asleep in the car on the way here. Oh, and the dog's here as well. They can't go home because someone needs to keep an eye on Claire tonight.'

Dee turned round fully, her mouth open in shock. 'I can't imagine you bringing a dog home to this precious house of yours.'

Where the hell did that come from? He got on well with dogs, always had. But he didn't have time to argue the point. 'Anyway, I really do need your help.'

With a loud, aggrieved sigh Dee stood up.

'I'll carry Gabby in from the car and then her mother, if Claire doesn't wake up. She's got concussion and has also taken painkillers that have knocked her out. Her shoulder was dislocated, you see, so it's very sore. I'd really appreciate it if you'd help me with the dog first and then with unloading the car. We'll put them in the bedroom with the twin beds – well, it's the only other one furnished, and we just have to put some sheets on the beds. I think they'll feel better when they wake up to see one another.'

'OK.'

No snide remarks, he noticed. Wonders never ceased. 'There are bags of clothing to go up to the bedroom, plus a computer and allied pieces, which can go in the dining room for now. Oh, and there are a few other bits and pieces of food, which can go in the kitchen.'

'How long are they staying? Why did they have to bring food? We're not exactly short of it. You could feed an army at short notice, the amount of frozen stuff you keep in stock.'

'I don't know how long they'll be here for. A day or two, I suppose. Depends how quickly Claire recovers. But Gabby didn't want to leave anything behind because they've already been burgled. Their rented house is a ramshackle place, easy to break in to, you see, with no close neighbours.'

He ran one hand through his hair, pushing it off his face. He couldn't think of anything else he needed to tell her now, so said, 'Come on,' and set off back to the car.

After Luke had lifted Gabby out, his daughter grabbed the dog's lead and started murmuring soothingly to her.

The little girl didn't stir as Luke carried her into the house. He hesitated then put her into an armchair in the sitting room. The dog dragged Dee across the room and plonked herself down beside Gabby, as if on guard.

'I think you'll be safe to let go of the lead now, Dee. We'll close the door of this room after I bring the mother in. Don't leave any of the outer doors open, though. Helly is an escapologist.'

The dog turned to grin at Dee as if she knew they were talking about her and his daughter gave her another stroke, her face soft with pleasure. Whey hadn't he realised how much she loved dogs? Maybe he should get one for her.

'I'll bring Claire in now.'

'Right.' Dee picked up a cushion and wedged Gabby into the armchair, so that she couldn't fall sideways.

'Good idea.'

Claire stirred and murmured something as he carried her in and set her down on the sofa, but went back to sleep. She was lighter than he'd expected, too thin. The dog jerked to her feet, hesitated, then stayed beside the child, as if keeping guard on her was her top priority.

Dee watched all this and forgot that she wasn't speaking to him. 'Who are they, did you say?'

'This is Claire, the woman I knocked over.'

For once the bored, world-weary teenager expression was missing from Dee's face. 'Do you know her?'

'No. Never met her before in my life.'

'And you brought her back here why?'

'Because she's been injured and desperately needs help – they both do. At a guess I think she's escaping an abusive husband. And look how thin she is. From what the daughter let slip, I'd guess she's not been eating properly.'

Dee stared at him as if she'd never seen him before. 'I never thought of *you* as a Good Samaritan.'

'I'm not. I just . . . don't like to see decent people in trouble. Especially children. And these two are having a very tough time of it, from what Gabby's let slip. Will you help me get the back bedroom next to yours ready?'

Dee shrugged, which he took to mean yes, and followed him upstairs.

The beds didn't take long to make up and he put clean towels out in the bathroom next door. At least the random modernisations had included three bathrooms, old-fashioned now but perfectly usable.

After that, he carried the child upstairs then went back down for the mother.

When he came back Dee was already taking off Gabby's outer jacket. 'I don't think we should undress them. That might freak them out when they wake up. Bad enough to wake in a strange place, but not minus your clothes. They can unpack some clean clothes tomorrow from their stuff.'

'Right. Thanks. Good idea.'

He tucked the child in and Dee did the same for the woman, then reached down to pat the dog again. 'We'd better let Helly out. Could you do that? They tell her to "be a good girl". Keep her on the lead, though. We don't want any more escapes.'

'We should leave a light on, or they'll panic if they wake up.'

Dee was nearest so switched on the bedside lamp, then took the dog away without any sarcastic remarks.

He followed her downstairs and heard her go down to the lower level and open the back door. He hadn't realised how practical she could be . . . when she wanted. She was almost a woman now, had only another year of school left.

When she came back he watched her start petting the dog again and saying soppy things to her. When Helly licked her nose suddenly, she chuckled. She was amazingly pretty when she chuckled.

How much of her life he'd missed! Damn Angie!

'She's a nice dog, isn't she, Dad? Friendly. She doesn't seem to be hurt.'

'No. It was the woman I hit not the animal she was chasing. Luckily I'd slowed down a lot by then.'

'I think Helly's hungry.'

'There isn't much dog food left and it looks like cheap, nasty stuff. Is there something in the pantry we can add to it?'

'Bound to be. I'll have a look.' She came out of the huge, old-fashioned pantry holding a tin of stewed steak. 'This should be OK for her, maybe mixed with some of that dry stuff of theirs.'

'She already had some pizza this evening, so we won't give her a huge helping.'

'She might have eaten, but she still looks hungry and she's too scrawny for a dog that size.' Without asking, Dee opened the tin and dumped half of its contents into a shallow bowl with some of the lumps of dog food, then filled another bowl with water.

Helly snapped that lot down in a few gulps and splashed water all over the floor as she quenched her thirst.

'Shall I make us a cup of warm milk?' he suggested.

'Yeah. Good idea.'

They watched a late news programme on the TV, then both yawned at the same time.

'I suppose I'd better let the dog out again,' he said.

'It'll be safer.'

He led the way down and called Helly to join him, then put on her lead, saying 'Be a good girl' once they got outside.

The dog sniffed her way round the nearer part of the garden, dragging him with her and ignoring the rougher ground at the rear, then did as required and pulled him back to the door.

Once they got inside, he frowned at her. 'Your legs and feet are all wet again, Helly.'

Dee came down from the kitchen. 'Get out of the way, Dad. I've found an old towel and a blanket. I'll rub her down then make up a bed for her here. We can leave the upstairs door open.'

'I doubt she'll stay. She seems determined to keep watch on that child. Let's see if she'll settle down in the bedroom with them.'

Helly condescended to settle down on the old blanket in between the two beds.

'She's a nice dog, aren't you, darling.' Dee bent to stroke the dog and she nuzzled her, then they left their guests alone.

'Have you had something to eat?'

'Of course I have. It's nearly ten o'clock, Dad.'

'What? So it is. The pizza's worn off and I'm hungry again, so I think I'll grab a bowl of muesli.'

Dee lingered to chat to him, something she didn't often do. 'They're all three of them very thin, aren't they?'

'Yes. I think they've been extremely short of money.'

'And yet she has a new computer.'

'Gabby says her mother works from home.'

'Hmm. Wonder what she does.' She raised her arms above her head, stretching and yawning. 'Call me if you need anything else. I'm going to bed now.'

'Dee?'

She turned at the door.

'Thanks for your help.'

She shrugged and went upstairs. She did a lot of shrugging when communicating with him. But she'd talked to the dog non-stop when she was around.

*   *   *

He stood for a moment then decided to pour himself a beer. He'd more than earned it tonight. He sat sipping it as he watched a current affairs programme on television. What the hell had he got himself into?

His whole life was unsettled at the moment. All that was certain was that his days of rushing all over the place on business and working seven-day weeks were over now. The company he'd started many years ago had been sold. He'd done well, was proud of the conservatories he'd designed and built, but when one of the biggest builders of conservatories in the country had made him an offer, he'd decided to take it.

He didn't want to get into a fight with them for market share, didn't care about building his company up into a national chain himself or setting it up for franchising, either.

He'd never wanted to get super-rich, had just enjoyed creating attractive conservatories based on period designs that people could be happy using. He was set for life financially now, even if he never worked again, which felt very liberating. Well, if he said so himself, his designs had been good and so had the quality of the workmanship in the finished product. Indeed, the company he'd sold to said they'd buy occasional designs from him if he was still doing them.

He might finish off a few of his half-started designs, but he had other things he'd like to do now, including his main priority: getting on better terms with his daughter.

Maybe he'd get a dog, though. It'd be company and might help to bridge the yawning gap between him and Dee, who was still a stranger to him in many ways. He'd discuss that with her once he'd got Claire and Gabby sorted out. They could take in a rescue dog, perhaps.

And he needed to find himself a part-time housekeeper. He didn't enjoy domestic chores and wasn't fond of cooking, though he could do what was necessary to feed himself. But he'd have to find someone who wouldn't be put off by his daughter and her moods. Or by the clutter that the renovations would cause.

A Christmas carol on the television reminded him that the festive season was looming. Less than a month to go now. It wasn't his favourite time of year. Well, it wasn't much fun celebrating on your own as he'd mostly done over the past few years. He'd held office parties for his core staff. This year they'd also been a form of farewell. But he didn't socialise with his staff otherwise.

In fact, he didn't have much of a social life at all. He hadn't wanted to go out with other women for the first year or two after Angie left him. At first he'd been too angry with her and at the time had been struggling to keep his company in profit as he managed some necessary expansions. She couldn't have left him at a worse time.

After a year or two he'd tried online dating sites but found it embarrassing to deal with strange women. There hadn't been one that he'd have wanted permanently in his life. Some were pleasant enough, but there had never been that spark. Others had proved to be liars, posting glamorous photos on the dating sites, images that barely resembled them, and not telling the truth about themselves in other ways.

He'd stepped quickly back from most of them after the introductory date in a safe public place. He'd asked a few of them for a second date, but hadn't managed more than a few weeks even with women he'd quite liked.

Maybe he wasn't cut out for marriage.

But it was lonely living on your own.

It was also lonely, albeit in a different way, living with Dee.

Such a shame. He'd worked hard and was now comfortably off, which was very nice. Would his tentative plans and interests be enough to fill his life? Who knew.

He raised his glass to his reflection in a nearby mirror. 'Happy Christmas, you poor lost soul!' he mocked. 'May Santa bring you some nice presents.'

But the glass was empty, though he didn't remember finishing the beer, and he didn't want another one.

Anyway, he had to keep a clear head in case anything went wrong with Claire during the night.

He decided to put on a tracksuit because it might frighten her if a strange man in pyjamas came into her bedroom to check on her. He made sure the house was locked up and the security system was on in the garage, but didn't arm the system in the house. Then he changed and hung up his business clothes for what he hoped would be the last time.

Setting the timer on his watch for an hour, he lay down with a sigh. Each time he was woken by it, he went to check on Claire, finding to his relief that her breathing was slow and steady. She only half woke up when he shook her uninjured shoulder gently, answered his question about what her dog's name was correctly, and immediately went back to sleep.

Was she still sleeping because of the concussion or the painkillers? Or was she deep down exhausted? Probably a bit of each.

As the later winter dawn approached, he felt it safe to set the watch for two hours. He was rather tired himself now. And no doubt he'd be kept busy tomorrow.

Only it was tomorrow now. Give or take. He hoped the day went better than yesterday had.

Chapter Four

At Number 5 Peppercorn Street, Janey Torrington happened to be standing near the window as Luke's car pulled in next door. She was glad he was home. He'd asked them to keep an eye on his daughter while he was away, but she'd only caught one glimpse of Dee, who had come home from school wearing her usual scowl, gone in through the front door and slammed it on the world.

It felt strange to be asked to watch out for someone who was only a couple of years younger than yourself, but she felt much older than Dee after all she'd been through. She'd been raped and left pregnant at seventeen. You grew up quickly when you became a single mother and were struggling to make ends meet.

Strange, how an evil deed had left her with a sunny-natured daughter whom she loved to distraction.

She didn't understand why Dee seemed to treat everyone, herself included, so scornfully when she had such a nice father and a comfortable home. Janey had met others around that age who were similar. Glass half empty types? Or just teenage rebels? She hoped her little daughter wouldn't grow up with such scorn for older people and the world generally because there was so much to enjoy in life.

She yawned and decided to go up and read in bed. Winifred, with whom she shared this house, was still watching an old movie, waxing sentimental over it, and mopping away occasional tears at particularly emotional bits. Well, at nearly eighty-six, her dear adopted aunt didn't seem to need a lot of sleep and she well deserved her little pleasures.

After checking that Millie was all right in the next room, Janey got into bed, picked up her book, stared at the cover then put it down again. She felt sleepy and since she had to get up early in the morning to go to college, which meant taking Millie to the crèche first, this story would have to wait till next time to reveal more secrets to her.

In the morning, when she went down to the kitchen, Janey was surprised to see a large dog outside in their back garden, a golden Labrador busy sniffing its way round. Now, where had that come from? She always closed and locked the side gate. She definitely hadn't seen this lovely creature before.

The mystery was quickly solved when Luke from next door poked his head over the fence and called the dog. But although it wagged its tail at the sound of his voice, it continued exploring, nose to the ground.

Feeling amused, Janey went out to see if she could help.

Luke brightened at the sight of her. 'Sorry about my four-legged visitor trespassing. I'll buy a new panel and block that hole in the fence as soon as the shops are open. Helly won't hurt you. She's a friendly creature – too friendly at times.'

'Did you get her from the dog pound?'

'No, I have two guests and she belongs to them. Um, do you want me to come round and grab her or can you guide her back to the hole and I'll pull her through?'

Janey went up to the dog cautiously, to be greeted by furious wagging and a lick on the hand, so she caught hold of the collar and set off towards the fence. Helly seemed happy to walk along beside her and Luke had no trouble guiding her through the hole – and he too was licked enthusiastically as he bent down.

'Thanks, Janey. I'll put the wheelbarrow upside down across the hole till I can mend it. Come on, Helly. You shouldn't go visiting till you're invited.'

When Janey went back inside, she went across to Millie, who was sitting in her high chair busy covering her face with porridge. If that child continued to grow so quickly she'd soon outgrow the chair and need a booster seat on a normal chair. She was toddling about all over the house now, given half a chance, and they'd had to buy two stair gates to keep her safe.

By the time Winifred came into the kitchen from what had once been the servants' quarters nearby, Janey had washed Millie's face, put on their outer clothes and was ready to leave. She kissed the papery cheek of the woman she now called 'aunt', told her about the dog next door and left.

Another day's lectures and tutorials lay ahead, with Millie being well cared for in the college crèche. Janey was enjoying her studies, and if her exam results were as good this year as last year's had been, she thought she'd have a good chance of getting a place at university. Though how she'd manage that in practical terms, she wasn't sure, because they were too far away from any university here in Sexton Bassett for her to commute.

And even if they had a crèche at the university, she wouldn't be able to afford to rent somewhere, nor was she willing to leave Winifred on her own. Her aunt was very fit for a woman of her age, and fiercely independent, but even she agreed that she ought not to live on her own again.

If necessary, Janey would have to do her studying through the Open University and get a job. And though that would be second best, Millie's and her aunt's needs had to come first. Two years ago, she'd not have expected to have any chance at all of furthering her education – or known about her real father, who'd been living in Australia and come to England with his other daughter to find her when he discovered her existence.

She started the car her birth father had bought her and left for college. Her life was so much easier with her own transport. He was a clever man, and fun, and a great grandfather.

She sighed happily. You never knew what was round the corner in this life. But the changes of the past year had all been good ones. She was so lucky.

At Number 1 Peppercorn Street, Angus Denning was woken early by his phone buzzing. He got up, talking quietly, and tiptoed out, trying not to wake his wife. Nell had been working hard lately, because the woman managing the café in the small artists' colony they'd set up at the lower end of their grounds had had a heart attack and would not be coming back.

The former manager, Ginger, was helping Nell out, but both women had other calls on their time. Dennings, his ancient family home, took a lot of looking after and Nell had grown to love it almost as much as he did. Hopefully they would soon find a suitable café manager among those who'd applied for the job. But the interviews weren't till early the following week.

He chatted quietly to the person on the phone about a possible job for himself, not sure whether to be pleased or sorry about this. They always needed money to maintain the old house that had been in his family for several generations and as a troubleshooter for major IT programs, he could earn some rather useful chunks of cash. But he'd been intending to help Nell today, had been looking forward to them spending time together.

When she got up, he told her about the job offer. 'I'm sorry, love. We'll have to postpone our plans, I'm afraid. The money's too good to turn down.'

'Of course you must take the job, Angus. Ginger and I are coping.'

'Then I'll accept. It's an intriguing problem, I must admit, and shouldn't be happening. I shall enjoy sorting it out.'

She watched him leave. He'd be absent in spirit until he'd finished this job, she knew. He had amazing powers of concentration. Maybe that was why he was so successful.

It looked like rain outside, so she took a walk through the historic parts of the small stately home, the parts they charged people to look round. The beautiful rooms and their furnishings always made her feel good. It was a privilege to live here, a privilege to be able to contribute to the preservation of a historical treasure – and a joy to be married to Angus, after a disastrous first marriage.

She went upstairs and looked across towards the rear gardens of the houses at the top end of Peppercorn Street. Although Dennings was nominally Number 1, that was really as a postal convenience, she always thought, because it still stood in its own grounds, not quite on the street, surrounded by suburbia, a jewel in Wiltshire's historical crown with a garden that was heritage listed in its own right as well as the house.

To her surprise, she saw a dog jumping up as if trying to see what was on the other side of the back fence of Number 5. Had Winifred acquired a dog? She hadn't said anything about it when Nell collected the last lot of cakes Winifred had baked for the café.

The man who'd bought Number 4 Peppercorn Street a few months ago came out of the basement area and strode across to the fence, gesticulating at the animal. She could see his mouth moving but couldn't hear what he was saying. At a guess he was calling the dog home. It must belong to him.

She smiled as she watched it ignore him till Janey came out and grabbed it by the collar. She had a soft spot for Labradors. Most of them had such lovely natures.

She hadn't had much to do with the newest resident in the top end of the street, though she'd been briefly introduced to him. But she would no doubt get to know him better when the finer weather came. He had a teenage daughter, too, who seemed to wear only black when she wasn't in school uniform. It'd be nice to have some young people around again – even dressed in perpetual mourning.

When she had time to socialise again, she'd invite the newcomers to tea. But first she'd have to find a new manager for the café.

Chapter Five

Luke took Helly back inside the house, trying to scold her, only it was hard to scold such a friendly animal, who made you laugh by panting loudly and wagging at you whenever you spoke to her.

He looked up as he heard a sound from the visitors' bedroom and hurriedly shut the dog in the kitchen before running up the stairs. If that was Claire waking up properly, she would wonder where she was and probably be upset not to recognise her surroundings.

Dee peered out of her bedroom as he reached the landing and he beckoned to her, guessing that her presence would make their guest feel safer.

Next thing he knew Helly came bounding up the stairs to join them. How had she got here? Surely he'd shut the kitchen door? He'd have to check the catch. Before he could stop her, the dog had slipped past his outstretched arm and disappeared into the bedroom where her owner was.

* * *

When Claire woke up she felt much more alert. She looked round, frowning as she found herself in a strange room where a lamp was shining beside the bed even though it was now daylight. She tried to sit up, but the room spun round her so she let her head fall back onto the pillow, such a lovely soft pillow. Lovely sheets against her cheeks, too. Quality always showed.

Where was Gabby? In sudden panic she turned her head from side to side, letting out a long breath of relief when she saw her daughter to her right, lying in another single bed, sprawled out like a starfish as always when she was fast asleep.

As she tried to figure out what was going on, Claire remembered the accident. Then things got a bit vague. Someone had come into the bedroom during the night and asked her questions.

Before she could make sense of it all, there was a sound from the door and Helly padded in, coming to stand by her bed, nearly wagging the clock radio off the bedside table.

She grabbed it and said, 'Sit!' before she dared let go of the clock again.

The dog looked at her reproachfully, as if this wasn't fair.

'*Sit*, Helly!'

With a sigh Helly obeyed her.

Claire sat up again, this time slowly, and found that if she didn't make any sudden moves, the room didn't spin round her.

'You seem to be properly awake this time, Claire.'

She froze and stared across towards the door. 'Who are you?'

'Luke Morgan. We were in an accident together.'

'Oh, yes. I remember you. Where am I now, though? I was in hospital last time I—' She shook her head, relieved that he'd stayed where he was, near the door. But she still felt nervous.

'You're in my house. You agreed to come here, but you didn't wake up last night after we left the hospital. And this is my daughter. You were asleep when she helped me bring your things into the house.'

A teenage girl stepped out from behind him, smiling tentatively. 'Hi. I'm Dee. How are you feeling today?'

Relief ran through Claire and she immediately felt safer. 'I'm much better, I think, just a bit confused as to how I got here. But I, um, need to use a bathroom before we talk any more.'

He stepped back and gestured to the right. 'There's one next to this room, which you and your daughter can use while you're here. We put out some towels and toiletries for you. Would you like a cup of tea?'

'Yes please.'

He stepped towards the stairs. 'Give me a call when you've finished and I'll bring you one up. Or just come down to the kitchen if you prefer.'

She checked that Gabby was still asleep, then turned to go next door, but moved too quickly and staggered, so had to let Dee steady her.

The bathroom was very old-fashioned but had all the necessary amenities. She locked the door before using them and afterwards stood frowning at her reflection in the mirror, thinking how awful the bruise on her forehead looked.

Why had he brought her and Gabby here? Were they

safe? Of course they were. His daughter was here.

She felt too unsteady to clamber in and out of the bath to have a shower, so made do with a quick wash. She couldn't resist using the hand cream, which smelt faintly of flowers.

When she went back towards the bedroom she had to steady herself with one hand on the wall and her right shoulder hurt when she moved it.

What had they told her at the hospital? Oh yes – she'd dislocated her shoulder in the accident and they'd put it back in place. Perhaps Luke would have some aspirin or something for the pain.

She could see that Gabby was still fast asleep, looking peaceful and rosy.

Dee came back as she prepared to let go of the door frame and walk across to the bed. 'Shall I help you across the room?'

'I'll be all right if I take it slowly, but thanks anyway.'

'I just want to say: it must feel strange to find yourself here, but don't worry. You'll be quite safe. Dad's all right. For a man.' Then she left the room.

He might be all right, but why had he brought her and her daughter to his home? That really worried Claire. She was a complete stranger and the accident hadn't been his fault, so he had nothing to feel guilty about. Surely no one could be so altruistic?

He must have brought her straight here from the hospital. She'd have woken up if they'd gone to her home first. Which meant her computer was still in that horrible little bungalow. She'd be lucky to find it still there when she went back.

He appeared in the doorway, holding a mug from which steam rose. 'Dee said you'd finished in the bathroom, so I thought you might like that cup of tea now.'

As he put it down beside her bed, she blurted out, 'I need to get back home quickly. Would you be able to give us a lift if I wake Gabby up?'

'Why? Is something wrong?'

'My computer's there. It could be stolen. It's the only way I have of earning a living at the moment.' She daren't get a job openly, too much chance of her ex finding them through it. If she could just keep out of Martin's way for a while, surely he'd give up trying to interfere in their lives? Or rather, interfere in Gabby's upbringing. He had such old-fashioned views about children and couldn't even talk to Gabby without lecturing her.

'No need to worry, Claire. I brought your computer here last night, brought all your things, actually, because I didn't trust that flimsy front door of yours to deter anyone. Gabby packed your clothes as well as her own.'

It was a moment or two before Claire could put any words together, she was so surprised by this. 'And I didn't wake up while this was going on?'

'No. You were in the front seat of the car. I kept an eye on you. When we were loading your things, you stirred and murmured something a couple of times, but you didn't really wake up, not even when I carried you up here. I think whatever they gave you for the pain had made you dopey on top of recovering from the anaesthetic.'

'Oh.' She reached up to rub her forehead, forgetting the bruise and winced. So did he.

'I'm so sorry about the accident. I couldn't stop the car in time.'

'My fault. I was panicking, thinking I'd lose Helly if I didn't catch her. She'd been shut up in the house for too long and needed a run. But one of the lads who hang around the building sites after the tradesmen have left started throwing stones at her and she took off running.'

'Well, you don't need to panic any longer.' He gestured to Helly. 'She seems happy enough here, and she's been out into the garden this morning, so you can just concentrate on resting and getting better.' He held out the mug. 'I hope you like English breakfast tea.'

'Thank you. I like any sort of tea.' She cradled the mug in her hands then took a cautious sip. It wasn't too hot, so she drank a couple of mouthfuls, then glanced at her daughter, who was still fast asleep.

'They sleep like logs at that age, don't they?' he said. 'My daughter was the same.'

'Yes, they do. Um, do you have any painkillers?'

He snapped his fingers. 'How stupid of me! They gave me some at the hospital and I forgot to bring them up.'

'I don't want such strong ones. How about a couple of aspirins?'

'Can do. You're probably right not to take something strong unless you absolutely have to. I won't be a tick.'

When he returned, she took the pills from him and swallowed them, before lying back on the pillow, feeling tiredness roll across her like waves on a shore. She held out the empty mug, afraid of dropping it, and he took it from her.

Helly took up her position on the floor between the beds again.

Claire snuggled down and said thank you, literally unable to keep her eyes open any longer.

That nice girl had been right about one thing. She did feel safe here.

Luke went back upstairs half an hour later to check on Claire, but she and the child were sleeping soundly, with the dog still lying between their two beds.

He went back downstairs and read the morning paper for a while before getting his breakfast. He preferred real newspapers to reading them online and enjoyed a leisurely start to his day.

As he was finishing his meal, he heard slow footsteps on the stairs and hurried out into the hall in time to see Claire making her way carefully down the last few steps, holding on with her left hand and keeping her right arm against her chest. It must still be painful to use. Perhaps she should wear the sling they'd given her?

When she got to the bottom of the stairs, she let go of the bannisters then immediately grabbed them again. She must still be a bit dizzy.

He already knew that she was fiercely independent, but since he didn't want her to have a fall, he moved quickly to steady her. When he offered her his arm, she hesitated visibly for a moment, then took it to cross the hall. She let go the minute she was able to take hold of the back of a kitchen chair.

He watched to make sure she was safely seated before he moved away. 'You're still dizzy, aren't you?'

'A little, not as bad.'

'I see you've changed your clothes. Do you want the others washed and dried?'

'I can do that if you'll let me use your washing machine.'

'Were you listening to what they told you in hospital? You're to avoid using that arm for the next few days.' He let that sink in, then said, 'It won't take me a minute to put your things in the machine once Gabby has got up.'

From the stubborn expression on her face, he guessed she wasn't going to let him do much for her. She was too independent for her own good.

'Would you like another cup of tea? Or do you prefer coffee? Or there's apple juice.'

'Apple juice, please. Where's your daughter?'

'Dee went back to bed after you did, which is over an hour ago now, to grab some more sleep. She's definitely not an early morning person. Is Gabby still asleep?'

'Yes. She got up to use the bathroom, which is what woke me, then went straight back to bed. Um, I know I'm in your house, but where is it exactly?'

'It's in Peppercorn Street.'

She looked at him blankly. He sounded as if he thought she'd recognise the name but she didn't.

'It's in Sexton Bassett, which is in Wiltshire, and the street is quite well known locally. It leads out from the town centre and ends near a small stately home on a couple of acres, which you can see from our back garden. We're at the top end, Number 4. I didn't bring you here without asking, by the way. You'd agreed to come and stay for a day or two once we'd got some clean clothes for you both.'

'Ah. Yes. I vaguely remember that.' She gave him a rueful smile. 'Only I didn't mean to do that. I was going to insist on staying at my own home.'

'Now why does that not surprise me?' He smiled

back at her. 'Not a good decision, though. You were concussed and not thinking clearly. Your eyes are much clearer this morning, if that's any comfort, even if you are still a bit dizzy.'

'My head's aching.'

'Even after the aspirins you took earlier?' He looked at his watch. 'Better not take anything else yet, though, but you should have something to eat, don't you think?'

'I suppose so. I don't feel hungry. Do I remember correctly that you brought my computer here?'

'Yes. Gabby and I packed all your possessions except for some crockery.'

'Oh. And did you lock up my house carefully?'

'Yes. For what that's worth. That house will hardly keep out the rain, let alone a burglar.'

She looked embarrassed. 'It does have a couple of leaks, but it was all I could afford to rent. I'm sorry to have given you so much trouble. I feel a lot better this morning, so we can get a taxi home after Gabby gets up and—'

'You're not better enough to manage on your own. You're still as white as a sheet and what's more, you're favouring that arm. My daughter will come pounding down the stairs any minute, so I'm going to make some more toast. She'll grab something to eat then rush off to school. She likes to stay in bed till the last possible minute. I thought we'd leave *your* daughter to wake up in her own time.'

Claire gave him another assessing stare then looked round the kitchen. 'No wife?'

'I'm divorced, have been for years. You?'

'Divorced. Two years ago.'

'Is your ex the one you're hiding from?'

She gasped. 'How did you know that?'

'It seems pretty obvious. New name. Things Gabby said.'

'Oh. Well, yes. He's being a – nuisance. I'm trying to stay out of his way.' After another of those long pauses, she added, 'Thank you so much for your help.'

She didn't sound particularly grateful but he didn't comment on that. 'Fruit and toast suit you?'

'Anything. Thank you.'

He started getting things out of the fridge and saw her looking round the room, studying it.

'It's quite an old house, isn't it?'

'Yes. Too big for just me and Dee, really, but I fell in love with it on sight. It was built in 1910 and is going to need quite a bit of modernising, which I shall enjoy doing. I'll have to get some help with that, but there's no rush. I want to do it *right*.'

'Did I see some stairs going down another level from the back of the hall?' She rubbed her forehead. 'I'm not quite sure which of the images in my mind are true and which are the result of the anaesthetic and painkillers.'

'Yes, you did see stairs. There's a slight slope along this part of the street, so we have a semi-basement which contains the former kitchen and servants' rooms. Winifred next door doesn't have that because her house is at the top of the slope, but the first four houses do. The last owners of this place were quite elderly and they had trouble with the stairs, so they closed off the lower part and put in a kitchen and utility room up here. They'd given up driving so didn't need to use the garage. I've opened up the basement again because I'm making a start on the back garden and obviously I do use the garage, but we don't use the rooms down there for anything.'

'What I've seen looks lovely. I miss having a bigger house. I don't miss living with my ex, though.'

'Does Gabby miss her father?'

'No,' she said so sharply he stopped asking questions.

Chapter Six

As Claire was eating a belated breakfast, Helly got up suddenly and padded out into the hall, standing looking up the stairs and giving a low woof. She put her spoon down. 'Gabby must be waking up. I'd better go to her. She'll worry if she doesn't know where I am.'

Luke stood up. 'Stay there. I'll call up to tell her we're down here.'

But there was the sound of voices then Dee came clumping down the stairs. 'Gabby's just using the bathroom. I told her to come down to the kitchen when she's finished.'

She stopped to pat Helly then snatched a piece of toast, smeared on some butter and ate it in a few rapid bites. Her mouth still full of the last of the toast, she picked up an apple and a banana, shoving them into her backpack. 'Bye.'

He grinned at Claire's surprised expression as his daughter slammed the front door behind her. He murmured his usual, 'Have a good day, Dee!' adding, 'I always say that, though she never hangs around to hear it.'

Claire couldn't help smiling as she pushed her empty bowl away and dealt with a piece of toast in a more civilised way. 'Talk about swift departures.'

'Yes. She's got it down to a fine art. I make certain there's fruit and toast easily available and she buys her lunch at the school canteen. She's more sociable in the evenings. Mostly, anyway. Unless I say something that upsets her.'

'Teenagers can be very touchy. I have that pleasure to come.'

'Your daughter still has a delightful attitude towards the world. Make the most of it while you can.' He remembered how Gabby had held his hand and openly enjoyed every mouthful of the pizza.

Claire relaxed visibly at the compliment. 'She's the joy of my life, and amazingly resilient, considering. I hope she doesn't turn too moody in her teens.'

'Good luck with that. I'm told they start behaving in a more friendly fashion after a while. And she's only been back with me for a few months. Her mother just dumped her.'

'That'd upset anyone.'

'I like to have her back again, however grumpily she behaves. Look, please, do help yourself to more toast. There's plenty of bread in the freezer.'

As she took a second slice, the dog whined in its throat and nudged her elbow.

Helly had been sitting watching them, clearly resenting every mouthful they ate. In the end Luke couldn't stand those hungry eyes any longer. He got out the rest of the tin of steak and showed Claire what it was. 'All right if I put this in Helly's bowl? She ate the other half last night. I'm not sure whether you feed her once or twice a day, but she seems hungry again.'

'She could eat for England, that one. Typical Labrador. But we've had to be a bit, um, economical lately. I feel guilty about that but I haven't been paid yet for my last job and I have to watch the pennies.'

'What do you do exactly?'

'I produce computer graphics at the moment, either of my own design or according to someone else's rough sketches. I do anything that'll earn money, simple websites, whatever. Sometimes people want me to design their own paper and business cards as a matching set and I put them together. I've worked with the same small printing company for a few years. Plus I have a friend who does advertising and she kindly keeps me in the loop for jobs. The last job I did was for one of them but the company isn't a rapid payer, unfortunately.'

She sighed and stared into space for a moment or two, then said quietly, almost as if talking to herself, 'I used to run my own design business and make decent money, but Gabby and I have had to stay under the radar since I left my husband, so I haven't been able to set up a shopfront again.'

'How come you didn't manage to take much business equipment with you after the split-up?'

She shrugged. 'Martin had smashed it up, told me he wanted me home for Gabby like a *proper* wife. I only kept my laptop, because it'd been in for repair and of course I still had the software and stuff I'd stored in the cloud. Gabby and I were in a bit of a hurry to leave at the end, you see.'

'But your husband's stalking you now.'

She grimaced. 'My *ex*-husband. It's not me, it's Gabby that he wants back now. I don't think he'd actually hurt her or me, come to that, but he says he doesn't trust me to bring her up *properly,* whatever that may mean and he wants to make sure she knows what's right and wrong. He uses the word *properly* all the time, as if there's only one way to do things.'

'He sounds more than a bit mixed up.'

'Tell me about it. But we've managed to avoid him for several months now and she's been nearly her old self again.'

'That must make life horrendously difficult for you.'

'Yes. I'm not doing anything illegal, because I got custody. He's only supposed to see Gabby twice a month in a supervised situation. But in the early days he picked her up from school a few times without letting me know, or from his parents' house because his mother's always on his side. He didn't bring Gabby back till late. She's too frightened of him when he gets *that look* on his face to refuse to go with him.'

He looked so sympathetic she continued her tale. 'I panicked the first time he took her because I didn't know where she was, and called the police. He was furious. But he brought her back at bedtime. He didn't hurt her physically, but he shouted at her and she said she didn't like it.'

He could only stare at her, shaking his head slowly at the idiocy of some people. What did you say to something like that?

'At first I found somewhere near her school because she had a lot of friends there, but that didn't work out. I asked the teachers not to let Gabby go home with him, but he sneaked into the school grounds or caught her as she came out of school.'

'Not nice.'

'Mmm. I got a restraining order to keep him from doing it, only he doesn't pay it much attention and it isn't a big priority for the police. It was upsetting Gabby more and more, so in the end I moved away without telling him where we were going and she gradually got back to being her old self. Only he found us again, so we had to slip away a second time.'

She sniffed and smeared away a tear with the back of one hand. 'He boasted to me the first time that we'll never escape him for long. He says he's going to do his duty by his child until she grows up and marries, and I'd better not stand in his way.'

She stopped and looked at him as if puzzled. 'I don't know why I'm telling you this. I don't usually confide in people.'

'People say I'm a good listener. Go on.'

She gave him a doubtful look and he waited in silence for her to continue or not, then more words came pouring out, as if she was desperate to unburden herself.

'Martin's always been a bit of a control freak, but not like this. He used to get such a smug, arrogant look on his face when he brought Gabby back, and he whispered things to me before he left, about how he'll never let go and I'd better get used to it. The expression on his face when he says that really creeps me out.'

'He sounds as if he needs professional help and counselling.'

'Yes. But he doesn't break the law in any other way, and it's only my word against his about what he says, so he's got off with warnings about sticking to arranged visits.'

'Didn't you get any money in the divorce settlement?'

'I should get the major share of the proceeds from the house. He found a way to prove that it'd bankrupt his business to pay me out any other way, so I have to wait till it sells. Only the house has been on the market for nearly two years and it hasn't sold. I think he's making sure it doesn't. *He* won't be short of money, after all.'

'No maintenance payments for Gabby, even?'

'In theory yes, in practice no, except for a token payment once or twice when I took him to court.'

'Can't you take over selling the house?'

'That'd mean getting in touch with him again. I can't work out how to do that without giving him a chance to upset Gabby all over again. That's why we're so short of money.'

'Well, whatever you're doing with her now must be right, whatever he says. She's got excellent manners and she's a real charmer.' He waited a moment then added, 'You haven't finished your breakfast.'

She looked down and started to push the plate away, then pulled it back, muttering, 'I mustn't waste good food.'

He didn't comment on that. 'You'll stay here a while longer, won't you? You really aren't fit to look after yourself yet, let alone Gabby and Helly.'

Silence, then, 'One more night, then, if that's not too much trouble. I'm worried about leaving my house unoccupied. I didn't realise when I rented it that it'd be such a target for hoodlums and vandals. Not in the daytime, when most of the nearby industrial units are occupied, but after dark. Only I didn't have much choice. It was the only house I could afford. A flat wouldn't have been any use with Helly to think of and actually, she's a help when it comes to people annoying us. Looks fierce if Gabby gets upset.'

'Maybe you can find somewhere else once you get paid.'

'Maybe.'

She didn't sound hopeful. Well, it took a chunk of money to rent a house, he knew that.

Claire concentrated on her food, eating the last few bites of toast, even though she didn't look to be enjoying it particularly.

He picked up his mug of tea and took another sip. He'd found out more about her situation than he'd expected to, but didn't want to push his luck. It made him angry to think of that delightful child being put under such pressure.

Then there were footsteps on the stairs and he called, 'We're in here.'

Gabby came in, looking rosy and clean, not wearing her school clothes but clean jeans, top and sweater.

She gave a beaming smile the minute she saw her mother and went over to have a cuddle, then bent to speak to the dog and ruffle her fur, before sitting down to her breakfast.

'Am I going to school today?'

'No, it's too far.'

Claire sighed and seemed lost in thought still, so Luke took charge. 'There's some fruit salad and toast, Gabby. Do you want both?'

'Yes, please.'

'Yoghurt on your fruit salad?'

'Ooh, yes. I love yoghurt.' She ate slowly and with relish.

'I'll put some bread in the toaster for you, shall I? Then you can choose what to put on it.' He indicated the jam jars and butter dish near the breadboard and she went across to study the labels.

'Ooh, cherry jam! My favourite.' She spread some thinly on her toast.

He took the knife from her and put on a much thicker layer of jam, with chunks of cherries. 'That's more like it.'

'Thank you.' She went back to sit at the table, taking small bites of the toast and making happy little noises as she chewed slowly. Her hair was the same red-gold as her mother's, and just as wavy. They were an attractive pair.

After Gabby had finished eating, Claire reached for her daughter's plate and started to clear the table, so he said firmly, 'I'll deal with the kitchen. You're looking tired again. Before I start, let's find you somewhere more comfortable to sit.'

Between them, he and the child persuaded her to lie down on the sofa in the room he used mainly in the evenings and Gabby picked up the magazine from the Sunday paper, which was still lying on a low table.

When the little girl's disappointment with the magazine's contents showed, he remembered suddenly a box filled with children's books that had belonged to Dee. 'Just a minute, Gabby. I've got some children's books you might like to read. Why don't you come with me to find them?'

He led the way up to the attics and she looked round with great interest. 'I've never been in such a big old house before. Does anyone sleep up here?'

'No. We're just dumping things here till we can think what to do with them. The box I want should be over here. Ah, here it is.'

'What sort of books are they?'

'All sorts of children's stuff. I'll open the box when we get downstairs. I don't want anything to fall out. Oh, just a minute! Grab that carrier bag as well, would you? Can you manage to carry it down?'

'Yes. It isn't heavy.'

If he was right, there should be a drawing pad and some of the coloured pencils that could be moistened and act almost as paints in that bag, as well as other arty things.

When he opened the box of books, Gabby fell on them like someone starving to death, oohing and aahing over old favourites and pretty covers.

Claire smiled sleepily from the sofa as she watched her daughter choose a book and lie on her stomach on the rug in front of the gas fire to read it. The cool winter sunlight shone through the window and brightened the room.

He put the drawing materials on the small table next to the sofa. 'You and Gabby may both enjoy these, Claire. Dee was drawing mad for a while, then she fell in love with computers and forgot about drawing. Her mother refused to throw these away because they might come in useful one day. Angie was a real pack rat, could never bear to throw anything out. That used to drive me mad. I still haven't gone through all the things she dumped here along with Dee.'

'Thank you. You're very thoughtful.' But Claire made no attempt to pick up the pencils and when he peeped into the room a few minutes later, she was asleep again.

Gabby smiled and put one finger to her lips.

Which only reinforced his view that Claire was in no fit state to go home tomorrow to a dangerous area. How on earth would she manage to look after a child and dog in her condition? She ought not to drive a car with that shoulder. Determination could overcome many things, but not this.

If it were up to him, she wouldn't leave here till she was truly better. He'd wait till later to try to persuade her, but the trouble was, if she insisted on going home, he had no power to stop her.

He racked his brain to work out how to help her, but the only thing he could come up with was to fit a better lock on the door of that bungalow. He went out into his workshop and found a heavy-duty bolt in his 'might come in useful one day' box and put it in his car, together with the necessary tools. Just in case. It seemed pitifully little.

Why hadn't their house sold after nearly two years on the market? Something fishy there.

Perhaps he'd see if he could find out. He knew several estate agents around this and the nearby counties from when he'd been building conservatories for people. They might have contacts who could get the information for him.

That made him realise she hadn't told him where exactly they used to live before. To say she was sparing with information was putting it mildly.

Well, his time was now his own and if he chose to use it to help Claire and her daughter, that was no one else's business. He hated to see decent people in trouble.

On top of everything else, it would soon be Christmas. Goodwill to all men – and to women and children too.

Who was he kidding? This was nothing to do with Christmas, unless he could use the festive season as a lever to get her to accept help. He was interested in Claire as a woman, very attracted in fact. It was as if he was coming suddenly to life again in that way.

She wouldn't have told him so much about herself if she'd felt uncomfortable with him, would she? If he stayed in touch, maybe they could get to know one another and . . . who knew?

He was out of practice with women, would have to tread carefully, but maybe if they became friends, they could see what came of it.

He'd been lonely for a long time.

Chapter Seven

Tom Douglas watched his wife sigh over the happy family gathering that signalled the end of the movie she'd been watching on television. She wiped a few tears away and turned as he went to sit next to her on the sofa.

'That took my mind off my worries for a while.'

He put an arm round her. 'Which worries?'

'Which do you think? Oh, Tom, it'll soon be Christmas and Martin is hedging about whether he'll be coming to us this year.'

'To be frank, I'd rather he didn't.'

She looked at him in surprise. 'But he's our *son*, the only close family we have left these days. Who else would we spend Christmas with.'

'He might be our son but we don't see him all that often, do we? Last time he visited was in the summer and the way he went on and on about poor Claire and couldn't say a good word about her – well, frankly it sickened me. I was glad to see the back of him. I like her, always have. She's a really nice person.'

'Yes, but she did take his child away.'

'Because he'd started hitting her.'

'I don't believe that. Gabby was mistaken.'

'I do. We've seen him take against people before, and for no real reason. He was being so unfair to the poor woman. It's only a short step from that to hitting someone.'

Hilary looked even more tearful. 'I used to like her too. But if she's not bringing up that child properly, you can't blame him for worrying.'

'Claire has always been a good mother and well you know it. I don't believe that can possibly have changed. Look, we need to talk about our son, Hilary. I don't believe he's thinking straight and we should—'

He wasn't surprised when she cut him short. She hated to hear any criticism of her precious Martin. It was the only thing they quarrelled about.

She made a dismissive gesture with one hand. 'Let it drop. What is there to say that we haven't said before?'

'Things have changed. Martin's been avoiding us for months, except for a few quick phone calls to keep in touch with you. Admit it. We're not really included in his life these days.'

'He's been busy.'

'He's always been busy. He's a hard worker, I'll grant him that. What's brought this on today? Has he done something else to upset you?'

'It was seeing the family in that movie, especially the grandchildren. We've completely lost touch with our granddaughter and Martin says he doesn't have any recent photos of Gabby, even. We don't know what she looks like now. You know how quickly they change at that age. One of my friends has a granddaughter of the same age and she keeps showing me photos. You know what people are like with their mobile phones – always taking photos. And when she asks about Gabby, I've nothing to share.'

She gulped audibly and added, 'He says to leave it be and he'll sort it out soon.'

Watching her try to hold back tears made Tom say bluntly, 'I think we're going to have to go to the courts to get access to that child.'

'What? No! We can't do that, Tom. It'll upset Martin even more.'

'It might be the only way we get a chance to see Gabby.'

'Martin said last time that he didn't know where they were living now, so what difference would a court order make? He's so *angry* at Claire. And yet once he loved her so much.'

Tom wasn't sure that Martin was capable of that sort of deep love, but he didn't want to further upset Hilary.

'I keep hoping he'll meet someone else and move on, but I don't think he's dated anyone since they broke up. Has he mentioned anyone to you, Tom?'

'No. And he's not likely to get interested in another woman while he's obsessing about finding Gabby. To tell the truth, I'd feel more like warning any other woman away from him at the moment.'

There was silence, then she said softly, 'I don't know how to help him.'

'I don't think we can. What he needs is expert counselling.'

'He doesn't believe in it. And I'm not sure I do, either. I could never tell my thoughts to a stranger.'

He opened his mouth then closed it again. No, he'd better not tell her what he'd been thinking about doing lately. He should just do it. He wasn't going to lose touch with his grandchild if he could help it. Whoever he upset by his actions.

After all, Claire had never been unreasonable with them. He didn't think she would be now, either. If he could find her he'd tell her he wasn't on Martin's side in this.

'It's best not to interfere between husband and wife, Tom.'

'Only she isn't his wife now, is she?'

'He was talking about them trying to get together again last time I spoke to him.'

'They're divorced, Hilary. He's deluding himself – or trying to fool you.'

'But if they don't get back together, Gabby could grow up without us seeing her at all.' She burst into loud, noisy tears.

'Ah, come here, love.' He held her in his arms while she wept. But her anguish was the final straw. He was definitely going to do something about the situation. Nearly two years without Gabby in their lives was too long.

They sat there together for a while, then Tom looked at the clock. 'Come on. Time for bed. Leave it to me, love. I'll look into what can be done. I'm better at this sort of research than you are.'

'You won't do anything that'll drive Martin away?'

'Of course not.' And may he be forgiven for lying to her. Because he'd just about given up on Martin and what he was planning was definitely going to upset his son.

*   *   *

Finding a private investigator who had time to take on their case was more difficult than Tom had expected. He only found one who was available straight away, but he didn't take to the fellow and didn't want to place his family's happiness in such a man's hands. Not to mention the fact that this guy was charging twice as much as the others.

In the end he went to ask advice from a colleague whose son was a detective in the local police force. That led him to a semi-retired former policeman turned private investigator, who apparently only took on cases he thought were worthwhile these days. Tom liked the sound of this, so made an appointment to see him.

Surely it couldn't be all that hard to find a missing person in this digital age? Everyone was supposed to be only a few connections away from everyone else, weren't they?

When they met he liked Eric Bancroft at once. The PI seemed not only intelligent, but sensitive to the difficulties of their situation.

As the two of them faced each other across an untidy desk, Tom was just about to offer him the job when Eric said, 'One more thing. I have to warn you, Mr Douglas: if I think what I find out will harm your daughter-in-law and granddaughter, I'll stop my investigation and I won't necessarily pass on what I've found. Though in that case I will, of course, return your money. I've seen enough children destroyed by their parents' quarrels to tread carefully into people's lives.'

After his initial surprise at this, Tom had to take a few moments to think it through, then he nodded slowly. 'I can accept that, though I hope you won't give up on us. My wife will worry herself into a breakdown if this situation continues.'

'Better your wife be upset than a child of eight, don't you think? Anyway, if that's settled, I've got enough information to make a start.'

He offered his hand and Tom shook it.

'I've not given you all that much information. I don't want to try to get more from my son, though. It might make him suspicious.'

'No. He does sound . . . a bit chancy psychologically at the moment. But you've given me enough to make a start and I know where to look better than most. I'll get back to you in a day or two.'

After that Tom could only wait.

He didn't usually keep secrets from Hilary. It made him feel uncomfortable, but sometimes you had to grasp the nettle if you wanted something important sorting out. He'd learnt that when running a business.

Chapter Eight

As the afternoon moved towards evening, Luke kept a careful eye on Claire, relieved to see that she seemed more alert. He offered some information about himself, telling her of his regret that he'd not been allowed to be a real part of Dee's upbringing for the past few years. But it brought nothing more in return.

While it was still light, he took Gabby and the dog outside to throw a ball around. They had trouble getting it back if Helly managed to intercept it, but the child's cheeks grew rosy and her laughter pealed out several times as they played.

When Dee got back from school, she didn't vanish into her room, for once, but came outside to join them, throwing the ball a few times. She stayed around even after they came inside, which pleased him. She chatted mostly to Gabby, and the younger child hung on her every word. Dee also petted the dog occasionally and she too stayed near her.

When Claire asked about her day at school, to Luke's amazement, Dee told their guest all sorts of details, including which subjects she liked most and the fact that she was thinking of going to university if she could get a place on a science course.

Why hadn't she told him about that?

And why had she shot a quick glance at him as she said it, as if expecting him to protest or disagree about what to study?

He joined in. 'I always liked science at school myself, so it's good to see you do too.'

'But they didn't encourage girls to study science in your day, so you're bound to feel differently about it.'

'I expect a lot of it's changed since my day, but you're wrong. I always thought people should study what interests them, whether they're girls or boys. There were plenty of girls doing science in my day. I'm not *that* old, for heaven's sake.'

When she frowned at him as if she didn't know whether to believe this, he asked outright, 'Why did you think I wouldn't approve of you studying science?'

'Mum said—' She broke off.

He had always vowed not to say anything bad about Angie, but he nearly broke that vow then. There was an awkward silence till Claire intervened.

'You're not that old, Luke, roughly my generation, and we weren't all sexist in those days, Dee, I promise you. Even my father's generation weren't all that sexist about what we studied at school.'

Luke held his breath. Would his daughter take offence at that? She seemed to get into a huff so easily.

'What did *you* study?' Dee asked Claire.

'Computing, IT stuff generally with a couple of subsidiaries in art. I was torn between the two areas, but my father thought IT would be much more likely to lead to jobs, so he urged me to concentrate on that. He was a good father and he was probably right, but one day, when I have more time, I'll take up art again as a hobby.'

'Why isn't your father helping you and Gabby now?'

Claire stared into space for a moment or two, then said quietly, 'He died about ten years ago. Hit and run accident.'

'Oh, that's terrible. What about your mother?'

'She's married again and gone to live in Newcastle with her second husband. We've drifted apart. She's got three stepchildren and several step-grandchildren now, whom she loves dearly. She does a lot for them. Martin always made it difficult for me and Gabby to have much to do with her, pushed us apart. When things settle down again I'll try to rebuild bridges with her. She knows I'm hiding from Martin.'

Luke said it before he could stop himself. 'Can you not go to take refuge with her now?'

'That'd play into my ex's hands. He keeps an eye on her, in case I go there. Before I blocked him completely, he used to send me photos of her that he'd taken sneakily when he was travelling round there for his job, and taunt me about him seeing her and me not. She's mentioned seeing him in the distance at shopping centres sometimes but said he's never come across to speak to her.'

'He sounds like a weirdo,' Dee said bluntly.

He saw Gabby take a quick look at the older girl, obviously struck by that succinct summary – which Luke agreed with too, actually.

'Let's play with those board games,' Dee suggested and took Gabby off to set one up on the kitchen table.

When they were alone again, Luke asked, 'Is your ex a weirdo?'

'Yes. And he seems to be growing weirder as each year passes.'

'That's hard on you.'

'Yes. He started making threats last time he found us and, well, I don't want to put Mum in danger. I email her sometimes and thank goodness I can do that without leaving a trace for him to pick up on.'

'You must miss being with your family at Christmas.'

She sighed and blinked her eyes furiously. 'Yes. Last year was – very quiet.'

'What about the other grandparents, the ones on Martin's side? What are they like?'

'Martin's mother is besotted with him, thinks he hung the moon in the sky and everything is my fault. I'm never quite sure what his father is thinking. Tom's pleasant enough but he's rather reserved. I daren't risk contacting them, even though they used to be very fond of Gabby, because I'm sure Hilary would tell Martin where we are.'

Luke didn't think he'd ever met someone so completely on her own in the world. And yet Claire was a kind woman, the sort who should have a lot of friends. Dee had taken to her at once.

He really wanted to help her. If only she would let him!

She looked at him now as if she knew what he was thinking and for a moment it felt as if they were connected, meant to be friends, more than friends, perhaps. Then she changed the subject abruptly.

'That's enough about my problems. It doesn't do to dwell on them.' She raised her voice again. 'It's getting late, Gabby. Finish that game then get ready for bed. You can take a book up with you and read for a while, if you like.'

When they'd put the game away, and Claire had gone up to settle Gabby, Dee came to get a glass of water. 'I think I'll pick up my emails.'

She disappeared into the small room at the back of the house before she could be left alone with her father, shutting the door firmly behind her.

That upset him.

What had he done wrong? Or, as he was beginning to wonder, what had his ex been saying about him?

The trouble was, he couldn't discuss it with Dee because in spite of being suddenly abandoned by her mother, she still fired up in defence of Angie at the slightest criticism.

He envied Claire her loving relationship with Gabby. He didn't think Dee had any idea how much he loved her, and had no way of making her understand that.

Half an hour later Claire looked at the clock. 'I think I'll follow Gabby up to bed. I'm tired now. I can be ready to leave at whatever time suits you tomorrow, Luke.'

He risked another plea. 'How about staying on for a few more days? You're still not fully recovered and I think Dee's enjoying having some female company. I've not seen her so chatty since she came to live with me. She usually vanishes to fiddle with her computer straight after tea.'

'She's been very good with Gabby, playing all those old-fashioned board games.'

'She's surprised me, I must admit. I didn't know she was so good with little kids. So . . . how about you two staying a bit longer?'

Claire shook her head. 'No. Thanks for the offer, but I can't impose on you. I have to stand on my own feet or – or it won't feel right. I didn't always do that when I was married and after we broke up I vowed I'd never act as a doormat again.'

'I can't imagine you being a doormat.'

'I was sometimes, especially when our quarrelling was likely to upset Gabby. Martin used that against me very skilfully.'

'A few quiet days without worry would help you, though. That arm is still painful, isn't it?'

'Yes, but I live by brainwork not physical labour, so I don't need to do anything that puts it at risk and . . . Luke, I really need to get back to work.'

Her voice was so determined, he gave up trying to persuade her. 'Then there's one small thing I think I can do to help you. I've got an old bolt lying around in my garage and I can fit it to the inside of your front door.'

She opened her mouth to refuse, then shut it again. 'Very well. Thank you. That would be helpful, I must admit. You haven't said what time you want to leave.'

'About ten o'clock. It doesn't matter if it's later.'

'Ten it is. And Luke . . .'

He waited.

'I'm extremely grateful for all you've done for us, truly I am.'

'Will you at least promise me that if you're in trouble, you'll come to me for help?'

'Um, thank you for that offer. Yes, I'll bear it in mind.' She stood up. 'I'll just let Helly out before I go up to bed.'

He doubted Claire would turn to him, whatever happened. She was one stubborn woman.

And very attractive when her green eyes sparkled with determination. There was something going on between the two of them, however much she tried to ignore it. You could usually tell when someone was attracted to you.

He wished . . . oh, he wished for lots of things. Maybe he should write a letter to Santa about them. Only about three weeks to go to Christmas now.

Would Dee agree to do any Christmassy things? He hoped so.

In the morning, he heard Claire get up early and have a shower. By the time Dee left for school, his guest was ready to go home with all but one bag standing ready near the front door. She'd carried them down one-handed. The boxes containing her computer were waiting for him to carry out because they needed two hands. At least she hadn't tried to deal with them.

When she came into the kitchen, he said, 'You seem ready. I can drive you back straight after breakfast, if you like.'

'Yes, I'm all packed, so we might as well.'

He made sure his guests had a good breakfast, but refused to let her help clear up. 'I can do that later. You've enough on your plate.' Then he got out the box of food he'd prepared. 'You brought some food with you, so it's only right you take some back.'

She opened her mouth to protest, then said, 'Thank

you. If you'll put the computer stuff in the car, I just have to get Helly.'

'I'll carry those boxes out, then go and bring her in for you while you check upstairs.'

But when he went out into the garden, he couldn't find the dog. His repairs to the fence between his house and Winifred's were still intact, so he'd have to check the rest of the perimeter.

Claire came to the door. 'Gabby won't be a minute. Oh. Where's Helly? Is something wrong?'

'I think Madame Houdini has escaped again. There must be a weak spot in the fence somewhere else.'

'I shall have to tie her up very carefully when we get back.' She came out to join him. 'You do the back fence and I'll check the other side.'

When Gabby came to the rear door, Claire called to her to wait in the kitchen and fetch Luke if anyone came to the front door.

'Aha! Here's the new escape hatch!' he called from the back fence. 'I think I'll have to replace the whole fence. The wood looks OK but it's completely rotten in places.'

She came across to look at the hole Helly must have made and peer over the fence. 'No sign of her. Do you know the people whose land this is?'

'I've been introduced over the garden fence by Winifred next door and we wave when we see one another, but I've not had much to do with them, been too busy settling in and dealing with Dee. The house is called Dennings.'

He tugged a nearby piece of the fence half-heartedly and stumbled backwards when it came away in his hands.

'Look at that.' He tossed it aside. 'At least we now have an escape hatch that's big enough for humans to get through. Shall we go a-hunting?'

She stepped through the gap and he followed her into the grounds of Dennings. There was no sign of Helly nearby, though.

'I think we'd better visit the big house and introduce ourselves before we go any further,' he suggested. 'We can't just tramp all over their land and they may have seen her.'

'I'll tell Gabby to come and stand by the back fence where we can see her in case Helly comes back on her own.'

How careful she was about her daughter!

That done, they set off down the gentle slope towards the pretty little manor house.

Angus Denning stretched and yawned, then stood up from his computer. Done! He needed to move his body more often. He'd let himself get stiff again.

Nell was looking out of the kitchen window. 'Hey! That dog's come back.' He went across, putting an arm round her shoulders as he too stared out. 'It's not doing any damage. Maybe it'll go home of its own accord.'

'Angus Denning, we are not risking it digging holes in my newly planted garden. There are bulbs and seeds in that area, lying peacefully waiting for the spring. Grab a jacket. We're going out to catch it.'

'Slave driver.' He picked up a few shreds of the ham she'd been chopping up. 'It might come to us more easily with a bribe.'

Outside the dog stared at them for a moment then continued to sniff its way across the garden. Angus walked forward, shaking the ham, and it suddenly whipped round as if it had smelt it.

Crouching, he held out a piece of the meat, but even though it licked its lips, it didn't take the ham from him.

Then someone called, 'Helly! Come here at once!' and two people came hurrying across the garden to join them.

The dog moved across to the newcomers, wagging its tail vigorously.

Angus stood up, popping the ham into his own mouth and saying a bit indistinctly, 'Luke, isn't it?'

'Yes. This is my friend Claire. Angus – Claire – Nell.'

The woman gave a quick nod. 'I'm afraid the dog is mine. I do hope she hasn't done any damage.'

'No. She seems to be enjoying the new smells. She wouldn't take any ham from me, though.'

'She's been trained not to take food from strangers.' She grabbed the dog's collar as she came close, then winced.

Luke took it from her. 'Let me do that. You don't want to do any more damage to your shoulder.'

She turned back to Angus. 'I'm so sorry for the invasion. We were just going to leave when we realised she'd escaped again.'

'No harm done. Nice to meet you.'

He watched them walk away then they went back inside. 'Luke's friend doesn't look well and I think she's got some sort of shoulder injury. She's got a big bruise on her forehead, too.'

'I don't know Luke yet, but I'd say he's attracted to her from the way he looked at her. She was avoiding looking at him.' Nell chuckled. 'Which probably means she's trying not to be attracted.'

He put his arm round his wife. 'Well, now that's settled and I've repelled the fearsome invader, perhaps you'll find me something to eat.'

'Job finished?'

'First stage is sorted out but there's more to do. Only I got up really early and I think I forgot to eat breakfast.'

'You did. There was a bowl of soggy cereal near the kettle.'

'Ah. Perhaps you'll feed me something more substantial, kind lady.'

'Only if you sit down and eat it here. If I bring it into the office, you'll forget to finish it.'

'Such a bully you are.' He pulled her close, dropped a quick kiss on her nose and then sat down at the table, arms folded. 'Your word is my command.'

Luke fastened Helly's lead to her collar and they walked back towards the house.

'This fence is in nearly as shocking a state as the one at my place,' she said.

'I've got some pieces of wood. Maybe I can improve on your side fence a little.'

She stopped walking for a moment. 'Why are you being so kind to me? What do you want?'

'To get to know you better, become friends. I've been quite open about that. Do I have to have an ulterior motive as well?'

She flushed. 'I'm just – not used to altruistic kindness.'

'Call it an early start on the Christmas spirit, if you prefer. Or . . . the usual way a single man behaves when he meets an attractive woman.'

'Oh.' She had grown out of the habit of expecting

kindness from anyone and she couldn't remember the last time someone had called her attractive. She could feel that she was still blushing, so stepped hastily over the remains of the fence panel and hurried into the house. 'Gabby? Where have you got to? I said to wait by the fence.'

Gabby came out of the kitchen, peering over the bannisters to look down to the basement. 'I had to use the bathroom.'

'Well, get ready to go now.'

The child scowled. 'You said we didn't have to leave till ten o'clock.'

'Since we're ready we might as well go and let Mr Morgan get on with his day.'

'He said I could call him Luke.'

'Luke, then. Go and do a final check. Remember, if you leave anything behind—'

'—you lose it.'

'Exactly.'

It took all Claire's courage to hold her aching head up and walk out to the car.

She admitted to herself that she didn't want to leave either.

And that she found him very attractive.

Luke decided to use his old transit van to take them back because it was bigger than his car and he could not only fit their possessions in it more easily, but also the planks to repair the fence with and some tools. Fortunately, there was a bench with a seat belt at one side of the back where Gabby could sit and hold Helly's lead.

It took just over half an hour to drive to Bartons End and only Gabby did any chatting, commenting on places they passed or people she saw through the side windows, or else asking questions.

When Luke stopped at some traffic lights, he stole a quick glance at Claire without her noticing. She looked pale, but grim and determined, and he'd tried all the arguments he could think of to persuade her to stay, but failed to change her mind. Pity.

When they reached the village, Gabby said, 'The other children will be at school. Am I going there this afternoon, Mum?'

'No. You can go again on Monday. We'll tell them you've not been well. I'll write you a note and—'

Luke turned the corner that led to their house and jammed on his brakes. 'What the hell—?'

Before he could stop her, Claire had flung open the car door and jumped out, racing towards her house from the side, so he stopped the engine and said, 'Keep Helly in the car, Gabby.' He closed his door and that on the passenger side and left his car where it was, rushing across to where police tape was stretched across the entrance to the drive of her house.

On the drive sat the blackened remains of a burnt-out car.

Claire had come to a halt and was standing staring at it, one hand pressed to her mouth. Then her shoulders started shaking and she burst into tears, so what could he do but put his arms round her?

He could have wept for her. What a viciously nasty thing to do. Was it vandals or the ex?

She didn't allow herself to weep for long and when she pulled away, Luke let her go and held out his handkerchief.

'Here. Use this.'

'Thanks.'

As she began to mop her eyes, there was the sound of heavy footsteps crunching on gravel. He swung round to see a large man in a dirty overall and well-worn boots hurrying towards them from the nearby industrial units.

She quickly wiped away the last of her tears.

'You're the tenant here, aren't you?' the stranger said. 'I've seen you going in and out of the house.'

'Yes. I'm Claire.'

'I'm Bill Turner. Electrician. Shame about your car. The world seems to be full of vandals these days. What do they get out of destroying things, that's what I want to know?'

'When did it happen?'

'It must have been after everyone went home for the day, not last night but the night before. The woman in the end unit was working late and saw it burning so called the police. She didn't see who set it alight, though, didn't see or hear a car even. Well, it's pretty deserted round here after dark, isn't it?'

Claire sniffed and wiped her eyes, and seemed to be struggling for words, so Luke asked the obvious question for her. 'Did the police have any idea who might have done this? I mean, sometimes they know about local gangs.'

'I don't think so. They came round yesterday morning to ask if anyone knew where you were. Only, no one did. They also asked if we'd seen anyone loitering in the past few days. Only, again no one had. Pity.'

'Yes. Great pity.'

'They left these with everyone and said to tell you to get in touch with them if you came back.' He held out a business card. 'They want to know if you've got anything on your security camera.'

Claire took it from him. 'I'll, um, go and see the police after I've checked the inside of the house.'

'The police didn't go inside, said they didn't want to break down the door, but they looked in through all the windows and said the house didn't seem to have been trashed except for a brick hurled through the kitchen window. You should probably contact them before you go in, just in case there's any evidence to be found.'

Someone yelled across from the units that Bill was wanted on the phone and he left them to it, shouting, 'Good luck!' as he hurried away.

'That means someone did this the night you took me away.' She shuddered.

'We were lucky, eh? Got you away in time.' Luke studied her house in disgust. It was even more ramshackle when you saw it by daylight.

'I don't understand why the police said that. I don't have a security camera.'

As he studied the front of the house, the sun reflected off something above the door. If hadn't been for the sun catching it at just the right angle, he'd not have noticed it. He stepped to one side and then back again, studying it, then pointed. 'That looks like one to me.'

She looked at where he was pointing.

'It may be. But *I* didn't put the camera there and it definitely wasn't there when I left to pick up Gabby from school. I'd have noticed.'

She clapped one hand to her mouth and looked to be holding back tears. 'It has to be Martin who did this. He's used concealed cameras before to keep watch on what I was doing, so now I keep my eyes open and look round every day. It wasn't there that afternoon, I'd stake my life on that.'

'Oh, hell. He must have wanted to see your reaction to the burnt car. He has to be totally crazy.'

A small whimper of distress escaped her control. 'That means he's found us. What am I going to *do*? How can I ever get away from him permanently? I've been so *careful* not to leave a trail this time. Even my car is in a friend's name.'

'We'll work something out, but first, I'm going to get my small ladder out of the van and take that camera down. Maybe he's left fingerprints on it.'

'Ha! Not Martin.'

'Well, anyway, I'll make sure the camera's not showing anything about you from now on.'

When he got to his van, he turned to study the angles the camera would probably be able to cover. Good. Unless he was much mistaken, his van was out of its range, so if it had been broadcasting any images, her ex wouldn't be able to trace him by the registration or the logo on the side of his vehicle. He'd used the van in his former business and not bothered to get it repainted yet because he mostly used his car.

He made sure the child and dog were still all right, telling Gabby it'd be better if she stayed where she was. She was sitting hunched up, and her face seemed too old and careworn for an eight-year-old child. This pitiful excuse for a father obviously didn't care what stress he put them both under.

'What are we going to do without a car, Luke? We're too far from the shops to walk,' said Gabby.

'We'll work that out later. For the moment you're leaving this place and coming back to stay with me again. I've got plenty of room.' That was a no-brainer and whatever it took, he'd persuade Claire to do it, if only as an interim measure.

Gabby brightened a little. 'Oh, good. I feel safe at your house.'

'Don't let that dog out. We'll come back in a few minutes.'

As he set the ladder down at the front door of the house, he turned to Claire. 'I don't think he could have caught my van on that camera. It seems to be set to cover the parking area and entrance to the house, but it can't film round the corner into the side street, can it? Good thing I stopped short of the house when you jumped out of the van so suddenly, eh?'

She looked at him as if this made no sense to her.

'My van has a logo on it as well as the registration plate. He could have used either of them to trace me. If he hasn't seen it that means you should still be safe coming back to stay at my house. You shouldn't even try to live on your own till he's been caught. It's only one step from where he is now to really dangerous behaviour.'

He saw her shudder and let that sink in before continuing. 'He'll have a sophisticated security system plus me to deal with if he tries to get into my house.'

As she opened her mouth to protest, he said, 'I'm not taking no for an answer, Claire. You're both coming back with me and that's that. There are times to manage on your own and times to admit you need help.' He could see the moment she gave in.

Her voice wobbled as she asked, 'Are you sure?'

'Yes. Very. I'm not leaving you and Gabby at some lunatic's mercy.'

She swallowed hard. 'Very well. I'll come back with you. We'll try not to be any trouble. Just till I can work out what to do, mind.'

'But we'll go to the police first and tell them about your ex.'

'No. Martin will expect us to do that. He'll go and see them in a day or two, pretend to be worried about Gabby, might even persuade them to tell him where I am. He's loosened people's tongues like that before. He can be very convincing. Let's just . . . move on. It's only the loss of a car to the police, and an old one at that. They won't make finding whoever set fire to it a priority. And I paid for it so my friend won't be out of pocket.'

'But the police might consider an attack on a woman and child more of a priority if you tell them what was really behind it all.'

'I won't be able to prove it. Martin won't have left any clues, believe me. He's always thorough, good at details.'

She wasn't a stupid woman so Luke was inclined to put faith in her judgement about the situation. Anyway, she was right: the police were overloaded with cases. But *he* had time to spare. Not to mention a very secure house – well, it would be secure once the fence was fixed and the security system switched on again at night and when they were out. He'd been lax about doing that since Dee came to live with him.

He wanted to help Claire even more after this discovery. What that man was doing was . . . shameful. Any decent person would be disgusted.

He covered the camera lens with a cloth as he took it down, trying not to get his own fingerprints on it, and put it in the back of his car. It was quite a sophisticated model, must have been expensive. It might be useful as evidence, who knew?

'We'll go home now, eh?' He didn't wait for her to answer but half turned in his seat and smiled at the child. 'You all right in the back there, Gabby?'

'Yes, Luke.'

But even Gabby was subdued on the way back. The anxious look seemed to have settled on her face, all the bubbly chatter extinguished. He hated to see that, hated to see the way Claire was drooping, as if she was heavy with despair.

Some people seemed to stir up angst all around them, as he'd found to his cost. But his ex wasn't in the same league as this woman's ex.

Then a sudden thought cheered him up. Maybe he could persuade Claire to stay until the new year. They could spend Christmas together. That would help him with Dee, as well as banishing the loneliness.

Chapter Nine

As he was driving home, Luke saw a small country pub advertising lunches. It was an attractive-looking place and on impulse he turned in to the car park. 'Let's go in here and get something to eat. I'm ravenous.'

'Are you sure? You must have better things to do with your time than run round all day after me.'

'Actually, no. I've recently sold my business for a very handsome sum, so there's nothing else that desperately needs doing, except for arranging to have a new fence erected.' He held up one hand to forestall her protest. 'And I'd need that whether Helly was visiting me or not, so don't start feeling guilty about it.'

As they walked towards the entrance, Gabby took her mother's hand and after giving him a shy smile, slipped her other hand into his. She got him in the heart every time she did that. Such a small, soft hand.

Of course, the pub had its Christmas decorations up,

with a tree full of winking lights to one side.

Gabby stopped to smile at them. 'Isn't it lovely? We used to have a Christmas tree with lights on, didn't we, Mum?'

'Yes, love, and we'll have one again after we settle somewhere.'

'I might have one somewhere,' Luke said. 'I just dumped things I'd not be using when I moved into Peppercorn Street. I'd forgotten about decorating the house. We'll get Dee on to that and how about you help her, Gabby?'

The child smiled and gave a happy skip at that, the anxious look fading still more. It took so little to make her happy. She hadn't learnt to be greedy or to feel entitled to anything. That was refreshing, what Christmas was really about, being kind to one another, small joys.

There was a group in the pub having an early Christmas lunch party at one side of the big room, but they found a free table away from the noise and near a window. He went to the bar to get some big cards from below a sign saying '*Pick up your menus here*' and brought them across after ordering three lemon, lime and bitters on an impulse.

'We'll all choose our very favourite dish to cheer ourselves up.' He passed out the menus.

Claire shot him a quick glance and he put his hand over hers on the table. 'No cheating. Price isn't important. I want you to have your very favourite meal.' He could see Gabby brighten a little and he nudged Claire, giving his head a little jerk in her daughter's direction.

She quickly realised what he was telling her, and said, 'I bet I can guess what my daughter will choose. I don't have to think twice about mine either. I'd like a chicken curry. I haven't had one for ages. What's your favourite, Luke?'

'Rack of lamb with roast potatoes.'

They both waited as Gabby studied the menu, looking cheerful and taking her time before choosing a child's beef burger and chips, 'With lots and lots of tomato sauce.'

Claire mouthed 'Thank you' at him.

When their drinks were brought across from the bar, he apologised for ordering without asking what they wanted. 'It's my favourite non-alcoholic drink, one Dee and I both love, so I ordered it automatically.'

'I've never tried it before.' Gabby took a sip of hers and beamed at him. 'Oh, yes, I like it too.'

They could have been any family out for a treat. He'd even temporarily banished some of the anxiety from their faces, but it was still lurking in their eyes, and in the way Claire scanned the room from time to time.

But it would do them no harm to eat a good meal and he deliberately led the conversation into what decorations they would need for his house, asking Gabby's advice.

He caught Claire studying him as he did that, again with that faintly puzzled air. Well, as far as he was concerned Christmas decorations were mainly there to delight children. He hadn't bothered when there was just him, but now he had two children to think of and he'd enjoy making them happy.

'We'll stop and buy some proper food for Helly on the way back as well as for ourselves,' he said as they walked outside. 'What's her favourite meal, Gabby?'

She laughed. 'Any sort of food. Mum says her father must have been a magician because she can make food disappear so fast.'

The dog was fast asleep in the driving seat but when she

was woken by their voices, she sat up and put her paws on the steering wheel as if about to drive off, which made them all chuckle.

He kept wishing they really were a family, with the addition of Dee, of course. He'd always wanted more than one child.

Claire's ex hadn't deserved these two.

And they didn't deserve to be harassed. That could hurt as much as physical violence.

Now that he knew her better, it was his guess that Claire had been worrying about more than the dog when she ran out in front of his car.

Every time he saw the bruise on her face or Gabby's expression turn anxious, Luke felt anger sizzle through him at the man responsible for their troubles.

Every time he made them smile, he felt a sense of achievement. He'd have to see what a proper Christmas did for them all.

It took him a few minutes to realise that the thought of that was raising his own spirits as well.

Chapter Ten

As they turned in to Peppercorn Street, Gabby exclaimed, 'Hurrah! I like living here.' Luke could see her happy expression in the rear-view mirror. After the garage door had rolled shut behind them she relaxed even more and he heard her whisper to the dog, 'We're home, Helly. Home.'

Dee must have run down the kitchen stairs when she saw them turn into the drive because she came into the garage almost immediately to greet them, something she had never done before to Luke. After a quick glance into the van, she ran round it to open the back doors and help Gabby out, giving her a big hug.

'You came back. Oh, I'm so glad.'

'We had to. Somebody burnt our car.'

Dee gasped and looked at her father for confirmation.

'Unfortunately it's true.'

'Oh, how awful. You poor things.'

Helly began trying to push Gabby away from the van

door and he yelled, 'Don't let that dog escape! We haven't got a proper fence in the back yet!'

Dee grabbed the dog's lead and held her firmly. Then the child slipped her hand into his daughter's, looking up at her with adoring eyes, and that brought a lump to his throat. He prayed Dee would let her keep hold, and she did. Holding onto someone clearly meant a lot to that child.

He watched Dee stare down at their joined hands, then at Gabby's face and back again to the hands. She smiled too. Maybe the gesture meant a lot to her as well. She'd hardly touched him since she came home. She seemed to be holding the whole world at bay and he didn't know how best to break down her invisible barriers.

Could this child help him do it?

'Will you two take the dog out into the back garden before you come upstairs, please?' he called. 'She's been shut up for rather a long time. Don't let her off the lead, though.' He must get that new fence installed ASAP. He knew a guy who had just set up a fencing business and wondered if Josh would have time to do it straight away.

'Come on.' Dee moved towards the garden, still holding both Gabby and the dog.

Claire had also been watching them and turned to Luke after they'd gone. 'I'm a bit concerned about how close those two are getting. It upset them both when we left today. What will they do when we leave here after Christmas if they grow even closer in the meantime?'

'We'll worry about that when the time comes. There's always email to keep us in touch and who said we couldn't meet up from time to time? Actually, I don't want to break the connection with you, either.'

'Oh.'

'Look, since you came to stay with us my daughter has come out from behind her barriers and it's the first time that's happened in the weeks since she's been living with me. It makes me happy to see that and more hopeful about our future together. It's a two-way street between you and me, you know: you're helping me as well. You and your daughter have somehow provided a key to unlocking some of Dee's defences, and if this is the result of you being here, I hope you'll stay for a long time.'

'Oh. Well, I'm glad we're not merely a burden to you.'

'No, definitely not a burden at all.'

She too looked more relaxed as that sank in and added, 'And I'm quite a good cook.'

'Good. I can manage, but I'm very average. I'll let you take over some of the cooking if your shoulder will stand it, and I'll be your chopping up assistant if needed.'

He walked round as she got out of the van, picked up one of her bags and led the way up the stairs into the main house. He stopped before they went into the kitchen and dared to squeeze her hand. 'You don't need to be alone in the world, Claire, and I'm really glad to have you here because I've been lonely, too.'

He didn't need to say 'like you have'. He'd stared loneliness in the face many a time after getting home from work to an empty house, and could recognise it in other people. Fate had given him a welcome gift when it threw them together. He meant to give this situation a chance, see where else it could lead.

She touched his cheek in an almost motherly gesture and

gave him a gently luminous smile, so he continued to clasp her hand for a little longer. Then, not wanting to push his luck, he let go and led the way into the kitchen.

'Now, would you be able to put the kettle on and brew a pot of tea while I unload the car?'

'Yes.'

The fact that she didn't protest or try to help him unload probably meant that her shoulder was hurting again. She'd done too much today. He decided to make it plain that she wasn't fooling him, so when he brought up the first computer box, he said, 'If you think I haven't noticed you favouring that shoulder today, you can think again. It's bound to be hurting.'

'You don't miss a thing, do you, Luke Morgan?'

She hadn't said it as if she was all that upset, so he risked saying, 'I try not to. Please don't refuse my help, Claire.'

'You make it hard to. It takes some getting used to. I've never met anyone like you before.'

'And I've never met anyone like you, either. I mean that in a complimentary way. So brave about your difficulties.'

They had another of those moments of staring at one another in a silence filled with unspoken words, then he carried on unloading the car.

She put the kettle on, got out some mugs and found some biscuits.

He finished the unloading and caught her staring into space so left her in peace and went to unpack her computer and set it up again in the dining room.

When the two girls came in with the dog, rosy-cheeked and laughing at something, not only did the younger child look a lot happier, but so did Dee.

'Would you like a bedroom of your own, Gabby?' he asked. 'There's one next to Dee's.'

But that was a step too far. She shook her head instantly and shrank back towards her mother. He could have kicked himself for putting that look of panic back on her face.

'I was only trying to make you more comfortable,' he said softly. 'You can sleep where you want, standing on your head in a corner if that's what you prefer.'

She laughed at that and he dared add, 'This is a big house, but wherever you are in it, I'll hear you if you shout for help and I'll come running.'

'So will I,' Dee added, actually standing by his side and leaning against him as she spoke.

He suddenly realised that if he wanted one Christmas gift, it was to regain his daughter's love and trust, fully regain it. And if he could be granted two gifts, the second one would be to have Claire and her daughter staying on here . . . and who knew where that might lead?

He'd do what he could to make both wishes come true.

It had taken longer for Luke to unpack the computer and then do the physical work of setting it up than it would take her to unpack her personal possessions, Claire thought as she finished setting out the mugs. She hadn't even got a pretty outfit to wear for Christmas, nor had Gabby. Maybe they could find something in a charity shop. She'd got some good bargains in such places.

She didn't let herself dwell on that. It would be enough for them to stay safe for Christmas. She couldn't afford new clothes and Gabby didn't care about them. She wondered, as she had many times before, what Martin had done with all the clothes she'd had to leave behind. Gabby's would be too small by now, of course, but she'd owned some pretty outfits.

Had he destroyed her clothes and possessions? Probably.

Oh, get over it, she told herself. *No use pining over the past. Concentrate on the future.*

She finished fixing up all the connections on her computer and was pleased to get online again. As she checked her bank account, she relaxed still more. The payment for the big job had now been deposited. Thank goodness for that. She would be able to afford to pay for their share of the groceries while they were here, at least. She couldn't just take, take, take. Even from Luke.

The emails waiting for her were mostly spam or to do with business. There was one from the friend who was the nominal owner of her car, worrying about them. She sent off a quick email to say they'd found refuge with a new friend and had an accident with the car, but didn't give any details.

There was another message from her mother, telling her about a party she and Ralph were giving for Christmas and wishing Claire and Gabby could join them. They had a spare bedroom, and she could give them some petrol money.

Wasn't going to happen. She wasn't putting her mother at risk.

But she wished they could take up the invitation. Gabby should be going to family parties and having fun at sleepovers with friends. Instead, the poor child had been uprooted three times in the past eighteen months and had to change school twice. Who knew when they'd be able to settle permanently somewhere? Or for how long their next temporary home would be safe from Martin?

Then she noticed a PS on her mother's email below the pretty flower image that framed the signature: *Tom Douglas has been in touch with me.*

She stopped reading for a moment in shock. Why would her father-in-law want to get in touch? Was this another of Martin's ploys? She braced herself and read on.

> *He's worried about you and Gabby. He asked me to tell you that he's unhappy about what his son is doing, and he wonders if he could meet you sometime to discuss the situation. He'd not tell Martin about it.*
>
> *What shall I say to him? Or would you like to contact him directly? This is his email address. And what is his horrible son doing now? Surely Martin's stopped pestering you? I haven't seen him at the shops recently and thank goodness for that. Perhaps he's no longer coming up to the north on business.*

Claire didn't even try to answer the email straight away. She would work out what to tell her mother tomorrow when she wasn't too tired to say it tactfully. She didn't want her mother to worry about the latest incident.

But no way was she letting her father-in-law know where she was, or meeting Tom. Even if *he* didn't pass the information on to his son, his wife would if she got hold of it.

She doubted Hilary would have changed about that. The woman had never been able to see any real faults in Martin, often dismissing unkind things he'd done with remarks like, 'He must have been having an off day. We all have those. No one is perfect, you know.'

Pity she couldn't trust her in-laws, though, for Gabby's sake. Her daughter had mentioned them a few times at first after they fled from Martin. She hadn't said a word about them for a while now, though.

Christmas would probably remind the poor child of them again because her in-laws had always bought her lovely presents and made much of her. There would be very few gifts this year, like last year. Only what she could afford, probably a pretty top and a book. She wouldn't even dare let her own mother send anything but an email link to a gift token, because she didn't want even her to know where they were.

Martin had often boasted of his skill at hacking into accounts and had proved that his boasts weren't lies since they split up. Though he hadn't found her new account, thank goodness.

Where would she and her daughter go after Christmas? She couldn't impose on Luke for too long, however kind he was. Even three weeks was a big ask.

Well, she'd worry about that later. At least now she could give Gabby some sort of Christmas.

She hoped she would be able to help soften the difficulties between Luke and his teenage daughter while they were here. That would indeed help repay him, she was sure. He was a very caring man and she'd seen for herself how stiff Dee was with him sometimes.

Maybe she could bake a few special Christmassy things for them all as well. She wasn't a bad cook when she had the ingredients.

Christmas ought to be special, full of joy, a time for families to get together.

The security camera worked well and Martin had watched from a distance as his wife discovered her burnt-out car and burst into tears. Serve the bitch right for taking his daughter away from him, he thought gleefully.

Then a man came into view, putting his arm round Claire's shoulders in a familiar gesture, as if he cared about her. And she didn't pull away.

It felt as if Martin's skull would explode with anger at that and it took him a minute or two to regain control of himself.

Where was his daughter at the moment? She wasn't at school and they hadn't been at home for the last two nights or they'd have found the burnt-out car sooner. Had they been staying at this man's house? His daughter would presumably have been left to her own devices there while Claire cosied up to her lover.

He had to find out where she was and take his daughter away from her immorality. Had to make sure the child had a well-structured life again, with proper patterns of behaviour established.

The man walked out of sight, reappearing with a ladder. Surely he couldn't have – but yes, he had discovered the camera, damn him! The transmission suddenly blurred and cut off.

How the hell had they discovered it? He'd hidden the camera so carefully under the edge of the roof tiles, covering most of it with cobwebs and nearby muck.

Well, this was only a setback. He'd find them again, whatever it took.

He'd be the one to do the disappearing trick then. But with his daughter. And he'd have the money from the house sale, plus some other funds he'd put together in the past couple of years.

His move to another country would need planning in careful detail. Unfortunately, with it being near Christmas, the settlement would be slowed down.

He got into bed thinking, *Just you wait, Claire, damn you! You're in for a big shock. You're not taking my daughter away from me. I'm taking her away from you.*

He was still smiling as he felt himself slipping into sleep.

Chapter Eleven

Claire woke early and lay there, warmly cocooned, listening to the faint sounds of a sleeping household. Occasional louder noises drifted up from the streets: a car starting up or footsteps running along the pavement outside, as if someone was starting the day by exercising, even in the winter darkness.

She looked at the bedside clock, its numerals showing in bright green that it was six o'clock in the morning. She'd slept straight through the night, a very rare thing for her.

The lamp she'd left switched on in one corner showed that Gabby was still asleep in the other bed. This wasn't a school day, so presumably Dee wouldn't get up until later than usual. What time did Luke start his day? How long dare she linger in bed herself? She was tempted to stay for a while. Very tempted.

On the floor between the beds, Helly was watching

her but not trying to get onto the bed or ask to go out, thank goodness.

No one else seemed to be stirring, so Claire padded to their bathroom, marvelling at how warm the whole house was. Then she gave in to temptation and got back into bed, snuggling down with a happy murmur.

When she woke again it was nine o'clock, Helly was no longer there and Gabby's bed was empty with the covers thrown back.

She listened and could hear sounds from downstairs in the kitchen. Was Gabby there? Highly likely. She went to the top of the stairs and heard her voice. Since she trusted both Luke and Dee to keep an eye on her daughter, she had a quick shower and got dressed, looking at herself ruefully in the mirror. Her jeans were old, the top had been mended and the sweater darned, but they were clean and hardly creased at all, which was the best she could achieve sartorially.

Her shoulder was feeling a little better and her headache seemed to have gone completely, which was a relief.

She went downstairs to join the others, opening the kitchen door quietly and staying where she was, enjoying the scene before her. Gabby had her back to the door and was spreading jam with great care on a piece of toast, Dee was chatting to her and Luke was watching them both with an indulgent expression on his face. The dog was watching Gabby's every move in case any titbits fell down on the floor.

It was Luke who first noticed Claire's presence and gave her a lazy smile. 'Welcome to what's left of the morning, sleepyhead.'

Gabby turned round, rushing across to give her mother a kiss. 'Me an' Helly tiptoed out an' let you sleep.'

'Thank you, darling.'

Dee had turned round and was smiling as well. She was pretty when she smiled, or would be without the black clothes. 'Shall I make you some toast and get you some fruit? And do I call you Mrs Small or Claire?'

'Claire. Breakfast would be lovely. Whatever's handy will be fine, thank you.' She moved towards the table. 'I'm sorry to be so lazy, Luke. You should have woken me.'

'Why? You obviously needed a good long sleep and no one needed to go anywhere or do anything in a hurry. Sit down and relax.' He reached out for her hand and pulled her into the chair next to him. 'Our waitresses will see to the food.'

Gabby's giggle filled her with delight and before she could stop herself, she'd whispered to him, 'I'd give anything to keep her happy like this.'

'To keep both of them that happy,' he replied in an equally low voice, then added more loudly, 'We've decided to have a peaceful day and if you feel like a short stroll in the late afternoon, we can amble down to Saffron Lane. The café there does wonderful cakes, and it's Winifred next door who usually bakes them. Most of the tourists and visitors will have left by then.'

'Winifred's the older lady next door, right?'

'Yes. It's not everyone who can start a new career at eighty-five, is it, and a very successful one, too. She makes the most delicious cakes I've ever tasted and produces them for the café.'

'What's the draw at this Saffron Lane?'

'It's a small artists' colony set up by Angus and Nell – last year, I think. There's a group of six renovated houses from the early twentieth century. They were requisitioned for security work during World War II and not given back to the Denning family for several decades afterwards, so they escaped demolition and smaller houses being crammed together on the site. Strange how the effects of the war still linger in some places, isn't it?'

'Amazing.'

'The houses are now inhabited by artists of various persuasions, who are the main but not the only people selling their work in the gallery at the café. There are some beautiful things to see, even if we don't buy anything.'

'Sounds like an interesting place, especially if it's close enough to walk to.'

'It is. And there's a small museum on site, too, a secret communications centre from the war with hidden passages under it. The government set up places like that in case of invasion. This one was somehow forgotten and has remained completely untouched. It's rapidly becoming a feature of this town for those who enjoy their history. I've been meaning to go round it ever since I moved here. I don't know why I haven't.'

'Perhaps we'd better not go there, though, if a lot of people visit it. I don't want to run into anyone I know.'

'I think you'll be quite safe and we'll be going at the quiet time of day, after the rush has passed.' He grinned suddenly. 'Dee and Gabby have already decided they're going to pretend to be sisters whenever we go out, and that you and I have to pretend to be married.'

She was a bit surprised at this and must have shown it.

He shrugged. 'Your ex won't be looking for two sisters, will he? So to back up the girls, we have to pretend to be married. Besides, he doesn't sound like the sort of person to go to art galleries, even if he knew you were living in Sexton Bassett, which he doesn't. He won't have any way of tying you to this town.'

'Hmm. You're right. He's definitely not interested in art and he'd throw a fit at the idea of wasting his precious time at a gallery or museum. He's very scornful about artists, doesn't even care about books or movies, except for reference books. The only things he thinks worthwhile are science and technology, and their contribution to the shaping of the modern world. He can rabbit on for hours about that.'

'Rabbit on!' He chuckled. 'I like that expression. My aunt used to use it when people talked too much. Mind you, I do think science and technology are interesting and important, but they're not the only disciplines humanity needs. What I enjoy most is architecture.'

'Dad's an expert on the history of conservatories and he's going to write a book about it,' Dee put in.

He flushed and looked at Claire apologetically. 'I know quite a bit about conservatories because that was what my company built. I'd like to write a book on the topic, just a small book with photos – a coffee table book rather than a learned tome. I've collected some lovely photos over the years and people might enjoy looking at them.'

'Sounds interesting.'

'I think it is. Conservatories go back a long way, you know, though they weren't always called by that name: orangeries, greenhouses, sunrooms, take your pick.'

* * *

It was cute how he modest he was, blushing like that, Claire thought. And how long was it since she'd had an interesting, adult conversation as they were having now? She loved finding out new things so followed up with, 'How long ago did people start building conservatories, then?'

'Wealthy landowners built them from about the sixteenth century onwards; middle-class people didn't usually manage to get them till the nineteenth century, and there was an increase in building them around the 1970s for all sorts of people.' He broke off. 'Don't get me started or I'll bombard you with information and bore you to death.'

'I don't think you could ever bore me, Luke.'

'I hope not.'

They stared at one another again, well, they did until they were interrupted by Gabby clearing her throat to get their attention. 'Breakfast is served.' As Dee mimed applauding her, she giggled and put a dish of fruit salad down carefully in front of her mother.

'Thank you, darling.'

Dee placed a small pot of yoghurt nearby and said, 'This is the first course, Claire. Please save some room for the toast. Dad always buys the best jams you've ever tasted. He has a whole shelf of jars he's bought from farms and markets all over the country.'

He rolled his eyes. 'OK, I admit it. I have a weakness for toast with real fruit jam, not coloured, thickened sugar. So sue me.'

From the way he shot a quick glance at Dee, he seemed both surprised and grateful to have received a compliment from his daughter, Claire thought. Another step in the right direction.

Hadn't Dee shown her pride in him before? She ought to have done. He was a lovely man.

In the middle of the afternoon, Luke persuaded them all to put on their coats and scarves and go out for a walk.

Dee pulled a face. 'I'm not sure I want to go. Mum always said history wasn't very interesting.'

Luke looked so annoyed, Claire said hastily, 'I find historical places very interesting. Perhaps your mother hasn't had time to find good ones to explore.'

She saw the exact moment when Dee noticed Gabby's disappointment and was glad when the girl added in an off-hand voice, 'Oh, why not? I'll be in good company, whatever the place is like.'

The child's face lit up and Dee lost her grudging look, giving Gabby a quick hug.

That warmed Claire's heart, as did the way Gabby slipped her hand into Dee's as they walked along. She held her breath but her daughter was allowed to leave it there and the two girls began chatting about some pop star she'd never even heard of.

Dealing with teenagers could be like treading on eggs sometimes. You had to be very careful not to break the shells, because they were more fragile than they looked.

Luke also watched the interaction between the girls and had a sudden foolish longing for someone to hold his hand, Claire for preference. But of course she didn't. And he couldn't push himself on her.

He led the way down the slope from the top end of Peppercorn Street, walking briskly and pointing out the pretty entrance to the big house on the right, then going on to the small street on the left at the lower end of his land.

A car with four people in it was just pulling away as they arrived, leaving only one car parked there, so the café was almost empty. Nell looked up from behind the counter and smiled a greeting and mimed 'just a minute'. She put two mugs of fancy coffee on the counter and then got plates out and put pieces of cake on them, presumably for the two young women sitting in a corner.

'We'll look at the museum first, if that's all right with you, Nell,' Luke called to her. 'After we've done we'll come and try some of the chocolate cake that's winking at me from the display.'

'Good choice. It's my own favourite.'

He put the money for the museum fee on the counter and led the way upstairs. There they were shown round the communications room by a cheerful young man who lived in one of the houses, and he explained how it had worked.

After that, to both children's excitement, their guide asked if they wanted to go down into the secret passage below ground.

'Can we really?' Dee asked.

His daughter had completely forgotten to be bored from the minute they came up here, Luke noticed in amusement. Well, who could be bored with Gabby asking a dozen questions a minute and a real secret passage to explore?

When they returned to the café and gallery on the ground floor, they chose cake and drinks, then wandered round the displays as they waited for it to be served.

Gabby stood entranced next to a little metal ornament of an imaginary breed of dog whose tail was on a spring and wagged at the slightest touch. If she and her mother were still there at Christmas, Luke decided, he'd buy it for her.

'Dad.'

He turned to see that Dee was holding a bright patchwork cushion.

She shot him a quick but strangely hesitant glance. 'Could you lend me some money to buy this, please? I don't have enough with me. I'll pay you back when we get home, I promise. It'll be just the thing to brighten up my bedroom.'

'It's gorgeous but I'd much rather buy it for you as a present. You don't often ask me for anything and fathers do like to buy things their daughters . . . given the chance.'

She gave one of her almost-frowns as if surprised by this, then nodded. 'Right. Thank you.' But the slightly puzzled expression was back and it lingered on her face for a while.

He didn't let himself ask what or who had made her think he didn't want to buy her presents, but he could guess.

When they'd finished their snack, they walked slowly back up to Peppercorn Street. It had been a lovely outing and Luke wished they could do more of this, not only for his guests' sake, but to help build more connections between himself and Dee.

Her mother hadn't said anything about what Dee was to do at Christmas and anyway, as far as he knew, Angie was still in Spain. He hoped she wouldn't invite Dee to spend the holidays with her. He was enjoying getting to know his daughter better and was mentally starting to plan their Christmas.

He hoped Angie would leave Dee with him permanently, though you could never tell with her. He didn't want to have to go to court to keep his daughter with him, didn't even know whose side Dee would be on about this. But he wanted her to stay, wanted it so very much.

Maybe he should consult his lawyer and find out where he stood.

Maybe he should ask Dee what she wanted before he did anything. Did he dare? What would he do if she said she wanted to go back to her mother?

It'd make for a very miserable Christmas to be without her, and it'd upset Gabby a lot.

Tom's PI visited him at home one evening to report on his preliminary findings. He arranged it for the night his wife met friends for a meal and natter. He preferred to discuss things in private rather than try to take in sensitive information in a noisy venue like a pub.

He asked Eric to park in the street and not to come in until he'd seen Hilary drive away. He didn't want his wife to find out what he was doing, because she'd try to stop him helping Claire. She was most definitely on Martin's side. It was a good thing he'd warned Eric, because she left at the last minute, even later than usual.

Eric didn't waste time on greetings and refused a drink. 'Let's just get on with our information sharing then I'll leave you in peace. It's been a long day. First, I've traced the house where your daughter-in-law and granddaughter were living, but they'd just moved out, I'm afraid.'

'Oh, dear. Do any of the neighbours know where they went and why?'

'There aren't any neighbours; it's an area that's being redeveloped and the other houses have already been knocked down. The house is part of the old industrial estate, really, so I suppose that's why it wasn't knocked down with the first batch of old houses. But it was pretty obvious why your daughter-in-law left. There's a burnt-out car standing on the drive, nicely decorated with police tape, and someone's thrown a brick through the kitchen window at the rear.'

Tom stared at him in horror and his voice came out croaky. 'They weren't hurt, were they?'

'No.'

'Do the police have any idea who did it?'

'No again. There aren't any gangs known to be operating in that area, for the simple reason there isn't much left to steal. Even the industrial units are half empty because they're going to be knocked down and the area redeveloped too.' He paused and added, 'But you and I may be able to suspect who did it.'

Tom knew, he just knew it was Martin, so all he could do was nod.

'You'll be shocked to see what a poor state their house is in. I was surprised anyone had been allowed to live there at all. See for yourself.' He held out his phone, heard the gasp that greeted the photos. 'Look at the next one. It's the remains of their car, which is owned by someone called Pam Dixon, apparently.'

'She's a friend of Claire's, if I remember correctly. Not that they saw much of one another after the marriage. The divorce wrangling made me realise how Martin had gradually stopped his wife from associating with her former friends. Claire fled to Pam's house when she first left my son, I gather from what he's said since and what he threatened to do to both of them one night when he must have been drinking, he was speaking so wildly.'

The PI stared at him. 'You said they *fled*. That's a strong word to use. Why didn't you tell me things were that bad when we first spoke? And what exactly has he been threatening to do to them?'

Tom stared at the floor, shaking his head, feeling embarrassed. 'I was ashamed to use that word. Unfortunately it's very accurate. My granddaughter gave the game away when she told me how they had to creep out of their home with only the clothes they could carry, then take a taxi to Pam's place.'

'Didn't they have a car?'

'Apparently Martin kept both cars in his own name.'

'Does he often threaten to hurt people?'

'Um, sometimes. But he hasn't done it to my knowledge. I thought it was, you know, just spoken in anger. But if he set that car alight . . .'

'It's a criminal act. And actually, it's not normal behaviour to make such threats, whether they're carried out or not. Nor is it normal to treat a wife like that. And what exactly did he threaten the night he was drunk?'

'To get rid of Claire permanently and raise his daughter on his own somewhere far away from bad influences. And . . .'

'Go on.'

'To make Pam sorry she ever crossed his path.'

As Eric opened his mouth, Tom held up one hand in a stop gesture. 'You don't need to tell me that this isn't normal. I've been looking it up online recently, reading about it, trying to understand my son's behaviour. And I know the way things are getting worse isn't a good sign.' To his dismay, his voice wobbled and he had to stop speaking and pull himself together.

His companion gave him a sympathetic look. 'Hard to face in your own family, I should think.'

'Yes. Very hard. Even now, my wife won't admit to anything but minor faults in Martin. *He could be a bit kinder. He's only trying to look after his daughter.* I don't know how to make her face what he's turned into. I'm hoping what you discover will help me do that. And though he definitely needs professional help, he'd fly off the handle and storm out if I even hinted at it.'

'If he's the one who set their car on fire, he needs help rather urgently now, I should think, whether he wants it or not. We don't want him to move on to violent acts towards his wife, do we? These damaged people can be very unpredictable.'

Tom closed his eyes for a moment, trying to find a reason for hoping it wasn't Martin who'd set fire to Claire's car. No, he mustn't fool himself. Who else could it be? He had to accept that, had to face up to it.

So he said it aloud. 'Yes. You're right. It can only have been Martin. Look, will you carry on with this, Eric, and try to find out what's happened to them? They might need help, or money, or protection. Whatever else we do or don't do about Martin, we have to keep them safe.'

'Doesn't Claire have any family to turn to?'

'There's her mother, but she's remarried and when I

contacted her recently, she said she doesn't know where they are either, though she at least has their email address. She won't give me it, though. The most she'd agree to was to pass on a message from me.' He paused, then repeated his plea. 'You will carry on with this?'

'Yes, definitely. I think this is a worthwhile case, one where I can make a difference.' Eric stood up. 'I'll get back to you in a day or two, probably by phone or email. This first time I wanted to see with my own eyes how you took the bad news. Some parents never do face up to what their children have turned into as adults, and I've learnt not to waste my time on them when I can be helping someone who will co-operate.'

He paused on his way out to put his hand on Tom's shoulder and ask sympathetically, 'You going to be all right?'

'I have to be, only I can't help wondering what I did wrong as a father,' Tom admitted.

'I'd say probably nothing, now that I've got to know you a bit better. You seem sane enough to me, and I'm a pretty good judge of character. If it's not their upbringing that's warped them – though that does happen – I think it can be hard-wired into some people to turn violent, or else they've developed abnormal behaviour because of chemical imbalances, often caused by taking drugs, or it can even be the result of accidents or events causing physical and mental damage.'

He gave a little shrug as Tom opened the front door and added, 'I try to keep up with research but medical science is still struggling to find the best ways to deal with many mental health problems. One day they'll have a much better idea of how to treat these damaged people.'

Tom nodded. 'One hopes so. In the meantime I'm truly grateful for your help. Don't forget to send your bill.'

'I will once I've really achieved something.'

When his visitor had driven away, Tom went back into the house and sat for a long time worrying. 'These damaged people,' Eric had said. What could have damaged his son? Was there any hope of helping him?

Hilary wasn't due back for another hour and he wondered yet again whether to say anything to her about this. If he did, would she believe that Martin could be responsible for a burnt-out car or that Claire had needed to flee from him more than once?

Probably not.

So he'd better wait a little longer to tell her. He'd need proof, overwhelming proof that she couldn't dismiss.

Chapter Twelve

On the Saturday morning Bill was in his workshop repairing an old fridge. He'd picked it up on the street verge for nothing, after checking it out and realising how little was wrong with it. He'd sell it later at a knock-down price and still make a good profit.

When a man came to the entrance to his unit and called out, he stood up and moved forward, easing his shoulders, thinking it was a customer.

Instead the man showed him some ID stating that he was a licensed private investigator. 'I wonder if you could spare me a few minutes?'

'What for?' Bill glanced impatiently back at the fridge.

'I'm working for a client, trying to trace the woman and child who lived over there at the house with the burnt-out car in the drive. Shocking thing to see, that.'

Bill was surprised and a bit suspicious. In all the months the woman and child had been living there, no one had visited them that he'd seen. 'Who wants to find them, then?'

'Her family. They're worried about her safety.'

'So they should be, letting her live in that dump for months. It's not safe round here at night unless you've got a good, monitored security system. I've had things nicked in broad daylight, with me working at the back, even. I'd not like one of *my* female relatives to live over there on her own, let alone a young child.'

'I agree. She should be at home with her family. Did you see her come back after the accident to the car?'

'That wasn't an accident, that was deliberate vandalism.'

'Well then, things are even worse, if you're right. Did you see her come back?'

Bill shrugged. 'Might have.'

The man suddenly looked angry, more angry than you'd expect from a PI investigating a case.

'What the hell does that mean? She may be in danger and if you're not telling me something, when you could have helped me find her, you may live to hear bad news and then you'll bear the guilt of that.'

Bill was beginning to dislike the fellow, whose smile was glassy and as false as he'd ever seen. If he was a PI, you'd have expected him to stay calm, surely, so that he could weigh the facts. Only, if he had police ID, surely he must be legit? 'There's nothing to tell. I don't know where they went, and I only ever spoke to them once in all the months they've been living over there, because they kept themselves to themselves.'

'But you noticed them come back this time?'

'I keep my eye on everything that's going on round here and the torched car made me more watchful than usual.

Besides, the police wanted to get in touch with them, so I was passing on a message.'

'The police? Just for a burnt-out car?'

'And the damage to the house. Threw a brick through the window, them sods did, afterwards. I tell you, this area is going downhill fast and I'm moving out myself in a couple of weeks to somewhere safer and busier.'

'What exactly did you notice about them? How did they get back here without their car? For heaven's sake, man, give me a bit of help. I'm trying to keep a little girl safe.'

'Well . . . a guy drove them home.'

'Can you remember anything about him? What sort of car was he driving, for instance?'

'He was driving a transit van with a logo on it.'

'What logo?'

'It belonged to that company that does conservatories. Can't remember their name, but a neighbour of mine had one built by them. Really good job they did for him.'

'What's the name of the company?'

Bill could see the van in his mind but not the name on it. 'I can't remember. Didn't notice that. Sorry.'

'Describe the logo, then.'

'It looks like a rough sketch of a conservatory, grey on the white of the van.'

'Is that all you remember?'

His voice was harsh and he didn't seem at all grateful for the help. Bill scowled at him, regretting now that he'd shared any information about that poor woman. 'Yes, that's all. I've got to get back to work now.'

He watched the man walk away without even a thank you. That seemed strange and his suspicion about the fellow deepened. Where was his car? How could he have got here without one? There was no public transport in the area now.

And Bill suddenly realised another thing: how did the man know the woman had been away from home when the car was torched?

Feeling worried that this chap might have some connection with whoever torched the car, whatever the ID seemed to say about him, Bill ran back into his unit. After locking it up, he drove off in the direction the man had taken, pulling his cap right down to hide his face.

There was only one road still usable, so he had no trouble finding the so-called PI, who was striding along. He overtook him near the far side of the group of industrial units, driving straight past and turning off the road to park behind one of the new houses that were half built. He cut the engine and slid down in the seat to watch where the fellow went.

The man seemed lost in thought and didn't notice Bill. When he stopped, he looked round as if to check there was no one nearby to see him, then quickly got into a big car parked behind a group of tradespeople's vehicles. It was as if he didn't want to be connected to the car.

Bill wondered if he was being foolish and the guy really was trying to help that poor woman, but hey, it wouldn't hurt to get a photo of that car's licence plate, just in case. He quickly did that, then slid down in his seat again before the man drove away.

Should he follow? No. He had work to do. But he couldn't help wondering why the fellow hadn't wanted to be seen after asking questions openly about the woman and child. None of this seemed to make sense and Bill was feeling uneasy about what he'd told him, wished he'd said nothing about the logo.

Should he go to the police? No, there was nothing definite to tell them. There had been ID shown to him, after all, and it had looked legit.

But at least if anyone ever came around asking questions, he'd be able to give them the number plate information which would lead them to the man.

No, nobody would come asking. There hadn't been a sign of the police since the car got burnt. It was only a minor incident to them. He was worrying about nothing. He'd been watching too many crime shows on TV.

He continued to work on the fridge, but he still couldn't get the incident out of his mind, couldn't stop worrying about the woman and child, hoping they were safe.

Ah, he'd be glad to get out of this place, damned glad. It was making him paranoid about security. And he wasn't alone in that. The other people who were still working here said the same thing, especially since the car had been set alight.

They were all being doubly careful, watching out for one another. It was bringing out the best in his neighbours. Must have been like that during the war – for decent folk, anyway.

Eh, that PI had left a bad taste in his mouth, he couldn't work out why. He might ask the others what they thought about it on Monday, particularly whether he should go to the police about his visitor or not. Always good to get a second opinion when you weren't sure what to do.

* * *

When he'd finished the job he'd been working on, Bill hesitated then phoned his best mate and asked him if he fancied a drink.

'Bit early for you, isn't it?'

'I've got something on my mind. Wouldn't mind asking what you think. Just a half.'

'OK. Usual place?'

'Where else?'

At the pub they discussed what had happened and his friend sat frowning, then said, 'I think you should have gone to the police.'

'I couldn't decide.'

'Do it. Burning that woman's car is really bad news.' He drained his beer. 'Come on. We'll do it now.'

The policeman at the counter took notes, frowned and said, 'You're sure about the car number plate?'

Bill pulled out his mobile phone and showed him.

'Can I download that?'

It all took longer than Bill had expected, but he felt better for doing it. Even if they didn't catch that guy, he'd done his best, hadn't he?

You had to feel comfortable inside your own head.

He clapped his friend on the back. 'Thanks. I'll shout you a drink next time.'

On the Sunday, Luke insisted on them all going to an outlet centre to buy some Christmas decorations, but Claire was reluctant to take another day off working, reluctant also to go to such a crowded place.

'I really should be getting on with my next job. The offers slow down for a while after Christmas so I need to do every job I can now.'

'It's still the weekend. Don't you ever take a day off?'

'Not often, no. And I've had a couple of days off because of my shoulder.'

'Well, do it this once for me. I want to decorate the house properly, make it seem like Christmas for Dee – and for your delightful daughter. Aw, come on. We're not likely to bump into your ex at that shopping centre. He lives two hours away, you said. The outing will only take an hour or two.' He paused, then added slyly, 'If you come with us, Dee will let herself enjoy it. Please.'

'Don't you have any Christmas decorations at all?'

'No. I thought I had but I haven't. Angie took the good stuff with her when we split up and I have a vague memory of throwing the rest away the first Christmas that I was on my own. I've not bothered with decorations since. It didn't seem worth it when there was just me.'

Claire kept being reminded that Luke needed company for the festive season just as much as his daughter did, though he might not admit it. He'd been kind to her so the least she could do was return the favour.

From chance remarks he'd made, she was beginning to think he'd been a workaholic after his wife left him, and a very lonely one at that. By choice, or to fill the empty hours? Or because he wanted to make a lot of money? No, he didn't seem to care all that much about money, hardly ever referred to it and didn't live luxuriously.

Although she'd missed adult companionship, she'd not been as lonely as he obviously had, because she'd had Gabby and they'd had fun together in a quiet way, with old-fashioned card games and paper games like Consequences. It sounded as if he'd not even had regular access to his daughter.

When he told the girls what he was proposing, she watched her daughter unobtrusively.

Gabby's face lit up with joy and she jigged up and down on the spot. 'We're going to have a Christmas tree. A real Christmas tree?'

'A big one,' he promised rashly.

'Oh, Luke, that'll look so pretty. I've seen pictures of them in people's houses.'

'Haven't you ever had one?' Dee cast a quick suspicious glance at Claire, as if ready to accuse her of ill-treating her daughter.

Gabby shook her head. 'My dad didn't like them and he gets grumpy if you don't do what he wants, so we didn't bother. All he did was put a wreath on the outside of the front door. It was quite pretty, though it got a bit dusty, but it didn't light up or anything. And you couldn't see it at all from inside the house.'

Claire immediately felt guilty. Once they'd left him, she should have made more effort to decorate the house as other families did. But she'd been so short of money at times that it'd been hard even to buy a present for Gabby. It wasn't that she hadn't been able to get small contract jobs, but in winter the rents and power bills had been so high they'd eaten a big hole in what she earned before she even started buying food and clothes.

Luke smiled at the two girls. 'Well, I haven't had a Christmas tree for years either, so we'll treat ourselves to one and to some all-new, all-shiny decorations to brighten up the whole house, even the bedrooms. It'll be fun putting them up, won't it? You're coming with us to help choose them, aren't you, Dee?'

The older girl had been smiling at Gabby's excitement and this time she took the child's hand, instead of the other way round. 'Of course I am. Can I, um, have some decorations for my bedroom as well, Dad?'

'Yes, of course. I'm counting on you two to help me make the whole house beautiful.'

As Gabby waved her hands about and jumped up and down again, Dee grabbed her hands and swung her round and round till they both crash-landed on the sofa, out of breath and laughing.

Claire felt a lump in her throat at that.

Luke clapped his hands together to get their attention. 'Right, then. We can leave as soon as you lot are ready. We'll go to that big shopping centre on the outskirts of town, shall we?'

'Yes. Come on, little sister, let's get our coats on.'

Gabby gave one of her gurgles of delight. 'Yes, big sister.'

They ran out, pushing and shoving one another.

'It's like a miracle with those two.' Luke looked at Claire and when she didn't say anything, he nudged her. 'Don't you think?'

'Oh, yes.' Her voice came thick with happy tears but he didn't comment, thank goodness.

This whole situation was a miracle for her, too. She hadn't felt so relaxed in ages, or lived in such a comfortable house.

'Let's simply go along with their fun and games. No warnings about not getting involved, no worrying about saving pennies. I've not had anything to spend my money on for years, and the more I earned, the less I could be bothered to spend. And please . . . don't just stay for Christmas but into the new year and we'll celebrate that, too.'

And heaven help her, she couldn't say no. 'All right. As long as Martin doesn't find us, that is. I don't want to put you and Dee in danger.'

He instantly became serious. 'If he does turn up and start causing trouble, you should think about making a stand, Claire, getting the police involved and finding a permanent way to stop him. You can't spend the rest of your life on the run. He has no right to do that to you. You don't deserve it and neither does Gabby.'

'I can't afford to pay lawyers for the necessary help and what's the point when he doesn't pay attention to restraining orders and the police only scold him for it because he hasn't hurt us?'

'I can pay for better help for you. No, wait. Listen to me. Do you know how much I sold my business for?'

'I'm not after your money,' she said sharply.

'I know that. You wouldn't be here if you were, believe me. I've learnt to spot gold diggers a mile away, to use an old-fashioned phrase for women after me for my money.'

'Oh.'

Then he told her how much he'd sold the business for and she gaped at him in shock. 'You're a multi-millionaire!'

He shrugged, his voice low and persuasive. 'For what that's worth. Money in the bank doesn't bring happiness, though, believe me. Let me do this for you. I'm benefitting from it emotionally as much as you are. Look at how Dee was dancing around just then. She and I had been living together but emotionally apart for weeks before you came.' His last words had come out choked and he had to pause a moment before continuing.

'This time, I'm going to keep Dee. I'll be seeing a

lawyer on my own behalf about that – well, I will if it's what she wants, too. I've not spoken to her about it yet but I will, and soon, to make sure it's OK with her. She's nearly grown up. If I'm very lucky, I'll be able to enjoy the last of her childhood and help her into adulthood, then stay connected even after she goes off to make her way into the world.'

He waited and when Claire said nothing, his hopeful expression began to fade.

She couldn't say no to him, just couldn't. 'Very well. Till the new year. But you'll let me pay our share of the housekeeping expenses while we're here, won't you?'

'I've got a much better idea. Why don't you take over as head cook? You talk as if you're a good one. I'm not. Oh, I've learnt to prepare adequate food for myself, especially quick and healthy salads. But I wouldn't know where to start with the preparations for a Christmas feast.'

'I'd enjoy doing that.'

'You won't get off lightly, because I want a real, home-made Christmas cake, mince pies, bowls of nuts – all the trimmings you can think of.'

She joined in, sharing her own favourites. 'And add a gingerbread house to your list. The girls will love helping me make one.'

'So will I. Hansel and Gretel, here we come.'

'I like making mince pies best, though. Not the plastic-looking ones you see in the shops, all in neat rows, all identical, all tasting . . . pleasant, but more like sugar than fruit. I like to see lopsided ones that children have rolled out and decorated with extra twirls of pastry. And they should have *good* fruit mince in them, a mixture that I've put together myself and soaked in port for a few days.'

'Ooh, yum. You're making my mouth water.' He leant back and beamed at her. 'Is that agreed then?' At her nod, he added, 'Then I'll appoint myself chief bottle washer and do the clearing up after meals as my share of the chores.'

She swallowed hard and confessed, 'Even now, I hardly dare hope for a Christmas like you describe to happen. We've just under two weeks to go.'

'It will if we try hard enough. We'll *make* it happen. And we won't let anyone stop us. Agreed?'

She looked at him. Did she dare allow herself to hope for a little joy for herself and Gabby? A little voice kept repeating in her head, *Oh please, oh please. Just go for it.*

She answered the voice with a mental vow: *All right. I will. I'll do it.* Then she said it aloud and saw his face brighten.

When the girls came back, she asked, 'After we come back from shopping, who wants to help me make fruit mince and then in a few days, make some batches of mince pies with it?'

Dee looked at her in surprise. 'I thought you just bought jars of fruit mince from the supermarket.'

'No. You put fruit together, with chopped walnuts and *real* dried fruit, not brown sweet sludge, and then you put port wine into it. After that you have to turn the bottles of fruit mince upside down a couple of times each day to let the port percolate through the fruit. You two will be in charge of doing that.'

They both cheered and jigged about shouting, 'Yes, yes! We'll do it.'

Best of all, Dee completely forgot to stand on her teenage dignity.

'And you have to be in it too, Luke. We can't leave you out of the fun. You have to roll out pastry and make mince pies as well when the time comes.'

She could see it now: four of them in the kitchen, laughing, bumping into one another, making preparations for a real family Christmas. What more could you ask for?

A shiver ran down Claire's spine at this thought.

She could also ask for a complete absence of fear, a sure knowledge that Martin wouldn't be coming after them, or was that a step too far?

Then she shook away those negative thoughts and let herself dive into the first preparations for a joyful family Christmas as they explored the cupboards and looked for suitable ingredients and baking equipment. There was very little of either to be found.

'Right. We need to make a shopping list.'

Dee rushed to find paper, Gabby tagging along behind her, and they set to work.

Chapter Thirteen

The shopping centre was crowded, with small children dashing about and slowing people down, since it was the weekend. Claire kept an eye on Gabby, who hadn't been in a big place like this since they left Martin. But her indomitable daughter took it all in her stride, watching wide-eyed, asking questions.

She still held tight to Dee's hand, however.

Luke nudged Claire. 'It's so crowded, you'd better hold onto me. We don't want our group to get separated. Dee, you two stay close behind us.' He took Claire's hand and they set off.

How long was it since she'd held a man's hand? Too long. This was . . . nice.

They found the perfect tree in one of the big superstores, and all right, it was artificial, all silver tinsel, but it was still going to be beautiful once they'd dressed it up.

Claire watched in amazement, feeling literally

breathless at the amount of money Luke was spending. But when she tried to protest that a smaller size of tree would be fine, and they definitely didn't need that many ornaments and strands of tinsel, he laughed and told the two girls to carry on choosing things.

In the end she gave up protesting and relaxed, allowing herself to enjoy every single thing about the day.

As they moved from shop to shop, everything was like a dream come true, right until the moment when a woman's voice called, 'Claire? Is that you?'

She stopped dead, clutching Luke's arm as well as his hand now as she stared in horror at a former neighbour from her time with Martin. What on earth was Lindsay Corton doing here, so far from home?

Lindsay came right up to her. 'Surprised to see me, Claire? Well, I'm even more surprised to see you. I thought you and Gabby had dropped off the face of the earth. Darren, look who's here!'

A man who'd been paying for something at the till turned round, saw them and hurried across to join the group. He studied Gabby intently and smiled at her, but gave Claire only a curt nod, not looking at all happy to see her.

Claire clung to Luke's arm, trying to hide her terror at the sight of them. The two girls seemed to pick up her anxiety and moved to stand close behind them, as if for protection.

Darren Corton was as close to a friend as Martin had ever had. They'd grown up together, worked in the same company for a time, gone for drinks after work together. Both had very rigid ideas about the world.

She couldn't get a word out, didn't know how to deal with this.

Luke half turned and bent to say something to Dee, then put his arm round her shoulders. 'Claire is so surprised to see you here that she hasn't introduced me. I'm her new husband, George.'

'Pleased to meet you.' But Darren didn't offer his hand and looked even more disapproving, clearly in no way pleased at this introduction. 'I must tell Martin we bumped into you – both of you. And does he know you've got married again?'

'No. It's none of his business.'

As he glared at her, his wife took over. 'You're looking good, Claire. Losing weight suits you. And who is this, not Gabby, surely? My, how you've grown. Your dad's really missing you.'

Dee kept her arm round the smaller child. 'I'm Gabby's new sister, Jenny.'

Lindsay said, 'Oh. How nice for you both.' But like her husband, she didn't look as if she approved of the new family situation.

'Do you live nearby, Claire? If so, we should meet for drinks. We're staying with an elderly aunt of mine for a few days. She's just come out of hospital.'

Again, it was Luke who stepped in. 'Sorry, but we can't. We're only visiting the area, staying with my mother for the weekend and taking the opportunity to do some major Christmas shopping, since this is our first Christmas together as a family. We have a party at my mother's tonight and then we go home tomorrow morning.'

Claire managed to pull herself together. 'Goodness, just look at the time. We said we'd not be more than a couple of hours, George. I promised to help your mother get ready for tonight. Nice seeing you again, Lindsay, Darren.'

'How about giving us your phone number?' Lindsay called after them.

She didn't answer, letting Luke lead them rapidly towards the nearest exit. The children didn't need telling to keep up.

They had to walk quite a way along the edge of the parking area, because this wasn't the closest exit to their car. They kept looking behind them but saw no sign of Lindsay and Darren following them, thank goodness.

As they got into the car, he studied Claire's face. 'You did well. Cheer up, we've got rid of them.' Then he turned round and said, 'You girls were magnificent! Anybody would have thought you really were sisters.'

'You know what? It feels as if we are.' Dee looked surprised at her own impulsive words.

Gabby beamed at him. To Claire's relief, she seemed to have taken the incident as a sort of game. 'I like having a big sister.'

Dee reached out a tentative hand to pat Claire's shoulder as if offering comfort. She obviously understood that Claire was upset by the encounter. 'We'll be all right, really we will. They don't know where we live.'

They drove round to pick up their larger purchases from the parcel pick-up at the rear of the store, then set off back. Claire would have just left the things and driven off, but Luke refused to do that.

He kept an eye on his rear-view mirror and she looked from side to side, but neither of them saw any sign of another vehicle following them.

*   *   *

When Claire and her new family had driven off from the parcel pick-up, Lindsay turned towards her husband. 'Clever of you to think they might come here, Darren. I've written the car registration down. A Mercedes, eh? He must have plenty of money.'

He started up the car again. 'I'm glad we saw them! I hate the way that woman has taken Martin's child from him. She deserves to lose custody for it.'

'Will he be able to find out where they are from the man's number plate?'

'Martin? He's brilliant at using the Internet to find things out. Of course he will.' He pulled out his phone.

She hesitated, putting a hand on his to stop him dialling. 'Just a minute. Are we rushing into this? I can't help wondering whether we really ought to interfere. Martin can be a bit . . . controlling. And they *are* divorced now.'

'Don't be stupid! He's had to take charge of what that fool of a woman was doing, for his daughter's sake. Of course we ought to tell him. If you can't help a friend, who can you help?'

He waited a moment, then dialled and waited, smiling grimly when his friend picked up. 'Martin? Yes, my aunt is improving, thank you. Look, I've got some useful information for you about your wife.'

'Ah.'

When he'd finished the conversation, Darren opened the car door and got out. 'We might as well finish our shopping. Come on. And stop looking so worried.'

'I'm still not sure we've done the right thing.'

'I am.'

* * *

When they turned in to Peppercorn Street, it felt to Claire as if they really were coming home. Then she got angry with herself for that. No, this wasn't her home and she mustn't think of it that way. It was going to be hard enough to leave here without allowing herself to get emotionally attached.

Then she admitted it to herself that it was too late to be sensible: she was already attached to this place, as well as to this kind man and his clever daughter – and so was Gabby.

Lindsay and Darren would undoubtedly tell Martin they'd seen her at the shopping centre and then he'd start ferreting around the district, might even chance on a clue and come after them. She'd never met anyone as persistent as he was when he wanted something.

Was nowhere going to be safe from him? What could she do to find a permanent hiding place? She'd been trying in vain to stay under the radar for nearly two years now and oh, she was so very tired of running away and being ultra-cautious about where she went and what she did.

Could Luke be right? Was it time to make a stand?

She didn't know if she had the courage to do that, or even whether there were any other legal ways of keeping her ex permanently away from them. Restraining orders hadn't worked. Only, if she didn't manage to get truly free of Martin, what would Gabby's young life be like?

That thought made her glance quickly at Luke as he turned in to their drive and waited for the garage door to finish rolling up. Did she dare stay here and face up to Martin?

'Don't,' Luke said, as if he could read her mind.

'Don't what?'

'Don't run away. You aren't alone this time. And I'm not penniless. I'll find help for you and pay for it.'

She closed her eyes, then opened them and the thought of what a lifetime of running and hiding would do to her daughter made her nod. 'All right. I won't run away this time. If you'll help us. I'm doing this for Gabby's sake.'

And at that moment it literally felt as if a load she'd been carrying on her shoulders for a long time had suddenly been lightened.

'Good,' he said. 'It's the right thing to do. She deserves a more normal life.'

She heard Dee's intake of breath from the back, but there was no sound from Gabby, and when she looked round, her daughter was asleep, her head on Dee's lap. It was probably better that she hadn't heard this conversation.

Dee gave her a long, serious stare, looking grown up, as teenagers sometimes can. 'Those people we met know your husband quite well, don't they? And they were obviously on his side.'

'Yes. They're long-time friends of his, especially Darren. They live near him.'

'I'm glad you're not going to leave. It's fun having a little sister, even if she is only a pretend one. I hope you don't mind?'

'Mind? I think it's wonderful.'

'Oh, good. I don't want to lose Gabby. She's such fun to be with.'

That remark seemed to set a seal of approval on Claire's decision. You not only couldn't let your child live in fear, you couldn't deny her important friendships like this one.

Luke's promise of support would make a huge difference, she was sure. Not just because of the money but because he was like a rock of sanity in a sea of craziness and muddles. Did she dare trust him, lean upon him?

She shivered, remembering what Martin had threatened in the months before she left: if she ever tried to leave him, he would take her daughter away from her for good. He'd made the same threat a few times, always with that confident smile on his face.

His threats had stayed with her, terrifying her as they were meant to do, because in all the time she'd known him, he'd never threatened what he couldn't carry out, never failed to achieve whatever it was sooner or later.

She wasn't going to let him take Gabby, whatever she had to do to keep her daughter safe. Gabby had been afraid of him towards the end. As had Claire.

What she didn't understand was why he wanted Gabby so badly. He'd had little to do with the practicalities of bringing up a lively young child, seemed to think you could switch a daughter on and off like a television set.

What had made him like this? His parents were decent people, but he was bad now, and getting worse.

The memory of that burnt-out car made her shiver every time she thought of it.

How different Luke was – how wonderfully kind!

When the garage door had rolled down and clunked into place, Dee woke Gabby and walked with her to the house door. 'Why don't you go up and fetch Helly from the kitchen, then you and I will let her out?'

As the child ran happily up the stairs, calling for the

dog, Dee remained in the doorway, saying quietly, 'Don't leave us, Claire. Whatever it takes. Things are better for all of us with you two here. Dad, don't let her and Gabby go away.' Then she went down the few steps to unbolt the door into the back garden and wait for the younger child and dog to come down from the kitchen.

Luke exchanged rather surprised glances with Claire. 'She's so grown-up sometimes.'

'She's a wonderful kid. I think she's been lonely too. I don't know your ex, but it sounds to me as if Dee has been rather neglected in the ways that matter most. She's well dressed but maybe not well loved.'

'I think so, too, now that I've got to know her. I didn't realise how bad things were or I'd have tried to do something about it sooner. And Dee is right: don't leave us, Claire. Please. We all seem better for being together.'

He gave her a quick, cheeky grin as he added, 'In fact I think you and Gabby are the best Christmas present we could have.'

She couldn't help sharing a smile with him, but tried to make him realise what it was like. 'I don't want to go, truly I don't. But Martin *will* come after us, and I'd never forgive myself if you and Dee got hurt, especially her.'

'I don't want that to happen, either. But you should take on board that I too can be persistent when I want something. Trust me on that. If we plan carefully how to deal with your ex, which includes consulting the best lawyers I can find, and upgrading security here, I'm sure we'll find a safe way through these difficulties for you.'

Gabby came clattering down the stairs with Helly just then, and when she and Dee had gone outside, Claire murmured, 'I keep being surprised at how like real sisters they are.'

'So do I. It's doing Dee a world of good and I always wanted other children.' When they went up to the kitchen, he went down to the rear window of the basement to keep an eye on them and the dog, and not until the trio had gone back upstairs did they resume their serious talk.

'Before we join them, tell me more about what Martin's like, anything that might help.'

'Whatever he's doing, he's very focused. He only seems to see the world in terms of his own needs and he's not good with people. He wanted a wife and family, so he courted me and we got married. I knew he wasn't good with words or romantic gestures, but he fooled me into believing he loved me. Now, for some weird reason, he's fixated on bringing Gabby up himself, keeps using the word "properly".'

'Because you've disappointed him, not lived up to unrealistic expectations, perhaps pushed your own ideas in the way of his life plans?'

'Yes, I think that's a good analysis. I hesitated to leave him, for Gabby's sake, because he really did seem to care for her. But he became so authoritarian that eventually I decided she needed more freedom and fewer restrictions: in other words, a normal life.'

'I presume you'd tried to make him see reason about her needs?'

'I talked myself hoarse, even suggested we get counselling. He was furious at that. I don't understand what made him change so much.'

'People do change when they're mentally ill.'

'I know. I worked that out, read about it online. But his

mental health must have got far worse since we left for him to have set my car on fire, don't you think?'

'Yes. I agree.' Luke glanced upstairs. 'I think we'd better go and spend time with our children now. Maybe we could talk it through and start making more detailed plans for protecting you both after they go to bed. One thing I'm determined about: we're not going to let this spoil their decorating party. We can be pretty sure your ex won't arrive here this afternoon.'

'No.'

'So we'll make a start by putting up the tree, but only after we've put all the food we've bought away and had a late lunch. I'm hungry even if you aren't.'

She nodded and went up to join their daughters.

She couldn't eat much, though, because the anxiety about Martin was back, shivering in her belly. And she could see that Luke had noticed.

But he said nothing and the girls were chattering on about Christmas decorations, so she gradually managed to push her worries aside temporarily and join in.

Thank goodness for Christmas! Who'd have thought? Last year had been lonely, but this year was full of promise.

Chapter Fourteen

Luke watched his three companions covertly while he ate lunch and chatted to them. Claire must be more terrified of her ex than he'd realised because she'd gone very quiet and thoughtful. He was worried, feeling that if she ran away again, she'd never stop running. And what sort of life was that for her and Gabby?

Or for him and Dee without them?

After they'd eaten, he wanted to speak to his daughter privately, so took charge of arrangements for the afternoon. 'Claire made the lunch, so Dee and I will clear up the kitchen. Gabby, will you please help your mother to unpack the decorations in the sitting room? If you remove the price tags and packaging, we'll be ready to start putting up the tree once we've cleared up here.'

'What fun! Yes.' Gabby found the kitchen scissors and brandished them triumphantly at her mother. 'Come on. There are a lot of things to unpack.'

Claire shot him a rueful glance over her shoulder as she was literally dragged away by her daughter.

When Dee was alone with him in the kitchen she said abruptly, 'They're frightened underneath it all, Dad. Both of them.'

'Yes. I could see that.'

'What should I do to help them?'

'The best thing you can do is carry on as you are, playing the big sister to Gabby. You're brilliant with her.'

'Oh. Do you really think so?' She blushed, something that didn't often happen.

He had to warn her, though. 'From now on, though, you should always stay close to her and keep an eye on your surroundings, for both your sakes. That father of hers sounds to be relentless.'

'He must be a nasty sort of person if he doesn't get on with Claire. She's really nice, isn't she? Doesn't talk down to me, or treat me like an idiot child.'

Who had been doing that to her? he wondered. 'Yes. She's very nice. After you and I have finished here, I need to talk to her on her own, if you don't mind. Can you keep Gabby occupied with putting up decorations in your rooms, then we'll all do the tree together? Tomorrow I shall look for a good lawyer and perhaps someone to help me protect them.'

'It's Sunday tomorrow, Dad. Will lawyers' offices be open?'

'Oh, damn! I'd forgotten that for the moment. But I do know one man who might help me find a bodyguard till we can work out how we stand legally.'

The last word made her gape at him. '*Bodyguard?* Are things that bad, do you think? Will that man actually attack them, Dad?'

'He might if they don't do as he tells them, especially Claire. He sounds – mentally unbalanced. I'll try to help them if there's a problem, but I'm not the world's most experienced fighter.' He spread his arms wide in a helpless shrug. 'I don't think I've got the killer instinct, which is why I'm thinking of hiring someone more experienced. Better to be too careful than find ourselves in trouble, don't you think?'

She nodded thoughtfully and continued to put things away. He waited for her to speak again.

'Um, I wanted to ask you about something else, Dad.'

'Go ahead. Ask anything you like.'

'Can I – would you let me live with you from now on?'

That had come out of left field and it left him gobsmacked. For a moment he could only stare at her. He'd been treading carefully, working his way up to asking the same thing delicately, terrified of rejection.

She swung away from him. 'Only if you want me.' Her voice had come out harshly.

He threw the tea towel on the table and grabbed her, pulling her towards him and holding her close. '*If I want you?* I've *always* wanted you. Always. Only, Angie made it difficult for me even to see you. There was frequently some reason for me not to visit when it was scheduled.'

'She used to tell me—' Dee gulped and clung to him, sounding tearful, 'that you were too busy, didn't want to come and see me. But as I got older I could tell she was being awkward about it on purpose, and I got to know how she looked when she was lying to me. I wasn't sure what you really wanted, though.'

'I wanted to be your father, preferably a full-time father. I kept myself busy because I missed you so much. But the money I made didn't make up for losing so much of your childhood.'

He put both hands on her shoulders and held her at arm's length so that he could look her straight in the eyes. She must have no doubt that he meant this.

'Dee, my darling daughter, I can't think of anything I'd like better than to have you living with me permanently. But will your mother let you do that without making a fuss? She was the one who was awarded custody, after all. And as we both know, she likes to get her own way.'

'Does she ever! She'll be with this new person for a while, so she won't care about me. But if it's like the other people she's got together with, after a year or so they'll start to quarrel, then split up and she'll turn back to me. It fooled me for a while when I was younger. I thought she wanted me more than them. But the last couple of times, I knew she was only fussing over me because she had no one else to fuss over. She didn't really care about what I wanted, only what she wanted. She really hates to be alone, even for an evening.'

She hesitated, then added, 'I've been reading about it online, and it sounds as if the courts take more notice of what older children want about who gets custody.'

'I've heard that too. We'll see my lawyer about you living with me as soon as we can get an appointment, as well as finding out about helping to protect Claire.'

When she didn't speak, he couldn't help adding, 'If you're really sure?'

Her eyes were bright with unshed tears. 'I am sure, Dad.

You've been treading on eggs with me since I got here, and I've been a bit wary, watching you, trying to work out how you felt. But lately I've started to believe that you really do care about me. You were right to go slowly, not press me. It takes time to get to know someone.'

He let out his breath in a whoosh. 'I'm glad, so very glad. I do my best.'

'And since you rescued Claire and Gabby, I've seen how you've helped them as well. How can I not trust you when you're so kind to everyone?' She gulped back a sob and tears began to run down her cheeks. 'I don't know you very well yet, and – and you don't know me very well. I lose my temper sometimes and say things I don't mean, but we can get through it . . . can't we?'

'Oh, yes. No one is perfect, but if the goodwill is there, things can be worked out.' He had to hug her all over again as he said that, and this time he dared to make a thorough job of it. She felt stiff in his arms at first, then relaxed against him, as Claire had done.

That was two people turning to him, wanting to be with him. And there was Gabby to love as well as Dee, yes, *love*. He'd had so much love locked away inside him for years and now it felt to be spilling out in a great, warm tide.

That felt wonderful. Abso-bloody-lutely wonderful.

And he didn't care if Dee saw that he was crying too.

As they both stopped and mopped their eyes, he said, 'This must be one of the most important conversations I've ever had in the whole of my life. And the most wonderful.'

'Me, too.'

Then Gabby came running in to say, 'We're ready. Everything is unpacked and—Oh! Is everything all right? You've both been crying.'

Dee went across to her. 'Everything's great! We've been crying with happiness, that's all. I'm going to live with Dad from now on. Aren't I lucky?'

She moved the younger girl towards the door and looked back to wink at him. 'Come on. Dad'll join us in a minute. Show me what you've been doing.'

Luke blew his nose, then blew it good and hard again. But it was a minute or two before he could regain control of his emotions and feel ready to face the others.

As he was about to join them, he remembered the question of safety and went into his home office instead to make a phone call to a security company run by a friend of his.

Rod listened as he explained the situation. 'Are you sure things are that bad?'

'Her ex not only burnt her car but put in a security camera to watch her reaction to that. He must be a real sicko. I'm worried that he might suddenly do something worse. I don't want them to get hurt and I'm not good at physical fighting, nor can I stay up all night keeping watch on the house, then keep an eye on things during the day.'

'Well, I know a guy who takes on occasional jobs. He's older and retired from the police force, but he works part-time as a private investigator. He's strong and very discreet, good at defusing difficult situations rather than getting into punch-ups.'

'Sounds perfect. See if he'll come and stay here until we set up something permanent.'

'You'll pay through the nose for full-time attendance.'

'What price my family's safety?'

'*Your family?* It's that serious with this woman, then?'

Luke didn't even have to think about his answer. 'It is if I can stop her running away. She'd do that not only for her own sake, but to try to save me and Dee from her ex. I want us all to be free of him permanently, so I'll be looking for legal help on Monday as well.'

Claire came across to him as he entered the living room where the decorations were now spread out. 'Everything all right?'

'Better than all right. This has been one of the best days of my life, in spite of our problems. I'll tell you about it later.' He raised his voice, 'Let's put that tree together, girls, before you do your bedrooms.'

'We've got some things for our bedrooms.' Gabby beamed at a pile of tinsel at one side.

'Good. But before we dress the tree up, we have to find something to stand it in, to keep it from falling over on us.'

However, the expensive tree came with a well-designed stand that was easy to put together. 'That shows how much I knew about artificial Christmas trees.'

Dee had recovered her spirits enough to give him a scornful eye roll. 'You should have read the information on the box more carefully, Dad.'

He grinned and shrugged. 'I stand guilty. You sort out what we buy next time.'

She jutted her chin at him, but smiled back at him as she spoke. 'All right. I will.'

When the furniture had been rearranged and the huge

silver tree set up in one corner, he helped Gabby up a ladder to fix the star at the very top, standing by her, holding it steady so that she couldn't fall.

After that Dee used the ladder to thread the twinkle lights in and out of the top branches, but waved him impatiently away when he tried to stand next to her. 'I've got a good sense of balance, Dad.'

Gabby hung the lights over the bottom branches, looking round in happy triumph as she finished. Finally, they all took turns to hang various glittering balls and ornaments on the tree.

'That's it,' Claire said after a while. 'It'd be gilding the lily to put any more decorations on it.'

Gabby sighed happily. 'It's gorgeous. Take a photo of it, Mum.'

So Claire got out her phone and did that.

They let Gabby switch the lights on the first time, watching her stand utterly still, her face so blissfully happy that her joy communicated itself to everyone.

'Me and Gabby will do our bedrooms now, then you oldies can come up and check everything.'

'Oldies, indeed!' He pretended to chase her and Gabby out of the room.

Their laughter echoed back, such a wonderful sound.

He came back looking happy. 'My daughter really likes you. I like you, too.'

'And I like her. Very much. She's a great kid.'

He took a risk for the second time that day. 'It's turning into more than friendship between us, I hope. I think we should see where you and I go for a while.'

'Are you sure?'

'I'm sure I want to give it a try. And on Monday we'll seek legal help to deal with the obstacles.'

She nodded, but her smile said as much as words could have done.

He waited a minute to tell her the other important thing. 'I'm going to order a takeaway meal for tonight and there will be an extra person to feed because I've hired a bodyguard.'

He tried to say this casually, but she wasn't fooled. She stared at him, the smile gone, her mouth open in shock, then asked in a croaky whisper, 'Do you know something I don't about Martin?'

'No. I'm simply taking the best precautions I can to keep us all safe. Remember, my daughter is involved in this as well, so I'm not doing this just for you and Gabby.'

She was silent as it all sank in, her eyes huge and fearful. 'Oh, Luke! It's horrible to think of that being necessary, isn't it?'

'Our bodyguard will stay mainly in the basement and on the ground floor level during the night, because that's how someone might get in. I'll tell the girls and introduce him to them, but we probably won't see or hear much from him after he's settled in, because he'll need to catch up on sleep in the daytime.'

When she didn't speak, he said, 'You've been afraid enough of Martin to run away twice. I would try to defend you if he attacked you, but though I keep myself healthy and reasonably fit, I've no particular skill at fighting. I've never had to do it, you see, didn't grow up in a rough area or go to a school where kids fought one another.'

'I've brought these troubles to you.'

'You've also brought joy to me, Claire, not only by your presence, but by helping me build a bridge to my daughter. I can't tell you how grateful I am for your help. She just asked me if she could live with me permanently. You can imagine how that delighted me.'

'Oh, that's wonderful!'

He waited a moment to let that sink in, then said, 'Now, we're in party mode today, remember. No work. No worrying. If I remember correctly, Gabby loves pizzas, but how does she feel about Chinese food?'

'She likes it when I cook it, so she'll probably enjoy it if you get a takeaway. She isn't fussy and luckily she doesn't seem to have any food problems about what she eats.'

'Good.' He checked the clock. 'I don't think those girls will be much longer decorating their bedrooms. It's mainly draping tinsel around.'

'You must have bought miles of it.'

He winked at her. 'And very useful stuff it has proved to be. Once it's been draped everywhere, we'll consult the menu and phone through an order. Do you like fizzy wine? Not posh champagne but I happen to have a rather nice fizzy plonk chilling in the fridge.'

'I haven't had any wine for ages, but yes, I do enjoy the odd glass.'

'Good.'

She looked a bit overwhelmed and asked yet again, 'Are you sure – about everything?'

'Absolutely sure. Aren't you?' He clasped one hand to his chest and said with an exaggerated pretence of anguish, 'Oh! Don't tell me you've been lying to me? How shall I ever get over it?'

'Stop that, you idiot.'

'All right. Let's enjoy tonight. Tomorrow we'll get serious again and start making plans for the future but today we party.'

Chapter Fifteen

The bodyguard turned up at the same time as the Chinese meal was being delivered. At least, Luke assumed that the man with the quiet face and watchful eyes was the bodyguard when he answered the door.

'Just a minute, please.' He took the paper carrier bag of hot containers from the delivery lad, and dropped a tip in his hand, then turned back to the man standing patiently to one side of the door.

As the delivery van drove away, he said, 'Rod sent me. I'm Eric. Apparently you need protection rather urgently, Mr Morgan.'

'Yes. Or more accurately, we may need protection.' Luke studied the stranger, who was older than him by at least a decade, but looked fit and muscular.

The man held out a card. 'Rod said to give you this.'

Luke checked that it was the business card of Rod's company, read the words on the back in his friend's handwriting and relaxed. 'Ah, good. We're just having takeaway and I ordered enough for you.' He held up the bag.

'Thanks. Very kind, but I've already eaten.'

'Well, come in.' He locked the door carefully, then quickly explained the layout of the house. 'Why don't you explore and we'll eat this while it's hot? I'd sort of assumed you'd keep watch mainly from the lower ground floor, which is no longer in use, but I can switch the heating on down there. It's up to you, really.'

'Sounds a good idea. I'll check it out.'

Luke hesitated before adding, 'I doubt anything will happen tonight, because it'll take time for this Martin guy to find us, but with two children in the house, I prefer not to take any risks. Claire and I will come and chat to you about the general background to this situation after we've eaten. I know Rod's briefed you, but you may want more details.'

He waved one hand. 'Just walk round, go anywhere you like then join us for a cup of coffee or whatever. I haven't furnished a couple of rooms yet and there's chaos in the attic.'

'Good idea. I'll do that.'

When he went into the kitchen, Luke explained quickly to the children about a bodyguard coming to sleep downstairs, adding as lightly as he could manage, 'Just in case there's any trouble from you know who.'

Three people stared at him solemnly, then Dee said, 'Good idea, Dad. I'm taking my hockey stick to bed tonight.' She stared challengingly at her father and mimicked his words, 'Just in case.'

Claire nodded approval. 'I'll find something for protection too. Martin can be – well, a bit rough sometimes.'

'I want something to hit him with if he tries to take me away from you.' Gabby looked at her mother. 'And I don't care if he is my father. I don't like him. He frightens me sometimes when he pulls me about. It's like a wicked witch has put a spell on him and he's turned horrible.'

Luke stared at the three females, who all looked very determined, and gave up any attempt to make light of what he was doing. 'There's no fooling you lot about possible dangers, is there?'

'Our car was burnt,' Claire said. 'We know Martin could cause serious trouble if he found us.'

'He's dragged me away from school a few times,' Gabby said. 'I didn't like it and I screamed for help but the teacher didn't try to stop him.'

'We'll stop him this time, I promise you.' Dee gave her another of those quick hugs and Gabby held onto her for a few seconds longer.

Luke thought it terrible that a child should feel like that about her father. 'We'll make sure you're all supplied with a defensive object before you go to bed, if it makes you feel better, though I doubt you'll need to use them with Eric on guard. Now, if we don't eat our meal it'll grow cold and that'd be a shame. The food from that café is always delicious.'

He began taking the tops off the containers and Dee got out some spoons and forks while Claire passed out plates.

It was all very normal behaviour on the surface, but the tension was there underneath.

* * *

Eric eavesdropped unashamedly outside the door of the kitchen, because that was the best way to find out the truth about what his clients were like. He'd been unable to believe his luck when Rod told him who he'd be guarding. Fate, blind chance, call it what you will, had tossed the people he was searching for right into his hands. How often did coincidences like that happen?

If they read about it in a novel, most folk would dismiss it as unbelievable, but he'd seen amazing coincidences a few times during his career as a policeman, as if fate was occasionally squarely on the side of law and justice.

Not very often, but more often than you might expect from sheer chance.

Since his retirement, he'd helped out on a few delicate cases that Rod didn't want messed up, if it could be prevented – cases that were worth sorting out. It was a wonderful way to semi-retire, picking and choosing which cases you worked on.

It particularly suited him that this job was about preventing violence to two children. Rod trusted him, knew he wouldn't get into a physical confrontation if it could possibly be avoided. But he would keep them safe.

He couldn't always prevent violence though. No one could.

The big unanswered question was whether he was going to tell Tom Douglas about this, since the two cases were so closely connected. No, not yet. This job would give him an excellent opportunity to find out what Claire Porter and her daughter were really like, not to mention the man she was now living with.

If Tom was doubtful about his own son, then Eric

needed to be even more careful than usual about giving him information that might leak to Martin.

When offering him the job, Rod had spoken very highly about Luke Morgan but Eric liked to make up his own mind about people.

The clatter of spoons on plates, followed by a reduced level of conversation in the kitchen, indicated that they were eating so Eric went upstairs, checking out the rooms and the layout of the house, peering out of windows and then coming quietly back down. He'd remember the house as a pattern of rooms in his brain, like a rough architect's drawing.

The lowest floor of the house felt rather cold and damp after the warmth of the upper levels and had a sad, neglected look to it, with thick dust on most of the shelves and surfaces. Switching on the lights one by one, he walked through the various rooms which had once made up the servants' quarters. It was bigger than some flats.

This would have been a busy area in those days, but now all was quiet as he checked it out, even looking for places from which he could watch the gardens outside without being seen.

You could never be too careful in a new place.

Once he'd gone round that floor, he felt the old-fashioned water-filled radiators, relieved that they were starting to warm up. Strange house, this, with the lower part at the back abandoned and old-fashioned, while the rest had been modernised about twenty years ago, if he were any judge.

He made sure all three outer doors were locked. The one furthest away from the stairs had been unlocked and creaked when he opened it, as if the hinges needed oiling.

He wondered how long it had been like that, but he was quite sure by now that no one was hiding in any part of the house.

He went back up the first half-flight of stairs to the door into the garage. That one didn't have a lock on it at all. Not good. He checked the door at the far side of the garage which led directly outside, shaking his head in disapproval. It might be locked but the door itself was a flimsy thing.

He'd suggest a few things, could fit heavy bolts and better locks himself, preferably before the following night. That ought to be enough to keep out an ex-husband coming here to cause trouble.

He thought Luke was right in his guess that the ex wouldn't have found out where Claire and Gabby were yet. You never could tell, though. Some people could be very cunning.

Thoughtfully he put on his night glasses and leant forward with his hands on a lukewarm radiator, staring out at the garden. It'd be easy enough to approach the house unseen from front or back but he'd be able to see anyone who trespassed clearly when wearing these.

Luke had been right to get help if Tom's son was potentially dangerous. Eric agreed absolutely that you couldn't be too careful where children were concerned.

With Christmas coming at the end of the month, there would be a lot more coming and going of strangers than usual, with deliveries of items bought online.

He'd go round after they all went to bed and check that they'd locked everywhere on the floor above, windows as well as the front door. Up a few steps here, down a few steps there. It was a strange house. He'd not like to have to navigate it for the first time in the dark, as an intruder would have to. That was another advantage their side had: they knew the terrain.

He heard footsteps coming down from the kitchen and turned as Luke came in to join him.

'Would you like to meet everyone now? I should warn you, the girls and Claire are intending to take weapons to bed, so don't be surprised if they brandish them at you.'

Eric blinked. '*Weapons!*'

Luke let out a huff of laughter. 'Yes, hockey sticks and rolling pins.'

Eric chuckled. 'Whatever makes them feel better. Should be peaceful tonight.'

'Yes. But if you think we need someone else to keep us safe as well as you, then we'll hire another guard from tomorrow onwards.'

'Might be a good idea. It's a big house, with a lot of doors leading outside. You could easily improve a few weak spots, though.' He explained.

Luke nodded. 'Do it.'

'I'll nip out to buy the stuff tomorrow, then.'

'We'll take down a mattress and bedding from one of the spare bedrooms so that you can rest tomorrow.'

'Yeah, good. I won't be sleeping tonight, though.'

Eric followed Luke upstairs, accepted a cup of coffee and was introduced to the others. Nice family group they were, even if they weren't really a family. He liked the look of them all. *Decent* was the word he used mentally. One of his favourite complimentary things to say about someone.

Then he went back down to the lower level and left them to it, though he'd be coming up and down to the kitchen and front door level during the night.

You did a lot of thinking on these night watches and as time passed, he couldn't help worrying about what to do about Tom Douglas, whether to tell him.

Did the man think his son was dangerous? He was certainly desperate to find his granddaughter again without the son knowing. The Christmas season could do that to you, make you want to catch up with people you'd once cared about. Eric was always glad that he got on well with his own family when he had to help people sort out the tangled and hostile relationships other people had to cope with.

Tom didn't seem a fool, though, not at all. If he'd hired a PI to find his granddaughter and asked Eric to keep what he was doing secret from his wife as well as his son, there must be a very good reason.

The night passed peacefully with no sign of anyone watching the house, let alone trying to get in.

The dog came down to check on Eric a couple of times when he moved about to keep himself awake. Lovely animal she was. But would she make a good watchdog? Probably not. She was altogether too friendly, even with a stranger like him. Pity. Dogs could be very helpful.

Luke and his guests stayed at home on the Sunday, planning over breakfast how to spend their time.

'Gabby and I can keep each other company if you need to get on with your work, Claire,' Dee offered as they finished eating.

'Would you mind? Only I'll get paid nicely for my present project, and it never hurts to build up some savings.'

'In case you have to flee?' the teenager asked bluntly. 'I thought you were going to stay here.'

'I am. But you never know what will happen or what you'll need. And anyway, I'm pretty short of money and Gabby's going to need some new clothes soon.'

Luke saw his daughter's embarrassment at this revelation and intervened. 'If you girls can keep an eye on each other, I'll keep an eye on the lower parts of the house and the gardens while Eric grabs some sleep. Don't try to leave the house, Dee.'

'We'll have to let Helly out.'

'When you do, come and find me first and leave Gabby inside.'

She nodded.

Gabby looked upset at that, but luckily Dee got out the board games and that distracted her.

As the morning passed, the games provided a break from reading or fiddling around on the computer and caused much laughter.

The sense of trouble approaching seemed to hover, though, whatever they did to pass the time. No one said anything about it aloud, but Luke could see that they were all braced for . . . something. Who knew what?

Why would that man deliberately make people afraid of him? he wondered. Or in his case, make him wary. Martin had been doing it over many years, from what Claire said. Luke had always hated bullies.

* * *

When Claire came into the kitchen part-way through the morning to make herself a cup of coffee, he checked again to make sure she hadn't changed her mind about consulting a lawyer and making a stand.

'No. I've not changed my mind. I can't bear to see that worried look on Gabby's face and when I think of such anxiety always being in the background, well, I can't bear it. If there's any chance of a permanent solution, I want to take it now that I'm not alone. Your offer of help has made such a difference to me and I'm truly grateful.'

He too had seen that look on Gabby's face. Dee was able to cheer the younger girl up for a while, but she always grew quieter again after their games and jumped in shock at sudden noises outside.

He noticed that Dee kept her hockey stick near the back door and took it with her when she let Helly out. Very sensible. But that meant his daughter was caught up in the web of menace and anxiety too, on top of her own worries about what her mother might do about her living with her father again.

His determination grew. He was going to free them all from their various worries – and before Christmas, if possible – and then they were all going to enjoy the festivities.

Was that possible? It had to be.

Tom Douglas fretted all weekend, worrying about what his son was doing and about Claire and Gabby's safety. He didn't think Martin would hurt Gabby, but he had a leaden feeling of dread in his belly when he thought about Claire because his son couldn't speak about her without wishing her ill and making wild threats.

Hilary dismissed what Martin had said as hot air, or letting off steam, but Tom wasn't so sure.

They hadn't heard from their son for a few weeks. His wife was starting to get worried about that and had mentioned once or twice that it wasn't like Martin not to answer her emails or phone calls, even though she'd marked them 'urgent'.

'Why have you been trying so hard to get in touch with him? What's so urgent?'

'He's our son and we haven't seen him for a while. I wanted to find out what he was doing with himself and invite him round for a meal at Christmas maybe.'

She frowned at her husband and added sharply, 'Last time he came here, you and he had sharp words about Gabby. Please don't get into that again.'

'I can't guarantee it, Hilary. Martin has grown . . . well, obsessive is the only word that comes to mind.'

'About what?'

'About wanting to find Gabby and take her away from Claire.'

'It's only to be expected that he'll miss her. He's her father and he adores her. He wouldn't be going on about it if Claire hadn't run off and hidden Gabby from us. It was cruel of her. Wrong.' She dabbed at her eyes.

He couldn't even pretend to agree with his wife about this. *Obsessive* was the right word for Martin and that wasn't a good thing to be. Hilary couldn't see it. Would she ever? Their son was the only thing they ever quarrelled about.

He worried about whether they'd be able to spend time with their granddaughter over the coming years if Martin didn't change. He doubted it and that made him sad.

He was beginning to think it wouldn't be safe for him to contact Claire, even if Eric did find out where she was hiding. If his wife found out, she might, no *would* pass the information on to their son.

His original intention had been to take Hilary somewhere safe and meet their daughter-in-law and granddaughter there. But if he met Claire and Gabby on their own and his wife found out, it could seriously damage their marriage.

Oh, hell. Sometimes there didn't seem to be any solution to problems.

Tom had hired Eric hoping for a reunion with Gabby to brighten up their Christmas. Instead it looked as if it was going to be another very quiet festive season, with just the two of them on the day itself.

Like last year.

When Hilary had wept in his arms.

On the Sunday evening, Eric received an email from a woman he'd asked to help him search for information after he'd found out who he'd be guarding. She was even better than he was at finding things out online, one of the best at that sort of work, in fact.

Sure enough, she had found a lead which he now wanted to follow up personally, so he went up to the living room to find Luke.

'All right if a colleague takes over the guard duties tomorrow morning? There's something I need to check out.'

Luke looked at him hopefully. 'Does that mean you've found something important?'

'Might have done. Don't know how important it is, but it's definitely relevant. As I said, I need to check it carefully first. Caitlin is highly competent, used to be a police sergeant. You'll like her and you'll be quite safe in her hands as long as you don't go out anywhere on your own.'

'Do as you think best. Hire anyone you need to. As I've said before, money is no object; it's safety I care about.'

Eric shot off an email and Caitlin agreed to come round to Peppercorn Street at seven o'clock the next morning and stay there as long as necessary.

He spent Sunday night keeping watch, but nothing disturbed the peace of the old house.

Chapter Sixteen

Caitlin arrived on the Monday morning, so Eric introduced her to Luke and Claire, who'd got up early on purpose, then briefed her himself, taking her quickly round the house before leaving her to look after security there. He was a bit short of sleep, but that didn't matter. He was used to it.

Bartons End was about an hour's drive away and Eric had no trouble finding the old industrial estate because it was starting to get light now. But there was no one at the units yet, so he went across to walk round the burnt-out car, which was still sitting in front of the dilapidated house Claire had lived in.

As he studied the blackened remains, he let out a low whistle. Whoever it was had done a thorough job of burning the whole vehicle. This had been a planned action, not an impulse.

He looked round the area, which looked like a war zone. She must have been desperate and very short of money to rent here at all. The house didn't even look fit for habitation and he'd bet that roof leaked.

He walked across to the nearest unit, which his research friend Elsa said was rented by the man who had made a report to the police. But Bill Turner had still not turned up, so Eric went back to wait in the car. It was a frosty morning and he was glad of his warm, down-filled jacket.

When another tenant arrived, Eric walked briskly across to ask about Bill, but the woman only knew that he didn't start work till around nine most days.

'Sorry not to be more help but I only took this place temporarily,' she said. 'I've hardly ever spoken to him, just a nod in passing.'

'Thanks anyway.'

OK. He'd guessed wrongly. Tradespeople usually started work earlier than other folk, but not this man apparently. Eric went back to his car. He could see people working on the new houses now at the other side of the demolition area, but this side was deserted apart from the woman's van. He sighed. He hoped Bill wouldn't be late.

It was quarter past nine before someone turned up in a large combi-van with 'Bill's Electrics' on the side. This turned in to the parking area in front of the nearest unit and a burly man with a shaven head got out. No-brainer that this was his man. After unlocking the double doors of the unit, the guy started unloading some empty cardboard boxes.

Eric got out and hurried across to him. 'Need a hand with those?'

Bill studied him intently as if suspicious then shrugged. 'Thanks. I'm not taking on any jobs today, though. I'm packing up and moving to another unit in a day or two. And I'll be glad to go. This place is like a morgue these days.'

Eric helped him carry the boxes inside. 'I'd be grateful if you could spare me a few minutes, though. I'm a private investigator and I need to ask a few questions about a man you were talking to on Saturday. Here's my ID.' He fumbled in his pocket for the card, with fingers that were stiff and cold by now.

Another shrug greeted that. 'He said he was a private investigator, too, and had ID that looked genuine. Only *he* didn't seem right, behaved really strangely. What's supposed to be your reason for coming here and why should I believe you?'

'My reason is probably similar to his, only I'm the genuine article.' Eric held out the ID card again. 'Look, if you don't believe me you can phone the police station in Swindon where I used to work. If you take a photo of me and email it to them, they'll vouch for me, I promise you.'

'Hmm. How did you know about me and that other chap?'

'I'm retired now but I still have friends here and there in the force. I'm trying to keep the woman who rented the house safe.'

'You're working for her?'

'Yes. Claire.'

After a thoughtful study of his face, Bill said, 'I will check with the police about you first, if you don't mind. There's an old saying that fits this situation: *Fool me once, shame on you. Fool me twice, shame on me.* Only it wasn't you who fooled me the first time, I will admit.'

'Why are you so sure he wasn't a PI if he had some ID that looked genuine?'

Bill explained about the car being parked away out of sight of the unit and the furtive way the fellow had behaved when going back to it, not to mention his bad manners.

'Have a look at this.' Eric took out his phone and found the photo of Martin that Tom had given him, holding it out for his companion to see. 'Is that him?'

'Oh, yes. That's definitely him. Who is he, then? His name on the ID was John Carter.'

'His real name is Martin Douglas. Phone up Swindon now and check on me, then we'll talk, if you don't mind. This guy is stalking his ex-wife and it's getting worse.' He gestured towards the car.

'If the police say you're legit, I'll be glad to tell you anything I can. It's been worrying me even though I reported the fellow to the police.' He gestured towards the burnt-out car. 'There was a small child living there. What if the car had exploded and injured her?'

'Yeah. That could have been a tragedy. Which is why I'm doing my best to help her stop the ex.'

'Well, if you're genuine, I'm glad someone is on her side. She must have lived a damned lonely life, her and that child. I never saw anyone else visit her.'

Bill made the phone call, sent the officer who answered a photo of the man standing beside him and got confirmation that this was indeed Eric Bancroft and yes, he was a licensed and well-respected PI.

After that the two men had a talk and Bill told Eric everything he knew, even agreeing to keep his eyes open for anyone else going near the nearby house or car, and taking down Eric's phone number.

'Don't say a word to anyone about this,' Eric warned

him. 'I don't want the ex finding out that I'm looking after that woman.'

'All right.'

Eric was very thoughtful as he set off for home. What he hadn't told Bill was that his friend said the police had a file on Martin Douglas, a file which included other stuff besides his harassment of his ex. Only they wouldn't say what that was about and had asked her to keep quiet and tell Eric to let them know quickly if he got any more information on Martin Douglas.

It was all turning out to be a lot more complicated than he'd expected.

Feeling guilty about not keeping in touch, Eric stopped the car halfway home to phone Tom, relieved when he caught his client at home.

'Did you find out where Gabby is?' Tom asked eagerly.

'I might have.'

'What does that mean? Either you've found her or you haven't.'

'I've still got something to check but your granddaughter is all right. That much I am sure of. I thought you'd like to know.'

'Yes, I do. Thank goodness. If anyone hurts that little lass, I won't be answerable for my actions.'

Eric didn't like the sound of this. Did he expect his son to hurt Gabby? 'What about her mother? Doesn't Claire's safety matter?'

'Yes, of course it does. But it's Gabby who's our blood relative, the one I care about most. Where has she been taken this time?'

'She's only about an hour's drive away from you.' He added a hasty, 'I think.' He didn't want to give away too much information even though Tom seemed a decent guy.

'Where exactly would that be?'

'I'll be able to tell you after I've checked the rest of the information. Have you heard from your son?'

'No. Martin doesn't contact me. It's his mother he speaks to.'

'Well, has *she* heard from him?'

'Not lately. He's not answering her emails or phone calls.'

'Could you let me know if he contacts her?'

'Why?'

Should he or should he not say something? Eric wondered.

'Tell me!' Tom said harshly.

'Turns out he set fire to Claire's car. That's a bit extreme, don't you think? I'm rather worried about his mental stability.'

'*Burnt her car!* Oh, hell. You're sure it was him?'

'Fairly sure, yes.'

'Why on earth would he do that?'

'Who knows what was going through his head? Look, I have to go now. I'll get back to you once I have more definite news.'

He cut the connection before Tom could protest, already regretting contacting him.

It might complicate matters if Tom said something to his son about burning the car.

When he got back to Peppercorn Street, Eric tried the front door, pleased that it was locked, and used his key to open it without ringing the doorbell to warn them.

By the time he got inside, Luke was already peering out of the small room nearby that he was using as an office and Claire had come to the door of the dining room.

Good. He liked to see them keeping checking on things.

'No problems?' he asked.

Luke answered. 'No signs of trouble. Bit of an anti-climax, actually. But I'm glad you're back now because Claire and I need to go and see my lawyer this afternoon. His secretary rang to say there'd been a cancellation for three o'clock, so we can go in for a preliminary consultation. We thought it might be best to leave the children here with the two of you.'

As laughter came from the kitchen, he grinned and gestured with one hand. 'I don't think they'll mind. It turns out Caitlin also likes board games. She's been winning hands down, too.'

'She always was good with kids.'

Claire smiled. 'Mind you, the girls are still carrying their weapons around. Those two are certainly prepared for trouble. I wonder if they'd actually use them, though.'

'You can never tell what someone will do if they're attacked.'

'Martin won't *attack* Gabby, surely. He's obsessed with her.'

Eric could only shrug. Since he didn't know this Martin he wouldn't even hazard a guess.

Caitlin came out of the kitchen to join them. 'Great kids you've got there, Claire and Luke.' She looked at Eric expectantly. 'How did it go?'

'I'll tell you about it. Do we want the kids in on this?'

'No,' Claire and Luke said at the same time.

'Not till we've heard it anyway,' she amended.

'Then we'll go into the dining room. There's room for us to sit comfortably there.'

He waited till they were settled to say, 'I checked your old house, Claire. Not a nice area.'

'Tell me about it. I hated living there. I hope I never see the place again!'

'I don't blame you. There don't seem to have been any more break-ins and no more windows have been smashed. The car's still standing with police tape across it. You'll have to have it taken away eventually. Have you contacted the landlord?'

'No, and I don't want to.'

'I can get a message sent to him that won't be traceable, if you like.'

'Would you?'

He nodded. 'Write the details down for me.'

'Why did you go there? Not to see the remains of my old car, surely?'

'I had word someone suspicious had been to see that electrician in the nearest unit.'

'Bill, you mean?'

'Yes.'

'And had they?'

'Yes. It was Martin. I showed him a photo.'

Eric heard her suck in her breath sharply and saw her mouth her ex's name.

'So he'd found us again. Does he know where we are now?'

'I can't tell. I've been wondering about those former neighbours of yours that you met at the shopping centre. Did they see your car?'

Both of them frowned, then Luke said reluctantly, 'I don't think so.'

'They could have followed us out of the shopping centre on foot and seen it, I suppose,' Claire said slowly. 'We tried to keep watch for them doing that, but who can see every single person in a huge car park?'

'I'm pretty sure they didn't follow us home,' Luke said. 'I watched all the traffic behind us really carefully and I even slowed down unnecessarily a couple of times to let people pass. No one lingered behind us. Why?'

'I'm thinking if they got your car registration, they could have told Martin about it. Would they have bothered to do that?'

Claire didn't hesitate. 'Darren would have told him straight away.'

'Then he'll probably trace you here. On the other hand, he won't know you have guards on duty, so I'd advise you to stay put, but improve your security. I doubt you'll ever be able to get away from him permanently unless you go to a women's refuge, so I agree with Luke that you should make a stand.'

'I've been trying to avoid going to a refuge.'

'I'll tell some people I know in the police that he's still stalking you. It's a women's unit and they'll be interested, believe me. And if you see any sign of your ex, you should call them immediately, Claire. I'll get you a name and phone number.'

She swallowed hard and Luke took her hand, holding it between his.

'We'll keep you safe,' Eric promised.

She sighed. 'We should tell the girls, I think. And

Luke, do you think we ought to go to the lawyer's this afternoon and leave them, or should we postpone that?'

'I think we should still go. We want as much legal backup as we can.'

'Caitlin and I will be here. We'll keep them safe.' It upset Eric to see a woman so traumatised by being stalked; he hated those who did that sort of thing with a passion.

Martin would have to knock him right out of the picture to get to those girls. Wasn't going to happen.

He looked at Caitlin. 'You can stay on too?'

'Try sending me away, my lad, and I'll camp outside. You're not the only one to hate the way some men treat their wives and children.'

Chapter Seventeen

After Tom had put the phone down, Hilary set the one in their bedroom gently back into its cradle, tears in her eyes. Tom was going behind her back and it sounded as if he'd hired someone to look for Gabby.

Only he hadn't discussed that with her or their son. It wasn't right. For all his faults, their Martin was Gabby's father and it was wrong of Claire to keep the child away from him. And wrong of Tom to act in such an underhand way towards herself as well.

It couldn't have been their son who'd burnt the car. It must have been vandals or a fault in the electrics. Martin would never do anything so despicable.

She heard Tom call out to her.

'Just going for a walk, Hilary love. Need to stretch my legs.'

Needed to think about what he was doing, more like. It was what he always did when he was worried about something – walked. Anger filled her and once Tom had vanished down the street, she picked up the phone again, shouting into it when the answerphone asked her to leave a message. 'Martin Douglas, I know you're there. Pick up this call at once. I've got something to tell you about Claire.'

The phone clicked into life. 'Hi, Ma.'

'Why haven't you answered my calls?'

'Been a bit busy looking for my daughter.'

'What have you been doing to Claire? Did you really burn her car?'

'Of course I did.'

She gasped. 'You didn't!'

'I wanted to make sure she couldn't run away again.'

She was shocked to the core. *Of course!* he'd said. As if there were nothing wrong with doing that. Her Martin. What had got into him?

'Make no mistake about it, Ma. I intend to get my daughter back, whatever it takes. She has no *right* to keep Gabby from me. You know how I love that child. And . . . I didn't tell you this before, but I can't have any more children.'

'Oh, no. What happened?'

'One of those things. I don't want to talk about it.'

'I'm so sorry, love.' She heard her own voice soften. She did know how much he cared for Gabby and now that she knew why it was even crueller to hide her from him. 'Well, it was wrong to burn the car, Martin, very wrong, and it sounds to me as though the police are on the lookout for you now about it.'

He laughed gently and confidently, with a patronising tone in his voice. She hated it when he treated her like that.

'They'll never tie it to me unless you give me away, Ma. You're the only one I've told about it and I know you're always on my side.'

'Well, of course I am. I'd never give you away, you know I wouldn't. But I still can't understand why you and Claire don't both go for counselling, sort out your differences and get back together again? If only for the child's sake.'

'I don't trust her and I don't *want* to get together with her again. What I do want is to get my daughter back and gain custody. Have you seen Gabby at all, or heard from her?'

'No.'

'How did you find out about the car, then? And why are you calling so urgently? Not that it isn't always nice to hear from you.'

'I overheard a phone call to your father. He's hired a private investigator to look for Claire.'

Silence, then Martin said slowly, 'Ah. Has this guy found out where Claire and Gabby are? What's he called?'

'I don't know his name. I was eavesdropping on a phone call, so I don't have all the details of what he's been doing. He sounds to be an ex-policeman and he said she was only about an hour away from here.'

'Well, that fits with something else I know. My friend Darren saw her at a big shopping centre. She was with a guy and introduced him as her husband.'

'She's got married again? *Claire has?* I don't believe it.'

'I wouldn't have either but Darren said they were holding hands and looking all lovey-dovey, so even if they're not married, they're definitely together. He got their car registration, so I'm onto it now. I'll find them, I promise you, and it won't take long. *My* daughter isn't going to be brought up by some stranger Claire's picked up. I'll make sure of that.'

She heard Martin breathing deeply, in the rhythmic way he did when he was calming himself down. She frowned. She hadn't heard him do that for years. Why would he need to calm himself down in that particular way again? His voice interrupted her thoughts.

'Anyway, it's nice to hear from you, Ma. How are you? No more health worries?'

'No. Just worries about you.'

'No need for that. I keep telling you I've got everything in hand, as that bitch will soon find out.'

Before she could urge him not to do anything rash, he said, 'Got to go now. There's a call waiting. Keep in touch. And let me know if you find anything else out.'

She clutched the phone to her chest for a good while before she put it down. He'd sounded so angry. Especially about his ex. Too angry. That worried her. They'd had a terrible time with him when he was younger, and had had to get professional help to teach him to control his temper.

Tears came into her eyes because he'd sounded vicious. She'd never heard quite that edge to his voice, or known him make such nasty threats. And he hadn't cared about burning the car. She had a sudden hope that he wouldn't find Claire. Or Gabby. At least, not until he'd calmed down again.

He used to take pills to help keep him on a level keel emotionally. It sounded as if he needed them again.

Did you ever stop worrying about your children?

She was left with the problem of whether to tell Tom about the conversation with Martin, but this would mean admitting that she'd listened in to his phone call, so no, she wouldn't do it. Not yet anyway.

Her husband hadn't told her about hiring a PI. She'd wait to tell him anything. But she would keep an eye on Tom from now on. It really upset her that her husband had gone behind her back like that.

Only, when she thought over what Martin had said, she couldn't help feeling more than a bit worried about the way he was talking, what he might be planning to do. She had no way of keeping an eye on her son, unfortunately.

Perhaps she could persuade Martin to come round for a meal so that she could see for herself how he was. She'd phone him again tomorrow and if he didn't pick up his phone, she'd leave a message inviting him to tea.

She tried to get on with her day but couldn't settle to anything. She kept changing her mind about whether she should she say something to her husband, but always wound up deciding not to. Well, not yet anyway. Not until he said something to her.

When he came back from his walk, he started talking about Christmas. Hilary had trouble hiding how little she cared about that. This Christmas was going to be just as bad and lonely as the last one had been, the way things were shaping up.

The day passed but Tom didn't say a single word about the PI. Not one word. That made her so angry.

As she often did when she couldn't settle, she started turning out a big cupboard in the spare bedroom.

When Tom looked at her, as if he knew something was wrong, she glared at him.

He opened his mouth to speak, then closed it again.

So she went into the bathroom and had a little cry. It was all such a mess.

Martin put down the phone and looked round his rented flat, scowling. It was a terrible place, far too small and looked messy with all his things crammed in. Claire was to blame for him having to live in such a hovel.

He smiled grimly. There was money waiting for her in the bank from the sale of the house, but she'd changed her bank account, hadn't she, and he had no idea – yet! – where she was currently living, so how could anyone arrange for it to be paid to her? The settlement people were searching for her and good luck to them.

She didn't deserve to get half the profits anyway, because he'd always earned more money than she had. And the house hadn't made the money he'd expected it to either, so he'd not wanted to sell it while prices weren't good. But that damned mediator had insisted because Claire needed the money.

If she did come out of hiding and get hold of that money, she'd only use it to run away from him. Ha! Well, see how she'd escape without a car.

Then he remembered the guy Darren had met – George, he was apparently called. Had she really married him or were they just shacked up together? He'd have to find out.

There would be plenty of time to do that now, but really he'd have been better to stick with his day job, which had given him a steady income stream without any risks. Only, he'd been sick to death of the idiots he'd had to work with and one day had lost his temper with one silly bitch – anyone with half a brain would have done, she was so stupid – and had given his notice when the HR people wouldn't get rid of her.

No one had tried to persuade him to stay, either. After all the years he'd devoted to the company, that sucked big time. Well, they were on his list, too, now. He'd make them regret it.

Though actually, he was making more money from his new venture than he had earned in that boring job. And Internet scams were rather amusing to arrange. People were so gullible. Especially older women. Of course it wasn't legal, so there was a small risk, but he didn't feel guilty or worried about that. If you asked him, anyone stupid enough to fall for what was promised in his phishing posts deserved to lose their money.

Besides, he was extremely clever and careful about how he did it and who he scammed. No one would ever be able to trace him.

It was a good thing he was doing so well, because the stuff he'd started taking to give him a clearer brain was costing him a small fortune. But you had to keep your mind clear to stay under the radar of the authorities and he would need the money from his long-term savings to start a new life with Gabby.

It suddenly occurred to him that his parents had a lot of old family silver, all stashed away in that cupboard under the stairs doing nothing. His father didn't even keep it in the bank.

They were stupid and gullible too. He must have had some earlier ancestors who had good brains and taken after them.

The silver would all come to Martin when his parents

died, so it wouldn't really be stealing to take it and put it to better use than sitting in a damned cupboard.

The lawyer's rooms were in Swindon old town and parking wasn't easy. Luke and Claire only just got there on time.

As the two of them had agreed, Luke did most of the speaking. He outlined their problems as succinctly as possible and they discussed the possible steps that could be taken.

'If you can't prove that Martin set fire to the car, it's going to be a bit difficult to get stronger restraining orders on him, I'm afraid.'

'I don't know what else I can do,' Claire said.

'Well, it's good that you've brought in professional help to protect Claire and Gabby, and Dee too, of course. And maybe this Bancroft guy will find some useful evidence for you. I've heard of him. He has a good reputation.'

'I'm glad to hear that,' Luke said.

'Now about the other matter, the custody of your daughter, Mr Morgan,' the lawyer added, 'that's likely to be more straightforward. She's sixteen now, old enough to have a say in who she lives with and you're a person of good repute. And you're not short of money, either, which never hurts.'

'No. It comes in useful.'

'What's more, since your ex dumped Dee on you without warning, before leaving for parts unknown, that adds to the strength of your case. Has she been in touch with either of you since?'

'No. Not a word.'

'All fairly straightforward then.'

The lawyer looked at the clock and turned back to Claire. 'It must sound bad to you, Ms Porter, with so many ifs and buts. But at least I know the general situation now and you've authorised me to act for you, so we'll go from there. I'll look into a couple of things and you can let me know if there are any other new developments – if this PI finds anything out, for instance.'

'Not as helpful as I'd hoped,' Luke said as he and Claire walked out to reception. 'But as Fillingham said – why do lawyers always have such exotic names? – we have good protection set up for Gabby. I think we can only wait now and see if your ex makes a move.'

'I seem to have spent a lot of time doing that.'

'Ah, Mr Morgan,' the receptionist said brightly. 'I have your bill here. Are you paying by credit card?'

Claire looked worried at that, too. Well, the money didn't matter, but she and her daughter did.

When they got home, Gabby flew across the kitchen to give Claire a hug, holding onto her mother for a while, rocking to and fro.

Dee watched and, after a moment's hesitation, sauntered across to give her father a quick hug.

She'd have pulled away again, but he held onto her. 'I want proper hugs from now on, Dee.'

She smiled up at him uncertainly, so he demonstrated what he meant. Her eyes were nearly on a level with his now. She was going to be quite tall. And pretty, however much she tried to hide that with her weird way of dressing.

It was all going well between them lately. He couldn't believe what a difference there had been since Claire and

Gabby came to stay with them. That child was very lovable. Even his daughter had been bewitched by her. He'd noticed Dee watching how their two visitors interacted with one another and looking sad. It was such a loving mother and child relationship. It did your heart good to see it.

He hoped Angie would continue to get on well with her new partner and leave him and Dee alone to cement their closer relationship.

Of course she would! She hadn't been with this person for long enough to have got to the quarrelling stage. It had always taken longer than this before. Why was he even thinking about that yet?

It was Claire's ex who was the main problem.

Chapter Eighteen

That evening, Angus Denning was taking a breath of fresh air in the moonlit formal gardens to the side of his house when he saw a man dressed in dark clothes and wearing a hoodie sneaking along by the hedge, trying to stay hidden.

Angus's first instinct was to call out and ask what the hell the fellow was doing in his grounds, but something made him move behind a nearby evergreen bush to watch him instead. It might be better to find out what was going on. Local people occasionally used the unpaved gravel road that led through his grounds and out past Saffron Lane as a shortcut. He didn't mind that as long as it didn't happen too often, but this man was behaving furtively and was tramping round the heritage garden.

The route the trespasser was taking led only towards the rears of the large older houses at the top end of Peppercorn Street. Was he planning to break in to one of them? He'd better not go near Winifred. At eighty-five she was something of a local treasure and they all watched out for her.

Angus patted his pocket, checking that he had his phone with him to call for help if necessary. Winifred might be wonderful for her age but she was too old to defend herself. And though Janey, who lived with her, was young and strong, she had a small daughter to look after as her first priority.

Damn! He hadn't brought his phone. Well, you didn't think of grabbing that when you were going out to stroll round your own patio to stretch your legs after a long day's work at the computer, did you?

He knew his grounds like the back of his hand, which paths led upwards and which places were likely to be littered with leaves that might crunch underfoot and give you away, so he moved silently. The other man was making quite a lot of noise, but at this hour of a chilly winter's evening, with rain forecast and clouds sailing across the moon, he wouldn't be expecting to meet anyone.

Feeling annoyed, Angus opened his mouth to shout to him to get off his land and not come back, but once again he shut it, because the intruder had stopped to take out of his pocket what looked like a pair of sunglasses and put them on. Sunglasses after dark? No, they must be night glasses. What else could they be? Why did he need those?

The man continued slowly forward till he was outside the rear of Number 4, or was it Number 5 he intended to break in to? Hard to tell from here.

No, it was definitely the new guy's house, Number 4.

Angus stopped a short distance behind him, expecting the intruder to try Luke's gate but he didn't, just stood by the fence, watching the house.

What the hell was going on here?

The garden lights at that house came on suddenly and the back door opened. The man stepped back hastily, crouching behind an evergreen shrub. Definitely up to no good.

There was a happy woofing and the big dog he'd met before came bounding out into the garden. The girl who lived there stayed in the doorway, calling to the dog to be a good girl.

The dog stopped dead but instead of squatting, she stiffened and began to growl.

The intruder began to back away. Why had he been watching a house where a big dog lived? Or hadn't he known about the animal?

Helly began to alternate barking hysterically with growling and the stranger moved more quickly, this time not going down the side of the big house but edging along the fence towards the top end of Angus's drive. He broke into a run once he was out of sight of the girl at the back door, still not noticing Angus.

A man came out of the house and began talking to the girl. Angus didn't recognise him. It definitely wasn't the owner of the house.

He made no attempt to follow the intruder on his own. Well, he'd not have caught up with him, would he? He wasn't the world's champion runner because he spent too much time working at his computer. Instead he called out to the man who was now patting Helly. 'Hey there! I'm

Angus Denning, owner of the big house. I was following an intruder and he came to stand outside your place. He ran off when your dog started barking.'

He moved slowly forward, hands held out sideways in an open, non-threatening position.

Luke came hurrying out of the house to join them.

'Is this chap Angus Denning, owner of that big house?' the man asked, his eyes still scanning their surroundings.

'Yes. Angus, this is Eric, who's helping me with security for a while. What's wrong?'

'There was a guy trespassing on my land. He was moving up through the gardens trying not to be seen. I was already outside, so my eyes were used to the dark and I could see him clearly. I followed him, wondering what he was up to. People don't usually take a detour to creep through my gardens.'

'No. Definitely suspicious.' The man nodded.

'He put on some night glasses as he came up to your house and then stood near the fence as if observing what was going on. When your dog came out, she must have sensed his presence and she started barking furiously. The guy ran away towards my drive.' He pointed. 'I heard him start running down towards the Saffron Lane end. You can't run quietly on gravel.'

Eric frowned. 'Why would he come up from the bottom part of your grounds to get to the back of these houses? It'd be quicker to come via the top end of Peppercorn Street.'

'Who knows.'

In the distance, through the still night air, they heard the sound of a car engine starting up somewhere down the hill.

'I bet that's him,' Eric said. 'I'd guess he parked there to make sure his car wasn't seen on a CCTV camera.'

Angus smiled. 'Well, he's made a mistake there. I have CCTV down at the lower end to guard the Saffron Lane workshops and café, and there's even a camera in the middle of the grove of trees. You'd have to know where it is to spot it. I can get the recording for you tomorrow, if you like.'

'You couldn't get it straight away, could you?' Luke asked. 'If it's Claire's ex, it means he knows where she is and we'd want as much notice as we can get of that.'

Angus looked at them in puzzlement. 'Her ex?'

'He's stalking her, set fire to her car recently.'

'Ah. Well, if we get any good views of him, I'll be interested too. If he's going to come across my land to annoy people, I'm involved in this, whether I'm his prime target or not. We have valuable artefacts inside Dennings and the formal gardens are heritage listed, so I don't want anyone creeping round them and trampling over the plants. Why don't you come with me and look at the recording now? I can also forward it to you afterwards.'

'Thanks. I'll do that, Mr Denning, if you don't mind,' Eric said. 'I know what Martin Douglas looks like and can give you a photo of him for future reference.'

'I'll come too, if you don't mind,' Luke said.

'I'd be glad of the company going back, actually. I think the intruder was alone, but you never know. A macho hero I'm not!'

The men enjoyed a brief discussion in low voices about the changing technology of CCTV cameras as they walked down the slight slope of the drive.

At one stage, Eric stumbled on some loose gravel and called, 'Stop!' He played his torch over the ground to the right-hand side of the track. 'Look at this mess. I'd guess someone fell over here recently and scattered the looser gravel at the edge.'

'It wasn't like that this afternoon or Nell would have noticed and mentioned it, because she was tidying the borders out here. My wife is the gardener in our house. I just do as she tells me.'

'Then it was probably Martin who did this. He was running in the dark over terrain he doesn't know, and you don't seem to have street lights along your drive. I'll come back tomorrow once it's properly light and see if I can spot anything of interest where he fell.'

'Perhaps we should walk to the bottom before we go inside and check that there's nothing else to be found?' Luke suggested.

'Good idea.'

They continued as far as the small grove of trees between the lower entrance and Saffron Lane. Here Angus pointed out where he'd positioned the various cameras, including one in a tree that was well camouflaged and looked like a piece of wood.

Eric played his torch over the ground beneath the trees. 'I doubt the intruder checked for them there. The earth is soft after the recent rain and there are no footprints. He may be good with technical stuff but he's not good at the details of burglary, is he?'

Luke joined in. 'He's a nasty type, even set a surveillance camera up to observe Claire's reaction when she first saw her car after he'd set fire to it. But that one was quite easy to spot. He's been stalking her and their daughter for a while. This is their third move to try to get away from him.'

Angus whistled. 'Bad man, eh?'

'Yes. How someone like that could father a delightful child like Gabby, I don't know. Perhaps she's a throwback to a more pleasant ancestor.'

They had reached the street just outside Angus's grounds by now. 'Let's see if we can find anything to indicate where Douglas parked the car.'

But there were only rows of ordinary-looking semi-detached houses, with a paved footpath along one side of the road. There were still lights on in several of the houses and a couple of cars parked on the street, but most cars were in the drives of the houses.

They walked up and down, but although the street was quite well lit, they found nothing to show where the intruder's car might have been parked.

As they stood looking back down the street from the far end, Angus pointed to the electricity sub-station. 'I think there's surveillance equipment at this end belonging to the council, because there are underground tunnels from World War II starting underneath their building. They lead to a small museum in Saffron Lane where the main entrance is. He'd have to drive past here to get to the main road, so the car might show up on their recording.'

'Will they share the information with us?'

'I can get in touch with a guy I know in the council's IT department tomorrow and say I had an intruder. He and I get on OK. I'm sure he'll let me see what they've got.'

'That'd be a big help.'

Eric started moving again. 'Nothing more we can do here

tonight. Let's go back to your place now, Angus, and see if your camera picked up anything to identify the intruder by.'

They went into the big house and viewed the footage, but unfortunately it only showed a figure wearing a hoodie and dressed in dark clothing running down the drive. The camera didn't cover enough of the street outside to see what sort of car he had, either.

'He looks to be quite tall, if we measure him against the end of the gateway, but I don't think we'll find out anything else about him, however much we enlarge it,' Angus said regretfully.

The two others stood up to leave.

'All right if I check that spot on the drive tomorrow?' Eric asked.

'Of course.'

'We'll have to hope there's something on the council recording,' Luke said. 'Thanks for your help, Angus. Much appreciated.'

The two men went back to Number 4 and brought the others up to date on how little they'd found.

Luke looked at Claire, sorry to see how pale and anxious she was. 'I must say, I didn't expect your ex to get here so quickly. His friends must have followed us and got Luke's car registration at the shopping centre.'

'What do you want me to do now?' Eric asked.

'You're the expert. I'll go by what you suggest.'

Eric looked at Caitlin, who gestured to him to continue. He was happy to do that but wasn't going to ram his ideas down their throats. People usually felt better if they were given the chance to make an input.

'Well, I suggest we assume it was Martin tonight. Who else could it be? In the morning, as soon as it's light, I'll go and search the area where he fell over, see if he left any traces. It isn't likely, but miracles do happen. I'll also report what happened to the police and discuss this incident with them. If they decide to get involved they'll want to take charge, but they have much wider resources than we do, so that'd be a bonus.'

Caitlin joined in. 'And looking at our own situation, from now on Dee shouldn't go outside on her own, even with the dog. I know she's sixteen, but the two of them shouldn't even be on their own inside the house if Gabby's father is likely to turn up suddenly. It's probably a good thing we have Helly. She sensed his presence tonight and may give us warning in future.'

'She never liked him,' Claire said.

Eric bent down to pat the dog, who seemed to have taken a fancy to him. 'I wasn't sure how good a watchdog she'd be, she's so friendly, but she did an excellent job this evening warning us. Her being here is going to make it difficult for him to get to the house without being noticed. We've got to ensure she doesn't eat anything someone else offers her, or stuff thrown into the yard, though.'

'I've already taught her that.' Claire looked at Luke. 'The only time she's broken the rule that I know of is when she took something from you.'

Gabby, who'd been sitting holding her mother's hand, said suddenly, 'That's because she likes Luke and he likes her. My father couldn't stand Helly and he tried to get rid of her. I saw him open the gate once and push her out, but she stayed nearby. Other dogs don't like him and I don't like him, either. I wish he wasn't my father.'

Eric saw Claire look at her daughter, open her mouth, then shake her head and close her mouth again, as if she'd changed her mind about what she'd been going to say. What was that about?

He saw that Luke was watching her and had also noticed her reaction, but gave another small shake of the head to warn Luke not to pursue this at the moment. It was better for people to give sensitive information when they felt it right, he always felt, and Claire's reaction had been in response to the way Gabby had spoken about her father, not to tonight's incident – or at least that's how it seemed to him. It might be something private that had occurred to her.

There was an uncomfortable silence as they all tried not to show that they'd heard the desperate unhappiness behind the child's angry words.

'Well,' Eric said eventually, 'you all look tired. You should get some sleep now. Caitlin and I will take it in turns to keep watch. I promise you no one will get past us during the night.'

'And Helly always sleeps next to our beds,' Gabby said. 'She makes me feel safer too.'

When the others had gone, Eric looked at Caitlin. 'I hate to see a child harassed and worried like that.'

'So do I. Let's hope we can catch her father.'

Once he'd driven away from the street where he'd parked his car, Martin shoved the hoodie back from his head, muttering, 'Damned dog! I should have killed it when it was living in my garden.' He'd thought about it many a time, kicked it when it got in his way, but had realised how much killing it would upset his daughter, who was too tender-hearted, thanks to the way her mother had brought her up.

He'd been very careful not to do anything which would set Gabby irrevocably against him. She was *his* daughter and even Claire had always respected his fatherhood claim and never mentioned the special circumstances. It was one of the few things he gave his ex credit for, that and her excellent physical care of the child.

She certainly hadn't raised Gabby as he'd ordered when it came to the social and moral side of things, though, and had dared quarrel with him about that sort of thing several times. In the end, he'd tried to thump a bit of sense into her. Only it hadn't had the expected effect. The guys he drank with sometimes were wrong. It was after that beating that she'd run away.

And to make matters worse, he hadn't even enjoyed doing it as the other guys had said he would.

Who could understand women? He was quite sure they weren't as intelligent as men on average, but of course you didn't dare say that these days.

Well, that was all water under the bridge. What mattered was that once again he had found out where she was living. Brains would win through every time. He now needed to work out how to snatch the child and where to take her.

He needed more money for his everyday expenses, though. He didn't want to dip into his special savings.

The antique silver pieces at his parents' house came to mind again. He'd accept his mother's invitation to pop round any time for a cup of coffee and make sure it was at a time when his father was out. He'd be able to find out easily whether they had installed a security system, like most other people did in their part of town.

They'd always been rather lax about that sort of thing, saying they had nothing worth stealing except their money, which was kept safely in the bank.

Well, don't be too sure of that, you lame-brained idiots!

His mother would believe anything he told her. He'd been fooling her ever since he was a child. His father was less gullible but he could still handle the old fellow. He just needed to take more care with him and not push him too hard.

He'd always thought that whatever he did to them served them right, for not creating him with a fully functional body.

Though he'd forgiven them somewhat when he realised how superior the mind was that they'd passed on to him.

Chapter Nineteen

At first light Eric went into Angus's grounds and followed as best he could the path the two of them had taken last night. He easily spotted the place where he'd stumbled. The intruder must have fallen heavily to have scattered so much loose gravel from the edge of the drive.

He was careful not to step onto that disturbed patch as he walked round it, studying it carefully. Was it possible – could that dark stain on a group of stones to one side be dried blood? It certainly looked like it. They weren't smooth pebbles but sharp-edged fragments.

After picturing how someone would have fallen when running, he decided it might have come from the side of someone's face or an outflung hand. Following a hunch that it had, he pulled out his phone and rang his former mates at the police station, explaining the situation, ending, 'I know you'd not usually come out for this, but I was told you're collecting evidence about this guy for other purposes. I'm pretty sure it's his blood.'

'Hold on. I'll just check whether there's anyone free.'

A couple of minutes later, he came back. 'You're in luck. Sam's in charge of the night shift. It was very quiet so they're just marking time till the end of their watch. And he has a real thing about druggies.'

'Druggies! You think this guy is into drugs?'

'Don't say I told you. It's quite certain he is, though not as a dealer, but a customer of someone we're extremely keen to snabble. We want to use your fellow to trap the dealer. Unfortunately he doesn't seem to buy supplies all that often and we haven't managed to catch him at it in such a way as to show evidence that'll hold up in court. Hang on again.'

Eric held his phone away from his ear as some Christmas music began to play. He hated the stuff. No, he wasn't dreaming of a white Christmas, thank you very much. And he didn't want any bells jingling in his ears. As for snow pitter-pattering, he could do without that altogether. It was a damned nuisance, snow was, if you asked him.

He glanced at his watch. This was taking longer than he'd expected but he hung on.

'Still there, Eric?'

'Yes, of course I am.'

'We're sending a couple of forensic officers out to check that it is blood and hopefully that'll help identify your intruder. It's a long shot, but *you* wouldn't have called us unless you're pretty certain about it. If it hadn't been a quiet night, we'd not have had anyone free for a minor offence, but as it is, we might as well look into it. Can you guard the site till then?'

'Yes, of course.'

'Be about half an hour.'

Eric ended the call, muttering, 'Should have brought a fur coat with me.' Then he phoned Caitlin and told her what he was doing. She said she'd hold the fort at the house, no worries.

He hoped the splatter of dark stuff would prove to be blood. Hell, yes. And then there was the council CCTV to check out.

While he was at it, he couldn't help hoping for the sake of that delightful child that a kindly fate was on duty in the universe at the moment, ready to send some bad luck to Martin Douglas.

On that thought, he looked up at the sky, mocking himself but still doing it and sending out his plea to fate, or whatever you called the force that was out there pulling the world's strings. *Please help them get free of him!*

'Go on!' he finished up in a coaxing voice. 'Give us good guys a break. Call it my Christmas present and I'll love Christmas from now on. I want Martin Douglas behind bars, and for more than stalking.' He too hated druggies.

He was glad no one could see what he was doing. Silly of him to act like that. Only, it didn't hurt to send out the right vibes, did it? He knew a few people who did that when something was important. If nothing else, it focused your mind on a problem.

It was a relief when his old mate Danny came out with the forensic officers to have a look round. By the time they'd parked their cars, Angus had joined them to find out what was going on in his grounds.

He must have seen Eric shivering, because as soon as he'd found out, he asked, 'Cups of tea any use to you?'

All four of them accepted the offer, not just Eric. There was a damned cold wind blowing.

'It's definitely blood,' the female forensic officer said suddenly, putting a few of the stained bits of gravel into a pouch as a sample.

They took several photos then the tea arrived and by that time Luke had come down to join them as well.

'This is just a minor incident, if anyone asks,' Danny said firmly. 'We happened to be in the neighbourhood when we heard about a peeping tom and since there's a child involved, we thought we'd have a look. Right?'

'Right. I'm not a gossip. When will you know what type of blood it is? We need a better restraining order to keep this Douglas fellow away from Claire and Gabby,' Luke said.

'We'll do the best we can, but falling over and bleeding isn't exactly an indictable offence.'

Just as suddenly as they'd arrived, the representatives of the law drained the last of their tea, got into their cars and left.

Angus and Luke stared at Eric, as if asking what was going to happen now.

He held out his arms in a helpless gesture. 'Let's get this straight. I'm not in the police force any more. I can suggest things to them or pass on information, and they'll listen because they know me, but I can't tell them what to do with it. They, um, already had an interest in this Martin fellow, I will admit, which helped bring them out. But this might not lead anywhere and things rarely happen overnight, so don't stop being careful and don't get your hopes up too high.'

'But don't stop hoping, either,' Angus put in quietly.

Luke nodded. An image of Claire's face came into his mind, something that kept happening. He had something else he was hoping for, too, he admitted to himself.

'If I can do anything to help, don't hesitate to ask me. I'll get on to my friend at the council about their CCTV camera as soon as the town hall opens.' Angus picked up the tray of empty mugs and went back into his house.

'You've got a great neighbour there,' Eric commented as he and Luke walked up the slope together.

'Him and his wife both. I agree. But the situation for poor Claire is frustrating and she's worried sick. I feel so helpless.'

'Yeah, well. We're all doing our best.'

Luke sighed. 'I know. Let's hope there's something on the council's CCTV recording.'

That same morning Martin parked nearby and began to keep watch on his parents' house, looking for an opportunity to catch his mother on her own. His father usually went out somewhere in the mornings.

When he saw the old man get into the car and drive off, he waited a couple of minutes then opened the front door and walked in without ringing the doorbell. Fancy leaving it unlocked! They must be getting senile.

His mother jerked in shock when he went into the kitchen. 'Martin! Oh, you did make me jump. Ring the doorbell next time, please, to let me know you're coming in.'

'OK. Sorry. I had a few minutes between appointments and thought I'd pop in because it's been a while. How about a quick cup of tea?'

He sat down and watched her put the kettle on, asking casually, 'Dad not around?'

'No, you just missed him. He had to meet someone.' He watched her lips tighten into a straight line.

'Oh, who?'

'How do I know? He didn't say.'

If they were at odds about something, he wasn't buying into it. He put up with her inane chatting for ten minutes, found out what he wanted, then looked at his watch and said he had to go, breathing a sigh of relief as he left the house.

He was twitching for some action. That stuff he was taking certainly filled you with energy. He loved that about it. But he'd stop taking it as soon as he'd got hold of Gabby. It wasn't a good example to set to a child, and anyway, it cost too much.

But he'd nearly used it up, had better get some more to help him see this through the next few days. His last few hits, it'd be.

Other people might get addicted. *He* wasn't the sort. He could stop taking it any time he wanted. No problem.

The next thing on his list was to get rid of that damned dog. It had given him away last night by barking. But its days were numbered and that was the last time it'd get in his way.

He needed a gun of some sort. He knew better than to offer the creature poisoned food. It'd never taken food from him and would probably bite his fingers if he put a hand near it.

On that thought, he stopped and took out his phone to ring the guy who supplied him with stuff. Maybe Alec would know about guns as well.

When he left home, Tom didn't go far, just down to the nearby park to phone Eric because he didn't want Hilary eavesdropping again. 'Any news?'

'Possibly.'

'Can we meet? I feel better discussing important things face-to-face.'

'Of course we can, but not at the moment. We think your son was prowling round the house where Claire and Gabby are staying last night, which means they're at risk again. I have to make that aspect my main focus for a while.'

'Oh, hell! What's got into him? He was never this bad before, though he was always an awkward sod.'

'Do you know his blood group? The intruder fell over while running away and we found traces of blood on the gravel.'

'Yes, I do know it.' Tom gave him the information.

'Thanks. I'll pass that on to my friends.'

'And about our meeting?'

'Could we leave that till tomorrow, do you think? There are a few things happening around here today.'

'All right. Do you want to fix a time now?'

'I'd rather do that later, if you don't mind. I'll ring you once I know my schedule.'

When he got near his home Tom noticed Martin's car parked in the street outside, hesitated, then drove past and waited round the corner, parking so that he'd be able to see the car leave through the bare branches of a shrub without drawing attention to himself. He didn't want to talk to his son until he was more sure of what was going on.

It was only a few minutes before Martin came out and drove off. The lower parts of the vehicle were covered in mud, which was unusual for him. He was usually fastidious about keeping the car clean.

Tom waited a few more minutes then went back home, seeing a few details in the kitchen that made him pretty certain Martin had been having a cosy tea party with his mother. He opened the dishwasher and peered inside. When Hilary scowled at him, he decided to speak out.

'Enjoy your cup of tea with Martin?'

She gasped. 'How did you know?'

He pointed to the caddy on the kitchen surface. 'You keep that type of tea only for him and there are two mugs in the dishwasher.' He opened the cupboard door. 'And you opened the packet of his favourite biscuits that you also keep only for him. You didn't say you were expecting a visit.'

'I wasn't. He popped in unexpectedly. We had a nice little chat.'

'Oh, good for you. The world is all right if you can chat to your son, and it doesn't matter what else he does, or who he does it to, eh?'

Her voice trembled. 'Tom, don't.'

'Don't what?'

'Don't be angry at me. He's my *son*.'

'He's my son too but that doesn't blind me to his faults.

He's been stalking Claire and making her life miserable ever since she left him. And recently he set fire to her car. She's so afraid he'll try to kidnap Gabby, she's taken refuge with a friend.'

Hilary's face went chalk white and she swayed, so he grabbed her, made her sit down, then got her a small brandy because he didn't know what else to do.

He didn't tell her any other details. He didn't want her passing information on to Martin about Claire and Gabby.

When Hilary had regained a bit of colour, he sat down beside her. 'You have to face it. Martin's acting so strangely, he may be mentally ill.'

She just stared at him, eyes brimming with tears.

'Please. I know you love him, Hilary, but don't turn a blind eye to the possibility of him trying to kidnap Gabby, for her sake. He wouldn't know how to look after a hamster, let alone a child. Claire always had to do everything in the house.'

He watched, praying she'd see sense.

There was silence for a few moments then she nodded. 'I'll agree to – to being more open to his faults, if you'll promise to take me with you when you see that PI again. I agree about making certain he doesn't try to take Gabby away from her mother, though I'm sure he wouldn't hurt her. He *loves* her.'

Tom hesitated because he didn't think Martin knew how to love anyone, but didn't like to push her too far. 'I promise.'

He hoped she would keep her side of the bargain. He thought she would, because she loved Gabby too.

He missed seeing his granddaughter so much. Wanted to buy her a Christmas present or two, had been looking in the shops. But what was the point unless he was going to see her?

As he put the phone down after his conversation with Tom, Eric heard the two girls singing Christmas carols in the kitchen and smiled. Lovely voices they had.

He was feeling worried about the police not managing to pin down Martin about this stalking.

He was even more worried when Angus dropped round to tell him about the council security recording.

'They got the car, but its number plates were covered in mud. The best we can do is a 6 and 2 in the registration number, and we could tell the make of car at least.'

'I'll have to see if a vehicle of that sort is registered to Douglas.'

Eric got a friend to check for him later, and it wasn't. It was registered to a C. V. Cummings, but when he followed up on the address, it proved to be bogus, a bigger street number added onto the end of a real street that wasn't that long.

In fact, the whole day was full of frustrations, which only made him more determined to find a way to catch Martin out.

Claire and Gabby deserved a more normal life – and if he had his way, that'd start with a normal Christmas this year.

He smiled. And Claire also deserved to get together with Luke. The fact that they were attracted to one another was obvious to anyone with even half an eye on the game. Them getting together could be one good outcome to this mess, at least. He certainly hoped so. His marriage had been very happy.

Luke's daughter had noticed the budding romance as well and was doing her best to give them time together. Eric liked that lass. From what he'd overheard, it sounded as if she deserved a happier life too.

He suddenly chuckled at himself. He was trying to act like Santa Claus and give everyone a happy Christmas, he who didn't even enjoy the festive season.

What would he get into next? He was enjoying not being tied to working for someone else and it was particularly good to be doing jobs that mattered more than departmental statistics, jobs that contributed to ordinary people's happiness. He'd had a few small successes working his own way in the past couple of years and hoped for a lot more.

Putting more happiness into the world was a very satisfying way to spend your retirement.

He wished his wife had lived long enough to share these years with him. She'd have loved to get involved. Eh, he missed her still, could hardly believe it had been five years now since she died so suddenly.

Luke swung round when someone knocked at his office door. Dee was hesitating near the door, looking nervous. 'Have you got a minute, Dad?'

'Of course I have. I've always got time for you.'

She returned his beaming smile, looking a bit embarrassed. She clearly wasn't used to expressing emotions. He was going to change that. 'What is it?'

'Um, Claire's trimming Gabby's hair. She says there's no

reason to look untidy, whatever's happening. I wanted to ask you about a few things.'

He gestured to a chair, surprised when she closed the door behind her. 'I think you're doing good job keeping Gabby's spirits up, Dee. Good for you.'

She shrugged. 'It's hard to keep her cheerful. She forgets for a while, but she's worried sick underneath it all. Claire's even more worried. The father must be a horrible man.'

'Yeah. I reckon. Anyway, you're doing brilliantly.'

'I suppose.' Silence, then, 'What's going to happen to them if we don't find a way to stop that father coming after them?'

'I don't know. It's not up to me to decide, but I'll help if I can.'

'You like Claire, though, don't you?'

'Yes. Very much. Do you mind?'

She let out an almost-laugh. 'Of course not. I love the way you two are with one another. No quarrels. No silly fusses and then making up, like Mum.'

She took a deep breath. 'Are you *sure* you'll still want me to live with you if, well, things work out with Claire?'

'Of course I am. What brought this on? Do I seem like I'd want to get rid of you?'

'No, but you're in love with her. Anyone can see that. You might not want me living with you playing gooseberry.'

'Oh, darling, of course I do. I want you *and* Claire *and* Gabby. I've plenty of love in me, more than enough for you all. I've been saving it up for years.'

She sniffed, fighting tears. 'That's such a nice thing to say.'

'I mean it.' He dared to lean forward and give her another hug.

She hugged him back and muttered, 'I love you too,' in a husky voice, then dashed out of the room.

She needed a lot of reassuring, he thought sadly. Angie hadn't been the best of mothers. He should have realised that sooner. And he hadn't been the best of fathers, should have made more fuss about being kept away. He'd never forgive Angie for that.

He was going to try to be the best father he could from now on, though. Oh, yes!

But first they had to deal with Claire's damned ex. Somehow. Whatever was needed. Luke didn't care what it cost, what he had to do. He just wanted it done.

He was determined to free Claire, so that they could explore their growing affection for one another. He wanted their children to consolidate the relationship that was building between them, too, and if things worked out as he expected he hoped they'd feel as if they were truly sisters.

Was it so much to ask?

That evening Tom took Hilary out for a drink at the local. He refused to take no for an answer. 'You'll only sit and brood, if we stay in.'

'There's a programme I usually watch on the telly.'

'Record it. We're going out if I have to drag you by the hair.' He did a pretend macho pose and it was so not him, he could see amusement soften her irritation with him.

'Oh, all right, you fool. Just for an hour.'

Fortunately they met some friends in the pub and the outing went on for over two hours.

When they got back, they found one of the back windows broken and various goods missing, including all the old family silver.

Hilary sat down and sobbed when she found the locked cupboard hidden under the stairs broken into and empty. 'We thought this cupboard wouldn't be obvious behind the vacuum cleaner. We were so wrong and Martin was right about this.'

'When were you talking to him about that?'

'Yesterday. It just came up, I suppose. He was saying he'd like to see the family silver again. I said I'd get it out from under the stairs next time he came.'

Tom gave her a quick hug, then phoned the police.

He felt fairly sure that it was Martin who'd broken in but when the police came, they said the footprints in the garden looked more like size twelve and Martin was size ten, so it couldn't be him.

'Looks like this person was an amateur, and didn't make any effort to hide his footprints, though he doesn't seem to have left any fingerprints. Well, anyone who watches TV knows not to do that. There is this, though. We found it on the floor under the stairs.'

The policeman held up a crumpled piece of dirty sticking plaster. 'Looks like it came off a recent injury, because there's some fresh blood on it. It isn't yours, is it, sir?'

'No. Definitely not.' He looked at Hilary and she avoided his gaze. 'Did Martin have a plaster on?'

'No.'

But he could tell she was lying.

When he was seeing the officers out, Tom made sure he was out of Hilary's hearing before he said, 'If you find the blood on this is B negative, you might take a look at my son. The police have another sample that might be his.'

'Your wife said he wasn't wearing a plaster.'

'She was lying. I can always tell.'

'Ah. Is he likely to have broken into your house? Don't you get on with him?'

'Might have been him. He's been acting very strangely lately.' He hesitated, then added, 'And he's stalking his ex.'

'What size of shoe does he take?'

'Size ten, but he could have worn a bigger size to confuse the issue. He's not stupid and I wouldn't put anything past him lately. I, um, think he's got mental health problems.'

'I'll add that information to the report, sir. Thank you for being honest with us.'

When he went back inside Tom said, 'I know you were lying. Was Martin wearing a sticking plaster?'

She shrugged. 'I said he wasn't.'

Don't keep lying to me, he thought, but didn't say it. What was the point? He started to clear up the mess of broken glass. Hilary sat down in the kitchen, staring into space and making no effort to help him.

'It's just one thing after another lately,' she said after a while. Then she went back to watching him clear up, not saying anything or telling him he'd missed a corner. Which wasn't like her. She usually fussed over every job in their immaculate house. And chatted to him if they were together in a room.

He could only hope Eric would come up with something, was even beginning to hope they'd lock Martin away and find out what was wrong with him. And whether it was curable.

That thought made him realise he should inform Eric about this break-in, just in case it was relevant. He'd do that first thing in the morning.

Chapter Twenty

Hilary said she had a headache and went up to lie down. After finishing the clearing up, Tom tried to settle to reading a book, but a few moments of fidgeting made him decide to phone Eric now and tell him about the break-in. He'd make sure the PI agreed to meet him early tomorrow.

And he'd take Hilary with him to the meeting. She was obviously starting to realise that there was something wrong with Martin. When their son had married Claire and produced a child, they'd felt so relieved, thinking he'd found his way in life and would now settle down.

But they'd been wrong, so wrong. As the years passed, poor Claire had started looking increasingly tense and unhappy, however hard she tried to hide her feelings when she was with them, while Martin had grown more and more aggressive, getting angry with her about anything and everything.

Oh, why dwell on that? It was past history. *What can't*

be cured must be endured. The old saying was right. The important thing now, Tom felt, was to make sure the future was better for Claire and that precious child, and for himself and Hilary to get on with their own lives.

He picked up the phone and contacted Eric. After a short conversation, during which he explained about the break-in and was very insistent about the need to have a face-to-face meeting, Eric agreed to meet him in a small town called Sexton Bassett. Only it had to be really early in the morning.

Tom felt guilty because he didn't tell Eric he would be bringing Hilary. He wouldn't tell her yet that they were going, though, would just wake her tomorrow and tell her to get ready. That way she wouldn't be able to tell Martin.

He realised Eric had said something. 'Sorry. I missed that. Could you please say it again?'

'I can only give you half an hour. I'm doing a security job at a house on the outskirts of town, but it's usually quiet at that time of day and I do have a colleague working with me, so I'll meet you in the library car park. It's in the town centre. You can't miss it. 7 a.m. is all I can offer.'

Tom was startled. 'But it'll still be dark then.'

'I know but that's truly the only time I can make and if you hadn't been robbed like that, I'd not even be doing so much. I want to hear all the details. Take it or leave it quickly. I have to get back to work.'

'I'll see you at seven, then.'

Tom set his alarm clock without telling Hilary and took her mobile phone out of her handbag so that she'd not be able to sneak a call to Martin. He put it on the kitchen surface and hoped she'd think she'd left it there, because he didn't want to add to what he was sure would be a stressful outing.

At half past five the following morning the alarm rang and the radio came on. He jerked awake, thinking, *Here goes!* He switched on the bedside light and waited till she was fully awake, then explained that he was going to meet his PI to discuss Martin and their break-in. 'If you want to come with me, you have fifteen minutes to get ready.'

'You're mad. What can we do at this time of day?'

'We can find out the facts about our son: ask questions, share information. You need to hear what Eric says as much as I do. And you need to meet him. He's a nice chap. I'm sure you'll trust him.'

'Why couldn't you have told me last night?'

'I, um, didn't want you lying awake worrying. Eric knows more than anyone else does about our son because he's been investigating Martin for a few days now. He's told me things I didn't know, things that have shocked me. We both need to face facts, however hard that is.'

'What things?'

'I'll tell you after we've spoken to Eric.'

She didn't look happy but got ready quickly. When she saw her phone, she snatched it up. 'How did I come to leave it down here?'

He wondered if she'd have phoned Martin if he hadn't taken away her phone. There wasn't time for her to do that now. He handed her an insulated mug of instant coffee and they went out to the car. He'd grabbed a quick drink while waiting for her. He was usually hungry in the mornings, but not today.

They hardly said a word on the hour-long drive to Sexton Bassett, but when they saw the sign with the town's name on it she said suddenly, 'You won't convince me that Martin's done anything really bad. Whatever this PI person says, our son's not wicked, just sometimes a bit impulsive and quick-tempered. He loves his daughter very much and misses her dreadfully. That's hardly a fault. Claire took Gabby away from him. She shouldn't have done that.'

He didn't answer. Hilary had been saying that to him for months, repeating it like a church litany. Who was she trying to persuade? Herself as much as him, he reckoned. He'd given up arguing about it, was hoping desperately that a few facts from someone else would help open her mind to the truth, that there was something wrong with their son and the way he was behaving.

He was quite sure Martin had been the one to rob them of the silver and that added a further dimension of pain to what was happening.

They found the library car park quite easily, but there was no car waiting for them.

As they pulled up, she folded her arms, scowling. 'What if this PI fellow doesn't turn up at all?'

'He will. And you'll like him. There's something innately decent about him. He's the sort of person you'd trust instinctively.'

'Ha! He's probably just acting, trying to take money off you. This must be costing us a fortune.'

'Worth every penny to get the truth, don't you think?'

'No, I don't.'

At three minutes after seven a car turned off the road and parked next to theirs. A man got out.

Tom did the same. 'Aren't you coming with me, Hilary?'

She let out a heavy sigh and opened her car door but still didn't get out, so he joined the PI, shivering at the chill, damp air.

'Who's that?' Eric asked.

'My wife. I've brought her with me because I'm having trouble convincing her that Martin's at fault. I'm hoping you've found out more about him. She needs to face the truth and then we can both move on.' He hoped.

Eric looked at him in dismay. 'Are you sure that's wise?'

'I'm not sure of anything at the moment. Our house being burgled has upset me big time.'

'She'll be reluctant to believe some of what I tell you. Mothers seem to be hard-wired to love and protect their children and they believe the lies told to them more easily than strangers might. Your daughter-in-law and granddaughter are already at risk. We don't want him to trace them here.'

'He wouldn't *hurt* them.'

'Wouldn't he? I'm not so sure. From what I've found out, I think he's on a serious downward spiral and needs medical help.'

Tom sucked in his breath at that, then turned round as he heard the car door shut.

Hilary came to join them at last, merely nodding when introduced to Eric, with that scowl still on her face.

Eric shivered. 'Let's sit in my car to talk. That's a damned cold breeze.'

Tom gestured to his wife to sit in the front and sat in the middle of the back seat, leaning forward between the other two.

Eric switched on the car's interior light and the small island of brightness in the wind-blown darkness of the car park felt intimate, as if it was encouraging the sharing of information.

The sky was starting to turn grey in the east now. He wished dawn would hurry up, was tired of short days and darkness by teatime, even more tired of worrying about their son.

He switched his attention to Eric, who started to explain about Martin's ongoing pursuit of his ex-wife and daughter, giving details Tom hadn't heard before.

Neither of them had known about Martin leaving his job. How was he making a living now?

When Tom laid one hand on Hilary's shoulder, she half turned her head to stare at him coldly, as if to tell him to get off, but he didn't remove his hand, and with a sigh she turned back to Eric, letting the hand stay there.

When the PI told them about Martin finding Claire's latest hiding place and coming to spy on her, Hilary only shrugged.

'He wants his daughter back. What did you expect? Any father would do that.'

'Other men don't thump their wives.'

'He'd been beating her?' Tom hated the thought of that, absolutely hated it. How could a son of his even think of doing that?

'That was apparently the final straw that made her leave him. She told me herself, and I believed her.'

Hilary let out a whimper of protest.

Eric waited a few seconds then continued, 'I also found out that Claire had to go to A&E three times before she got away from him. Once there were marks on her wrist showing someone had twisted it. It'd been hurt so badly, the doctors thought she'd broken a bone and X-rayed it. She denied being abused by her husband, but the doctor didn't believe her.'

'You're jumping to conclusions. She might have had a fall,' Hilary snapped.

'You don't get twist marks from a fall.'

Silence.

'She had her daughter with her and the child was also bruised, so Gabby was questioned by a nurse away from her mother. They believed her when she said that her daddy had hit her mummy and pushed her out of the way. She'd fallen while running away from him.'

Hilary swallowed audibly and there was no sharp comment this time.

Eric's voice was quietly emphatic. 'There is no doubt in my mind or that doctor's, Mrs Douglas, that your daughter-in-law was being abused, mainly mentally but also physically towards the end.'

'How come you were allowed to see the medical records?'

'The doctor at her local medical centre was worried about Claire and Gabby. She signalled her concern to the local police under a new initiative to combat spousal abuse. And when Claire and Gabby missed an appointment, she called at their home. A neighbour, who was also worried, told her they'd not been seen for a few days, so the doctor reported that to the police as well, and they went round to question your son.'

'What happened to confidentiality?'

'I used to be a police inspector and was able to find out about all that informally, because I'm concerned about their safety now, as well. I hope you won't give me away or I'll get into trouble.'

His wife was sitting hunched up now, hands tightly clenched in her lap, looking anguished. Tom's heart went out to her, but she had to know the truth, for Claire and Gabby's sake.

While they were speaking the sky had continued to brighten and there was now a greyish light and an occasional car driving past as the town woke up.

Eric looked sideways. 'I'm sorry to have to tell you this, Mrs Douglas.'

'I find it hard to believe some of it.'

Tom spoke gently. 'But you do believe it, don't you, Hilary?'

Before she could answer him, Eric's phone rang and when he saw who it was, he exclaimed in dismay, 'There must be trouble at the place I'm supposed to be guarding. That's all I use this phone for. I shouldn't have left them. Please get out of the car quickly. I have to leave.' He ignored them and asked the caller, 'What's the matter, Caitlin?'

At Number 5, Janey was woken just as dawn was breaking by her little daughter crying. She went into the bedroom next door to shush her, but Millie refused to be comforted and sobbed so broken-heartedly that her young mother lifted her out of bed. The dim nightlight that was always left on showed her that Millie was flushed so Janey decided to carry her down to the kitchen and get her a drink of warm milk.

She didn't bother to put any of the lights on. There was enough grey light now to see what she was doing and she could have found her way down those stairs blindfolded. Anyway, she didn't want to wake Winifred, who slept in what had been the housekeeper's quarters next to the kitchen and was a very light sleeper.

However, Janey stopped abruptly on the landing because she had seen something moving in the top part of Angus's grounds, just beyond the next-door garden's back fence, something that resolved itself into a man-shaped silhouette. No mistaking it. What was someone doing out there?

She blinked and took a good long look at the figure, staying where she was, hopefully out of sight, and jiggling Millie in her arms, which seemed to soothe her daughter. She didn't like the look of this. Why was someone standing looking at the houses at this hour of the morning?

No, looking at the next-door house.

Luke from next door had introduced her to Eric only yesterday and explained that his companion was helping guard his visitors. He'd also warned her to be careful herself at the moment, because Claire was being stalked by her ex, who was a violent man.

Eric had given her a business card and told her to phone him at once if she saw anything unusual, night or day. It didn't matter if it turned out to be a mistake. Better safe than sorry.

She gasped in shock as she suddenly realised what the man outside was holding: some sort of gun. Was it really? She strained her eyes, wishing it were lighter, but that shape couldn't be anything else. And he was standing in an unusual way, holding the gun like a villain in a bad movie might.

Definitely something to tell Eric about. She ran down the stairs and picked up the phone. It didn't ring for long.

'Hello?'

'Janey here from next door. Eric, there's a man with a gun standing near your fence at the back.'

'A gun? Are you sure of that?'

'Pretty sure. That shape is unmistakable, and the way he's holding it.'

'Leave it to me. Stay inside and don't go near any of the back windows from now on. I'm in town at the moment but I'll be back in five minutes at most.'

Winifred came out to see what was going on, and they decided to go into her quarters and stay away from the kitchen window.

Shoving the phone back in his pocket, Eric started the car. 'I have to go. There's a problem.'

Tom bent to close the door. 'Anything I can do to help?'

'Definitely not. Someone's standing outside the house with a gun. Please, Tom, go home and leave this to me. If it's your son, Mrs Douglas, I'll see they deal as gently as possible with him.'

'Come on, love.' Tom got back into his own car and when Hilary was sitting beside him, started up the engine.

'If you go home now, I'll never speak to you again.'

He gaped at her.

'Drive out of the car park and wait out of sight of that man. When he drives away, we're going to follow him. If it's our son, I intend to be there.'

'But Hilary, he said there was a man with a gun.'

'That's got to be a mistake. Martin doesn't own a gun. And even if what Eric said about our son hurting Claire is true and he's stalking her, I'm going to make sure that Martin gets the best help possible.' She sobbed but poked him in the arm and said in a choked voice, 'Do it! If you have any love for me at all, just do it, Tom!'

He hesitated. 'You're not to get in the way if the police are dealing with this.'

'Of course not.'

Hoping she would keep her word, he did as she asked. It was easy to follow Eric's headlights from a distance. He didn't switch on his own car lights and prayed he'd not meet any other vehicles. He was half hoping they'd lose Eric, but the street he turned in to was a long one and he didn't turn off it but went right up to the top, which looked to be a cul-de-sac, and stopped there.

Tom stopped further down and waited, watching the PI run into the garden and use a key to open the front door. He still hadn't noticed them following him, thank goodness.

They might wait and find out what was happening and if it involved Martin, but no way was he letting Hilary go near that house.

Caitlin came up from the kitchen to the hall as Eric went inside the house. 'Oh, it's you. Everything go OK?'

'No.' He told her what Janey had said, then ran up the stairs and took a careful look out of the landing window while Caitlin went to check from the kitchen.

As he was standing there Luke came out of his bedroom. 'Is something wrong?'

'Stay where you are!'

Luke stopped dead. 'What's the matter?'

'Janey next door rang to say there's a man with a gun standing near the bottom of your garden. That was about five minutes ago. I'd just nipped out to meet someone in town. Anyway, I've had a look out and he's still there. It looks like Martin to me, however carefully he's covered his face. There's something aggressive about the way that man stands. You can see it in all the recent photos of him that his father gave me.'

'Oh, hell, no! Is he planning to shoot Claire, do you think?'

'He must be planning to shoot someone or why bring a gun?'

Helly came padding across from Claire and Gabby's bedroom and nudged Luke. This was usually the signal for someone to let her out.

The two men exchanged glances and stared down at her.

'Or maybe he's planning to shoot your dog, since she gave his presence away the other night,' Eric said slowly.

'*Shoot Helly!* Has the guy gone completely mad? Would he really come here to shoot a dog?'

'He's certainly not thinking straight. Maybe he thinks if there's no dog around he can come back another time and kidnap Gabby.'

'Over my dead body.'

Claire came to join them. 'I heard what you were saying and I looked out of our bedroom window and saw him too.'

'I hope you didn't let him see you.'

'No. During the past two years I've learnt to be careful what I do.'

'Did you recognise anything about the man?' Eric asked.

'It could be Martin. You're right. He does stand like that. Only I can't be absolutely sure it's him because it's not fully light enough yet and he's got his face covered. If he's trying to keep out of sight, he's not doing a good job of it. Martin gets restless, hates standing still or having nothing to do.'

The dog nudged her and whined. 'Look, Helly urgently needs to go out. I can take her out on the lead at the front of the house. She's usually very quick in the morning. I'll bring her straight back in, I promise.'

Eric had a think, then nodded. 'As long as I can see this chap, whoever it is, you should be safe enough, Claire, but be as quick as you can, and try to keep quiet. In the meantime I'm going to phone the police. Luke, if you stand by the front door, I'll shout if he moves and Claire can come in.' He did not like guns, or the people who used them.

A couple of minutes later, Claire came back inside with Helly. She passed Eric on the landing on her way up. 'I'd better go up and wake the girls, tell them what's happening. They could sleep for England, those two could.'

'Tell them not to put any lights on.'

Luke followed her and they both stopped at the top as Dee came out of her bedroom.

'I heard voices. Is something wrong, Dad?'

'Don't put any lights on.'

'Why not?'

She stared in horror as they explained about Martin lurking outside and what they thought he was intending to do.

'Kill our dog? He can't. You won't let him hurt Helly, will you, Dad?'

'Of course not.'

Eric said in a low voice from where he was still keeping watch at the landing window, 'The police are on their way. This is a matter for them to deal with. I certainly don't carry a gun. I think we'd better phone Angus and warn him to stay inside his house as well. Do you have his phone number, Luke?'

'Yes. Actually, I know it by heart. I keep meaning to put it on my phone, but it's so easy to remember that I've never got round to it.' He recited the number and Eric keyed it in and quickly outlined what was going on to Angus.

When he'd finished the call, he said, 'You people should wake Gabby and it might be better for you all to wait in one of the front bedrooms. We don't want any stray bullets hitting you.'

'He wouldn't fire at the house, surely?' Luke asked.

'If he's on drugs, who knows what he'll do? Depending on what he's on, he could be hallucinating big time. And keep the dog with you. We don't want her getting hurt either.'

Dee immediately grabbed Helly's collar. 'Your bedroom, Dad?'

'Yes. You go in. We'll fetch Gabby.'

When they were all there, Luke shut the door of his bedroom to make sure Helly couldn't get out. She kept looking from one person to the other, as if uncertain what was going on, instinctively aware that it wasn't good.

He gestured to the bed. 'Why don't you girls get under the covers and keep warm? I'd turn up the central heating sooner than it's programmed to start, but the control box is in the kitchen and I think we'd better stay put here.'

The girls did this, sitting close together in the middle of the bed.

He flourished one hand at Claire. 'How about you and I get in at each side of these two? It's a six-foot wide bed. We'll all four fit in if we don't mind cuddling up, and I for one enjoy a good cuddle. But no tickling.' He waggled his eyebrows at the girls, who both giggled.

And, Claire thought, *if we're at the outer edges of the bed, that'll also make sure the children can't get out easily. Great organisation, Luke.*

She quickly went to the nearest side of the bed and slipped under the covers, then realised that she was next to Dee, not her own daughter. Smiling at the girl, she blew a kiss at Gabby across her as she pulled the covers up round their bodies.

When Luke got into the other side, he drew Gabby into a close cuddle and she went to him willingly.

That man was full of love as well as kindness, Claire thought. From what he'd said, he must have been very lonely. So had she, in spite of having Gabby to look after.

It was now light enough to see the little girl look up at him with such adoration that Claire got a lump in her throat.

Gabby sighed happily and brought tears to her mother's eyes by adding, 'This is just like being a real family, isn't it?'

Dee smiled at Claire, then turned the other way and winked at her father. 'Yes. It is. I like it.'

'So do I,' Luke said.

His next sigh wasn't a blissful one, though. 'I hate to

spoil this love-in, but I think we'd better keep quiet and listen to what's going on.'

But nothing seemed to be happening and after a few moments, Gabby sagged sideways against Luke and closed her eyes.

Soon she was breathing slowly and deeply.

The sight of her innocent face against Luke's pyjamas twisted Claire's heart strings. She saw him look lovingly at his daughter, on the other side of Gabby. Dee was now snuggling against Claire.

The whole thing brought a lump to Claire's throat. As her daughter had said, it felt as if they really were a family. She couldn't help longing for this to continue.

Did she dare hope for that?

Or would Martin spoil things for them again?

Did Luke really mean it about developing feelings for her? The last thing she wanted to do was take advantage of him if all he felt was general kindness and an obligation to help people in trouble.

The thought of Martin bringing a gun and staking out the house made her shudder and feel sick inside. Surely he wouldn't use it?

Chapter Twenty-One

Outside Martin shivered and cursed under his breath as he waited for the people in Number 4 to get up and let that damned dog out for what he intended to be its last ever attempt to 'be a good girl' – of all the stupid phrases to use.

He looked at the house sourly. Why were they still in bed? Lazy devils. He wanted to get this over and done with before other people were about.

But when he looked at his watch it wasn't yet eight o'clock, which accounted for the poor light. Perhaps it would be better if they didn't let the dog out till he could see more clearly. He didn't want to miss.

He began to practise his calming breathing, but it didn't seem to work very well today, because he'd taken some stuff and was all hyped up. Well, he needed to be fast on his feet to be sure of killing that dog and getting away without anyone seeing him.

But the slow minutes passed and no one appeared or

let the dog out. 'Come on!' he muttered. 'Come on, damn you.' He was ready. After that, he'd wait a few days and make preparations for snatching his daughter. He'd take her somewhere no one would ever find her again.

He glanced round. No one had seen him this time, because he hadn't come up through the grounds belonging to that nosey, interfering sod at the big house. He'd parked his car in the next street, which ran parallel with Peppercorn Street and had an alley connecting the top end of both streets. It ran along the side of Number 5 and didn't look as if it got much use. The paving was all cracked and there were dead weeds along the edges. The local council ought to keep their footpaths in better condition.

Pity he hadn't noticed the alley before. He should have studied the street map more carefully.

He wouldn't make that mistake again. He never made the same mistake twice. He was a better learner than anyone he knew.

He thought he'd heard a car draw up a while ago in Peppercorn Street somewhere near the top, but as there was still no sign of activity in the house he was watching, he'd relaxed again. Someone going to another house.

It meant people were starting to get up, and about time. He was cold and fed up of waiting. 'Come on!' he repeated.

'What is Eric doing at that house anyway?' Hilary muttered. 'Apart from that woman letting her dog out just after we arrived, there hasn't been any sign of movement there.'

'Who knows? He's probably waiting for the police to arrive and just keeping watch.'

'I should try to find Martin. I'm sure I could talk sense into him more easily than anyone else. I will if something doesn't happen soon. You know how impatient he gets.'

Tom didn't say anything but he clicked all the door locks on.

She jerked her head round to stare at him. 'What did you just do?'

'Locked the car doors. You're not getting out of it till the police have sorted everything out.'

The look she threw at him would have curdled milk. 'Even if I could help Martin to calm down?'

'Especially so.'

He was regretting following Eric now, whatever she'd threatened. He should just have driven her home.

They heard the occasional sound of cars further down the street, presumably people leaving for work. Then a large black vehicle drove slowly to the top and stopped in front of the house, followed by a police car.

Tom whistled softly at the sight of the occupants of the unmarked vehicle. 'It's an armed squad. Martin must be threatening to use the gun.'

'He won't do that. It's just bravado.' But Hilary's voice quavered and she looked at him as if pleading for him to agree with her.

He couldn't. Because he thought Martin must be in an agitated enough state to do anything if he'd gone to the trouble of acquiring a gun. Tom had never even touched a gun and he didn't have a clue how you got hold of one apart from visiting a gun shop.

Officers in dark outfits and what looked like bulletproof vests got out of the first car, their faces grim and determined.

Two of them ran to the top end of the cul-de-sac and disappeared down what looked like someone's drive.

A police officer got out of the second car and came across to them, so Tom wound down his window.

'I wonder if you'd mind leaving the street, sir. We have an incident going on and we don't want anyone to get hurt.'

Hilary answered before Tom could stop her. 'I think it's our son who's involved. I could talk to him for you, persuade him to give himself up.'

The officer took out her phone and relayed this information to someone, then put it away again, shaking her head.

'We'd rather you stayed out of it, madam. The man in question is in a very unstable state of mind, I'm afraid. I have orders to take away your car keys, sir. Please stay inside the vehicle.'

Tom took the keys out, handing them over, then closed the window. He turned in his seat to keep an eye on Hilary. He wasn't giving her any chance to get out and do something rash.

She sat scowling first at him then at the officer, who was still standing nearby as if guarding them.

Martin wasn't the only one in an unstable condition, Tom thought. He'd never seen his wife so upset. He'd better be ready to grab her if she tried to get out.

Caitlin, who was watching the street from the front of the house, saw the police cars stop and two dark-clad officers walk up to the top of the cul-de-sac. After a few moments, two others came towards the house, accompanied by a sergeant in uniform. They had guns in holsters. She called out to let Eric know they'd arrived.

'I'll go and let them in, Caitlin. You keep watch on the back.'

He opened the front door and let the officers come inside.

'Can you show me the intruder without him seeing me?' the female officer asked. 'And we need to know how to get out into the back garden.'

Caitlin took the male shooter and a uniformed officer downstairs while Eric showed the female up to the landing window, then waited nearby in case he could be of further assistance.

The officer stood watching what was going on outside, using her mobile to tell someone exactly what she could see.

She stayed on the phone, not speaking till he heard the faint sound of someone at the other end. 'OK. We'll do that.'

She put the mobile away. 'The other squad has got round to the back via the drive and is now behind him in the gardens of the big house. They're closing in on the guy as quietly as they can. He's not holding the gun at the ready and doesn't look as if he's used to handling guns, so hopefully their main job will be to keep him from escaping. I'm going downstairs now in case I'm needed.'

She paused to ask, 'Just one thing: where are the people who live here? We don't want them getting caught in any cross-fire.'

He explained about sending them into the front bedroom and telling Janey next door to make sure she and Winifred kept to the front of the house as well.

'Well done.' She peered out of the window again. 'If you ask me he's very jittery. I bet he's high on something. What's his wife like?'

'His ex-wife. Nice woman, nice kid, surprising that she's

his child. There's a dog as well, but it's shut in the bedroom with the family.'

'Good. Let's hope they have the sense to stay there.'

'They will, I'm sure.'

'Well, let's go downstairs and get it over with.'

Hilary couldn't stand the waiting any longer. She watched the uniformed police officer pacing to and fro in the street. She'd wait until the woman was at the furthest point from their car before she made her move.

She picked up her handbag, trying to seem casual.

'Do *not* think of doing anything except waiting here for the police to sort things out,' Tom warned her.

'I have to blow my nose, don't I? Or do you want me to sit here with snot dribbling down my face?'

She felt in her bag, took out her own car keys and used them to unlock the door, covering the sound with a cough. Then she kept them where she could grab them quickly. As the police officer again neared the furthest point of her pacing, she took hold of the keys and flung them at Tom, followed by the handbag. She was out of the vehicle before he could stop her.

Then she ran as fast as she could towards the house, yelling at the top of her voice, 'Get away from there, Martin! Get away!'

The police officer chased after her.

'Oh, you idiot!' Tom said softly as he watched.

She managed to get into the front garden of the house, still yelling at her son to get away, and slammed the gate on her pursuer.

*   *   *

At the same time as Hilary was preparing to escape, one of the officers creeping up the slope behind the man with the gun trod on a twig which snapped loudly enough for the sound to carry.

The intruder swung round, gesturing wildly with the weapon at the sight of them and yelling, 'Keep back! Keep right back or I'll shoot!'

'Police. Drop your weapon!' the officer called. 'Drop it and lie face down.'

But the man paid no attention and continued to wave the weapon about. 'No! I'm a crack shot. *You* back off. I'll get that dog if it's the last thing I do.'

'Dog?' one of them muttered to the other. 'What the hell is he talking about? Can you see a dog?'

'No. I can just see some nutcase threatening us with a gun. He must be hallucinating.'

When the first man repeated his call to surrender, Martin fired at him, but missed by a mile, then began yelling, 'Helly! Helly, come on out. Good dog! Good dog!'

'I reckon he's high on something. There's definitely no sign of a dog.'

The officers dropped to the ground, but Martin stayed where he was, pointing the gun to one side then the other, yelling and cursing at them, threatening what he would do if they came near him.

Another call to surrender made him raise the gun and aim it at them. A shot ploughed into the ground near one officer.

'That was too close for comfort.'

'He's not going to give himself up. Better see if you fire really close to him and make him drop the gun.'

His companion took careful aim and Martin yelled and dropped to the ground, but didn't let go of the gun. He rolled over and fired at them again but fortunately the bullet whizzed harmlessly to one side, as the others had done.

'Crack shot indeed,' one officer muttered.

'He might hit someone by mistake if he goes on firing so wildly. We'll have to stop him. See if you can hit him somewhere not fatal.'

His companion took careful aim, this time hitting Martin in the leg which made him screech with pain and roll about.

A woman's voice could be heard from the direction of the house, yelling at someone to get away from her.

The officers ran to the fallen man, one putting his foot on the hand still holding the gun while his companion twisted the other arm behind his back and then took the gun away from him.

He whipped round in surprise as the yelling started again, only closer this time, and a woman ran across the back garden of the house with a uniformed female officer chasing her. But the officer tripped and fell on the uneven ground, so the woman got out of the back gate and ran towards them.

'Get back!' he yelled, but she paid no attention and flung herself at them. 'Leave him alone! Leave my son alone!'

'Hell, it's his mother. What next? Pink elephants? Get her off me.'

But she'd seen the blood. 'He's hurt. You've shot him. Get off him, you brutes!'

To add to the weirdness of this incident, the woman's

arrival seemed to upset the injured guy all over again and he erupted into action, ignoring the pain and trying to get away from the officer aside.

He began yelling and screaming at her. 'Get away from me, you old fool. Get the hell away!'

'It's me, your mother. Martin, why are you doing this? Stop it!'

'I'd have shot them both and got away if *you* hadn't spoilt things. You always spoil things. Why was I cursed with a stupid mother like you? Get away from me.' And he somehow found the strength to fling her aside.

It took both officers all their time to hold him, because he seemed oblivious to pain.

The uniformed officer who'd been chasing Hilary grabbed her as she got up and marched her back towards the house.

Another officer came across, helping get cuffs on Martin. From then on he refused to move but continued to yell at his mother.

Hilary had stopped struggling and was weeping now as her son continued to yell curses and threats at her.

'He hates me. How can he hate me?' she whispered.

'He doesn't really hate you. He's probably high on drugs.'

Martin heard that and continued to glare at his mother. 'She's right. I do hate her. She's a stupid bitch and if I never see her again, it'll be too soon.'

'I don't know what he's on,' the female officer said to Hilary. 'But you don't often see them reacting this badly to drugs. He really doesn't know what he's saying, let alone mean it.'

But somehow Hilary felt quite sure Martin did mean it,

high on drugs or just high on arrogance. She covered her face with her hands, sobbing loudly, unable to bear the sight of him glaring at her.

The officer looked at her sympathetically. The poor woman had drawn the short straw in getting a son like this.

She looked round as someone called, 'I've contacted the emergency department at the hospital. An ambulance is on its way. I've warned them they'll need to sedate him before they can do anything to help him.'

'I hope they get here quickly.' She turned round as a man came out of the house to join them. 'Eric. Fancy meeting you here.'

He rolled his eyes. 'Yeah. Like *Gunfight at the OK Corral* today, isn't it? Look, you'll need to call Danny about his. Martin Douglas is a person of interest to them on more than one count.'

'OK. Thanks for confirming the identification. You're sure of who he is?'

'Yeah. I'm working for his father, who wants to trace him, and also for the owner of Number 4, who wants to protect the woman Martin Douglas has been stalking.' He looked at the still sobbing mother, hating to see her anguish, and lowered his voice. 'Hard on her, eh?'

He was thinking of putting his arm round Hilary, out of the sheer human desire to console someone in such extreme distress, when there was a shout from the side of the house. A man came across the back garden, moving slowly and carefully, with another officer's hand on his shoulder.

When they reached the woman, the officer said, 'All right. See if you can calm your wife down, sir.'

* * *

Tom put his arms round Hilary, feeling as if his heart was breaking. 'It's me, love.'

She clung to him, trying to speak but unable to get any coherent words out.

The officer whispered to him what Martin had said and Tom closed his eyes in despair. This would surely destroy her.

'Can I take her home?'

'She could be charged with obstructing the police,' the officer who'd accompanied him round the house said.

One of the armed officers looked across at Hilary pityingly. 'I don't think she should be charged. I think she's been punished enough. Anyway we'll know where to find her if we need her.'

'So can I take her home, then?' Tom asked again.

'Yes. But I think you ought to get a doctor to see her, don't you?'

He nodded and began to lead Hilary back to their car. She kept stumbling, hardly seeming aware of what they were doing. Tears were still running down her cheeks, so many tears.

When they got home, Hilary looked at Tom and said in a husky voice, 'He meant it. It wasn't just the drugs talking.'

'I know. Our son's turned into a sad, warped creature.'

Then she surprised him. 'I'm not going to let him destroy me, Tom. Or us. You won't leave me, will you?'

'Of course not.' And he took her into his arms again.

'I did everything I could, for years, tried to help him, tried to make him feel loved. But I couldn't get through to him. I needed to do my best, though, Tom, or I couldn't have forgiven myself.'

'Well, you did more than anyone could have expected, put up with a lot, so you can be proud of how hard you tried. It's medical help he needs now. I hope there's something they can do for him.'

'I think I'll need help, too, from a counsellor. I'll do whatever it takes to – to get better. If you stay with me. He was – hardly human.'

'That's my girl. I'm sure you'll cope if we get help. And just you try getting rid of me.'

She cried again, thanking him over and over. Then they sat down and held one another for a long time, not even making a cup of tea, just needing the comfort of a loving touch.

He wouldn't mind getting help from a professional counsellor, too, Tom decided, trying to hold back his own tears. He was feeling ravaged by this, too. How could you not be? His son was mad. On drugs. How could such things happen?

He didn't know. He didn't feel as if he knew anything.

It wasn't till later that Hilary said something that comforted them both.

'This means that we can see our granddaughter again. That's the only good thing.'

'If Claire will let us.'

'She will. I know she will.'

Eric and the sergeant went into the house once Martin had been taken away and everything had been dealt with outside.

'That poor woman,' the sergeant said. 'She'll need help to get over it. I doubt he's even sane enough to stand trial.'

'I hope they lock him up and throw away the key,' Eric said. 'I've no sympathy with people who take drugs. And that guy has made his wife and child's lives a misery for years. They've a chance now of making a happy life for themselves.'

He nodded as if that thought pleased him, then smiled. 'And if I'm not mistaken she'll be getting together with the owner of this house, who is a genuinely nice guy. If ever I saw two people in love, it's them.'

'We'd better go and check on them before I leave.'

They went upstairs and tapped on the door of the front bedroom, opening it slightly.

Four people seemed to be asleep in the bed and the dog was lying on a rug near the foot of the bed. It wagged its tail at the sight of them but didn't get up.

Luke opened his eyes and put one finger to his lips, making a faint shushing sound and jerking his head towards the others.

Eric moved backwards as quietly as he could and closed the door.

'Let's give them another hour or so before you speak to them.'

'I should get back to the station.'

'An hour won't make much difference. I'll make you a coffee and some toast if you're hungry.'

'I am, actually.'

Eric sniffed the air as they went into the kitchen. 'Ah, Caitlin. You wonderful woman! Is that coffee I see waiting for us?'

'What else? I used the good stuff and the fancy coffee maker. We've all earned it today, I reckon. Luke won't mind. Where is he?'

'Asleep. They all are.'

'They slept through it?' she asked in astonishment.

'They built good solid houses in the old days and solid wooden doors on the inside as well as the outside. We're leaving them for another hour or so. That family's been through a lot lately.'

He knew they weren't a family exactly, but they acted like one and he hoped they'd become one.

Just over an hour later, Luke came down to join them. 'Sorry about us falling asleep on you. It was so comfortable in that bed.'

'You were awake when I looked in.'

'Only just. I drifted off again. I presume you caught Martin?'

Claire followed him into the kitchen, yawning. 'What did we miss?'

It was the officer who spoke. 'Your ex-husband went crazy and started firing at the police. Good thing he's a pitiful shot and the gun had a silencer or he'd have woken the neighbourhood.'

'He used to hate guns, said he'd never held one and never would.'

'Well, he was holding one like an amateur today but he wouldn't put it down. They had to shoot him in the leg to stop him, or else he might have hit one of the officers. He's been taken to hospital. He's way beyond high on some sort of drugs, if I'm any judge. He'll be locked away for a good while, I'd guess.'

She stared at him then closed her eyes in sheer relief. 'Oh, thank goodness! Thank goodness!'

'Not sure if he'll recover from the drugs or how long it'll take. You'll be kept informed. We're just guessing. But if he's been annoying you as much as Eric here says, well, I'd say you'll be clear of him for a good many years, whatever happens to his own state of health. He shot at police officers, and that is a serious offence! And he treated his mother abominably. You should have heard the things he said to her. I doubt she'll ever speak to him again.'

'But she dotes on him. I thought he loved her, at least, though he argued with his father sometimes.'

'I'd not be so sure of her doting on him any longer after what he said to her. I felt sorry for the poor woman.'

'Oh dear. She's a nice person, didn't deserve a son like him.'

The two girls were hungry as usual and led the way downstairs for some food.

After Luke and Claire had explained what had happened, everyone looked at Gabby.

'Are you all right, love?' Claire asked.

She looked round at them all solemnly. 'Yes, I am. But I'll feel better if he's locked away. He's a horrible man. I wish he wasn't my father.'

Claire took a deep breath. The time had come to say it. 'He isn't your father.'

The silence seemed to echo round them as the others took this in.

Gabby frowned at her mother. 'I don't understand.'

Claire could feel herself flushing as she tried to explain the medical facts to her young daughter in front of a room full of people. 'He, um, he couldn't father a child. His body didn't produce the, um, seeds necessary. So we got a donor to supply them and well, you are the result of that and of me. I'm definitely your mother.'

Gabby beamed at her. 'Oh. I see. That's great news. We did about how babies are made in science at school. I know all the proper words for the body parts and how they all get together.'

Claire didn't know what to say to that. 'Right. Um, good.'

'So do you know who my real biological father is?'

'No. It was an anonymous donation.'

'That's a pity. I'd really like a proper father.' Gabby looked sideways at Luke as she spoke.

Dee let out a choke of laughter. 'You can't rush people into these things, Gabby. Give your mother time to recover from having to run away all the time. And she and my father need to get to know one another better. Who knows what will happen then?'

Claire changed the subject hastily. 'We'll be able to find somewhere decent to live now and not bother Luke.'

He held up one hand. 'No. We agreed to spend Christmas together and I'm not letting you go back on your word.'

Dee and Gabby looked at her anxiously.

Claire hesitated, then said, 'I don't want to impose on you.'

'We've already discussed that. It's not imposing. We love having you and there are benefits both ways. Anyway, these girls deserve a proper family Christmas, with your home cooking. You promised that. And I'm going to see that you give it to them.'

The police officer and Eric had kept quiet, but Dee and Gabby continued to watch Claire and Luke intently, heads turning from one person to another, looking as if they were at a tennis match.

When Gabby opened her mouth to say something, Claire saw Dee dig an elbow in her side and shush her.

She turned back to Luke. 'Are you sure you want us to stay?'

'Very sure.' His smile lit up his whole face. 'I'm not going to let you get away so easily.'

It seemed as if even the dog was holding her breath, waiting for Claire's answer.

Claire gave in to temptation. 'That'll be so lovely. Thank you.' But her eyes said a lot more to him.

The police officer and Eric took the opportunity to slip out of the room, smiling at one another.

Claire laughed as the girls erupted into cheers, then started dancing each other round the kitchen, singing, 'Christmas is coming, the geese are getting fat.'

'Stupid song, that,' Claire said.

Luke chuckled. 'Yes, but look at those two dancing to it. Isn't that a wonderful sight?'

'Wonderful.'

'Why don't we join them? I can sing stupid songs as well as the next person.' He grabbed Claire and began twirling her round the kitchen till she was helpless with laughter.

When the girls stopped singing for lack of breath, everyone collapsed onto chairs, panting.

'I can't wait for Christmas!' Gabby said.

'Me too.' Dee grinned at her father.

When they'd got their breath back and had something to eat, Claire took Gabby upstairs to get washed and dressed.

Once the two of them were alone, Dee fixed her father

with a very stern look. 'If you don't find some way to keep her here permanently, I'll never forgive you.'

'I'll never forgive myself. Don't worry, I'm onto it.'

'Good.'

Chapter Twenty-Two

The next week passed lazily, with shopping expeditions and secret meetings to discuss presents, as well as secret sessions to make Christmas cards, since at Dee's suggestion, everyone was making them, not buying them.

The few times they had to deal with the police were over and done with quickly.

Dee grumbled about having to go to school, but Luke insisted.

Gabby was looking forward to school in the new year. Claire had decided that it'd be better for her not to start at a new school yet. Besides, she would only miss a few more days of lessons.

At home, it was Dee who made opportunities for Claire and Luke to spend time together. At first, aware of what the girl was doing, Claire was embarrassed.

'Don't!' Luke said one day as she grew flustered about Dee's wink as she took Gabby out for a brisk walk.

'What do you mean?'

'Don't get embarrassed about what Dee is doing.'

'Oh, well. It's just – I don't want her to push me at you.'

'I do. I want it very much.'

Those simple words stopped her dead in her tracks. She looked at him and when he held out his hand, she walked across the kitchen and took it.

He tucked her hand under his arm and walked with her into the living room. 'This isn't a conversation I want to hold in a kitchen. It's too important.'

When they were sitting down on the sofa, he took both her hands in his. 'I want Dee to push you at me partly because it means she's agreeable to me chatting you up.'

That made her smile. 'Chatting me up. What an old-fashioned term.'

'I like it and I like doing it. That's the other part of what I want. But you're a hard lady to win. Do *you* want me to back off? I will if I have to, but it'll make me sad.'

'Why do you say that?' She still found it hard to believe he could care about her.

'Sad at losing this chance of what promises to become a real family, sad to risk you taking Gabby away from Dee. A little sister is the best thing that's happened to my daughter in years. And most of all, sad for myself if I lost you. I fell in love with you very quickly, you know, Claire. The genuine thing. I don't know why, but it just happened. And it feels so very right.'

He paused and asked again, 'Do you really want me to back off?'

She took a deep breath and let herself believe. 'No. I don't. I've rather fallen for you, too. I was just afraid of you feeling you had to continue looking after us.'

'O ye of little faith! I *want* to look after you both, you dope. That's very different from *having to*. But I also want you to look after me and my daughter. Mutual support and love and the whole shebang is what I want. Could we try it?'

Her doubts fell away and she raised his hand to her lips, seeing the joy bloom in his face. 'Yes, please, kind sir.'

'We must seal that with a kiss, but what's the betting the kids return and interrupt it?'

'I don't care. If you're sure.'

So he proved how sure he was in every tender way he could, kissing her, murmuring soft words of love, holding her close.

He thought he'd listened for the kids to return, but when someone cleared their throat nearby, he and Claire jerked apart in shock.

Dee and Gabby were standing there beaming.

'Now that was a good, long kiss,' Dee said. 'I hope I find someone who can kiss like that when I fall in love.'

'Does that mean you and Luke are in love, Mum?' Gabby asked.

Claire and Luke spoke at the same time. 'Of course it does.'

Then Helly jumped up to give Claire and Luke a few doggy kisses, and everyone chuckled as the two adults tried to fend her off and keep away from those licks.

It took a while because the dog seemed to sense the joy in the room and had grown wildly excited at this new game of pile-up-onto-the-sofa.

When it was Gabby's bedtime, Claire went up to say a final goodnight.

'Are you sure you're happy about me and Luke getting together permanently?' she asked, stroking her daughter's hair back and planting a kiss on her forehead. 'He won't be like Martin.'

'Of course I'm happy. Dee said you were in love, but it seemed to take ages for you to show it.'

'And you've no worries about anything else?'

Gabby hesitated.

'Go on. You know you can tell me anything.'

'Eric said Grandma Hilary was crying and crying, because Martin had been cruel to her.'

'Yes. I felt so sorry for her when I heard about that.'

'Are we ever going to see them again?'

Claire hesitated. 'Well, Grandpa Tom has emailed me to ask that same question. He says they still want to be considered your grandparents. He says they've missed you dreadfully.'

'I've missed them too. He was fun and Grandma Hilary was going to teach me to crochet.'

'So you won't mind if I invite them over for a small Christmas party?'

'I'd love it. Will Luke be OK with that?'

'Yes.'

'Oh, goody! And can we invite the people next door as well? Aunty Winifred – she told me to call her that – says she'll teach me and Dee to make cakes, and everyone says she makes the best cakes of anyone.'

'Angus and Nell, too.'

'We already know some nice people here.' Gabby snuggled down. 'I'm glad we're staying.'

* * *

When Claire went downstairs again, she found Luke and Dee chatting in the living room.

'Don't vanish yet, Dee. I've just had an important talk with Gabby. She wants Tom and Hilary to continue to act as grandparents and they want it too. And she's happy at the thought of a Christmas party, would like to invite them and—'

Two faces lit up with pleasure.

'Yes, yes, yes!' Dee came rushing across to hug her. 'You'll do it, won't you?'

'And invite Winifred and Janey, too?' Luke asked. 'Not to mention Angus and Nell? And a few other people I know. I can arrange to have it catered so that it's not too much trouble.'

'No way. I enjoy cooking. We ladies will prepare the refreshments and you, sir, can sort out the drinks.'

Dee came to thread an arm in Claire's. 'You and Gabby are the best thing that has ever happened to me and Dad.'

'And you're the best thing that's happened to me since Gabby appeared in my world.' Claire gave Dee a quick hug, something she'd started doing.

Luke noticed the tears of happiness in Dee's eyes before she turned and busied herself with some clearing up to hide them.

The next afternoon the doorbell rang and Dee went to answer it. It rang again before she could answer it and she sighed at whoever it was. Why so impatient?

When she opened the door, she wished she hadn't done, because her mother was standing there smiling at her. Oh no! Dee knew that sort of smile. Her mother couldn't have broken up with the new lover already, surely?

'Darling, I've come to collect you.' She waited and when Dee didn't move out of the way, she pushed her gently back. 'Don't keep me standing on the doorstep. It's raining in case you haven't noticed.'

'I'm not going with you,' Dee said. 'You dumped me here and it was the best thing you've ever done for me. I'm living with Dad from now on.'

'Don't be silly. We've spent most of our lives together. I made a mistake, I will admit, but I'll make up to you for that and—'

'I don't want presents. I don't want you to make up for anything. I just want to stay here.'

Dee was backing away when she bumped into someone. She turned and saw it was her father, so flung her arms round him. 'Don't let her take me away, Dad. Please don't let her ruin it all.'

Angie glared at them both. 'What have you been telling her about me, Luke Morgan?'

'I've not been telling her anything. She's got eyes in her head.'

She rounded on her daughter. 'Go and pack your things at once. I've found us a lovely new flat in London and—'

'I've only just settled in at this new school. I'm not changing schools again. And I'm *not* leaving Dad and going with you.'

Luke put his arm round his daughter's shaking shoulders and moved her gently along the hall. He caught a glimpse of Gabby standing in the kitchen doorway, looking worried. 'Go and tell your mother my ex has turned up, Gabby. We'll have to postpone that shopping trip.'

Then he took Dee and Angie into the living room and closed the door firmly. This was for him to sort out.

Gabby stepped backwards into the kitchen and bumped into her mother, who was standing behind her, unashamedly eavesdropping.

'It's Dee's mother. She's come to take Dee away. Don't let her do it, Mum!'

'I can't stop her. I'm not related to Dee.'

'But I've only just found her. She's my *sister* now! We've sworn it.'

'I know. Let's leave it to Luke, shall we?'

But Gabby had thrown herself onto a chair and was sobbing loudly.

In the living room, Dee was still clinging to him and Luke could feel her trembling. He indicated the sofa and Angie sat down on it, patting the place beside her and beckoning to her daughter.

Dee went to sit on one of the armchairs across the room.

'I'm taking her away from here and I'm never letting her near you again, Luke Morgan.' Angie's voice was vicious. 'You've poisoned her mind about me.'

He looked at their daughter. 'What do you want to do, Dee?'

'Stay here with you.'

'I have custody,' Angie pointed out, her voice acid sharp.

With a big effort, he kept his own voice level. 'I think by Dee's age, they're allowed to choose who they live with. I've spoken to my lawyer about that and he's going to arrange for it to be made official.'

'Well, if he hasn't already arranged it, I've still got custody and she's coming with me. I'll make sure we overcome whatever brainwashing you've been using on her before you have time to go through any legal channels, believe me.'

'I'm not stupid. I know how you've treated me,' Dee said suddenly.

'It was an emergency that made me bring you here.'

'No, it wasn't. You were dumping me for your new girlfriend,' Dee said suddenly. 'You've always ignored me when someone new came along. Only they don't stay, do they? Because you're too selfish to live with.'

'Don't you dare speak to—'

Dee talked over her loudly. 'Dad was really kind to me, even though I was grumpy and upset. And now, we've got a new family and—'

Angie looked puzzled. 'What do you mean by that?'

'Claire is going to live with us and Gabby will be my sister for real. It was all going brilliantly till you came and I'm not letting you spoil it.'

'You don't have the choice. I'm your mother and I have legal custody.'

'You keep saying that, but you never say you love me. You never care about what I want, only about how I can be there for you. Think I haven't noticed how other families do things?'

Angie's mouth fell open, then she took a deep breath. 'How dare you talk to me like that?'

'It's my whole life that depends on it, so I dare do anything.' She looked across at her father. 'You meant it, didn't you, about wanting me here?'

'Of course I did, darling. I want you very much.'

Dee didn't wait for him to say anything else but turned to her mother. 'How are you going to get me to go with you?'

'What do you mean?'

'I'll fight you every inch of the way. Literally. I will not live with you again. You don't care about other people, only yourself.'

'We'll see about that.' Angie stood up and grabbed her daughter's arm, trying to drag her up out of the chair.

Luke stood up too, arm outstretched to stop her.

But Dee tore herself away from her mother without his help. 'Don't, Dad. She'll try to sue you if you touch her. But she can't sue me.'

She found herself looking straight into her mother's face. 'I'm the same height as you now,' she said in amazement, then smiled. 'And I'm fitter. You aren't strong enough to drag me out.'

'But if I go and pack your things, you'll have to go with me when I take them away.' Angie turned.

Luke barred the way. 'You're not thinking straight. This is my house. I don't give you permission to go anywhere else except this room. And if you try, I'll have to be the one doing the dragging and calling my lawyer. I've listened to you ordering Dee about as if she's only a possession, and I've tried not to interfere, because this is her decision. She's decided she wants to stay here. And believe me, I'm delighted about that.'

'You've *bought* her off.'

'No. I haven't.'

'Well, she's coming with me till it's sorted legally, whatever it takes.' Angie took her daughter by surprise, grabbing her by the arm and twisting it behind her back so that Dee yelled in pain.

The door crashed open and Claire came in. 'I wasn't going to interfere, either, but I think you need a witness and not me. Fortunately Angus was in his garden so I called him in as well and we've been listening to you.'

She stepped aside and their neighbour moved into place beside her.

'Good idea.' Luke turned to Angie. 'Would you please leave my house now?'

She looked from one person to another and saw nothing except disgust in their faces. 'You'll be hearing from my lawyer and you won't win.'

'This isn't a contest. It's Dee's life that matters. Tell her again what you want, Dee. I won't stop you if you want to leave.'

Claire held her breath, waiting, almost sure what Dee was going to say but needing to hear it.

Angus leant against the door frame, arms folded.

Dee took a step backwards, wanting to put more distance between herself and her mother. 'I don't want to live with you again, Mum. I haven't been happy for a long time and I'm very happy here.'

The words seemed to echo in the room, and Dee saw the moment her mother started to believe her and Angie's shoulders sagged.

'But we've always lived together.'

'No, we haven't, Mum. I've lived in the same house as you and your lovers. But you mostly left me to my own devices. You provided whatever was necessary physically, but we weren't *together* in the ways that matter most. I'm not coming back and I'll run away if your lawyer tries to make me.'

Luke's voice was calm but firm. 'I'll show you out now, Angie.'

She stood for a moment longer, then swallowed hard and walked out of the room, saying, 'You'll be sorry!' as she passed him.

Claire and Angus stood aside as she passed and she glared at Claire. 'I suppose you're his latest. Well, you'll soon be out on your ear. No one lasts long with him.'

As Luke walked out to the front door, Dee crumpled and began to cry silently. Claire went across and took her in her arms, not saying anything, just making soothing noises and rocking her slightly.

'I did it,' Dee said after she'd started to calm down.

'Yes, but it hurt. She is still your mother and I'm sure she loves you in her own way.'

Dee turned as her father returned and flung herself at him.

Claire left the room quietly and went to the kitchen to tell Gabby what had happened.

Angus was already there, talking to the child. He looked up. 'All right now?'

'Yes. Thanks for coming. Should we need a witness we'll get back to you, if that's all right.'

'Fine by me. She's a very acid-voiced female, isn't she?'

'Even worse than I'd expected.'

Inside the living room, Dee was simply sitting on the sofa with her father, held safely in his arms, feeling warmly wrapped in his love.

'She doesn't understand,' he said after a while.

'She doesn't try to understand,' Dee corrected. She cuddled even closer. 'I love living here with you and I consider Gabby my sister.'

'She feels the same.'

'She's cute, isn't she? Always blurting things out, laughing at things. She makes me feel happy.'

'She captured my heart the first time I met her.'

'And Claire? Are you going to marry her?'

'I hope so. But leave the proposing to me, please.'

'Don't leave it too long then. It'd be good to feel certain of you both.' She reached across to pull another tissue out of the box and finished mopping her eyes. 'Phew! That was hard.'

'But you've made me very happy.'

'I meant what I said, you know. If any lawyer or judge tries to make me go back to her, I will run away.'

'It won't be necessary but I'm honoured.'

She nodded. 'That's settled. Now, I'm hungry. And I want to make sure Gabby isn't upset.'

'You make a great older sister.'

She gave him one of her cheeky looks. 'I do, don't I? I'd make a good step-daughter too.'

Epilogue

The Christmas party was to take place on Christmas Eve and start at five o'clock because of Gabby and Winifred, neither of whom were good at staying up late, being too young and too old respectively.

Claire and the girls bought new outfits for the occasion and Dee took charge of her father's wardrobe and told him what he should wear to look his best.

She'd hoped that he'd have proposed to Claire by now, but there had been no signs of it and he'd told her firmly to butt out, that this was something a man organised for himself.

Perhaps he'd do it at the party. Or after it.

The refreshments were prepared partly by the girls under Claire's supervision, with a few things bought in, as well as two cakes from Winifred. Claire enjoyed making a few dishes of the sort she'd not been able to afford for two years, showing the girls how to make them.

It was wonderful to see the two of them working so happily together, with Gabby's face showing utter concentration as she iced some small cakes and decorated them with faces.

Dee was following Claire's instructions with equal care as the put together some savoury nibbles. When the doorbell rang, she said, 'Oh, bother! I can't answer that.'

'I'll get it,' Luke shouted.

'Phew! Thank goodness. I've nearly finished these now. Don't they look nice?'

Luke stood in the doorway, smiling to see his daughter so engrossed in what she was doing. But he kept glancing down at the Christmas card that had arrived. He recognised his ex's handwriting and was worried it would bring more threats and take the edge off their Christmas enjoyment.

When Dee had finished making the nibbles, he said, 'It's a card for you. It's from your mother.'

'Oh. Will you open it for me? I'm all sticky.'

'It can wait till your hands are clean.'

Her eyes were pleading with him to open it for her, but he shook her head. 'The lawyer said she won't be able to take you away from me. It's safe to open it.'

She wiped her hands on her apron and took it from him.

Gabby came to stand beside her, as if to offer moral support and Dee steeled herself visibly to tear it open. She read it, swallowed hard, then read it again.

Looking up, she smiled sadly and said, 'She's made it up with that woman and since I'm not acting like a proper daughter to her, she will not appeal to the courts about leaving me here. I've made my bed and I won't find it as comfortable as I expect.'

'What a mean-spirited thing to say!' Claire exclaimed. 'She's acting like a spoilt child.'

Dee walked across to the kitchen bin and dropped the card and envelope into it. 'I'm not letting her spoil my Christmas. Or my life.'

She was quiet as she helped finish the preparations, then cheered up visibly as she and Gabby went upstairs to change into their new clothes.

By the time they came down, she was smiling again. 'Will you take a photo of us, Dad? I want to put it up on my page online.'

The photo was duly taken and came out so well, Claire immediately decided to have a good copy made to stand on the mantelpiece.

'I'm still angry at your ex,' Claire said to Luke as they in turn went up to change into their party outfits.

'She's like that. Fancy sending such a letter by courier on Christmas Eve.'

When she came out of the bedroom, he was waiting for her and let out a soft whistle of appreciation at her appearance. 'You look good enough to eat.'

'So do you. Dee has excellent taste in clothes.'

He grinned. 'Better than me, that's sure. I'd never have chosen this shirt, but it looks OK, doesn't it?'

'It looks great.'

When they went into the living room, both girls applauded.

Then they had some non-alcoholic punch before the guests arrived and toasted one another with it.

It seemed to Claire that the girls had a secret, but it was

the season for secrets so she didn't try to find out what they were planning.

Then the guests started arriving and the party got under way, with young Millie also sporting a party dress. The toddler lasted only half an hour, then fell asleep curled up on the floor beside the Christmas tree, whose lights had fascinated her.

Such nice people, Claire thought, watching as they mixed together easily, chatting and then finding someone else to talk to. She exchanged delighted glances with Luke every now and then.

Only one person had been left out and Helly soon let them know she wasn't having that by sneaking in when someone left the door open, nudging first Luke then Claire, after which she began slobbering happy kisses on any part of her people she could reach.

Luke fumbled in his pocket. 'I have a treat for her, because she brought us together.'

Helly swallowed the dog treat in one gulp and condescended to accept a second one, which was made of hide and hard enough to keep her busy for a while.

They and their guests laughed and the party continued.

At seven o'clock, Luke took Claire's arm. 'Have you got a moment?'

'Is something wrong? The food's OK, isn't it?'

'The food is wonderful. I have something to show you. It won't take long.'

He took her into his office. He was looking so nervous she wondered what the matter was.

Then he went down on one knee and said, 'Hang the

speech I'd prepared. Claire, my darling Claire, will you please marry me? And the sooner the better.'

She looked down at him, her eyes full of happy tears. 'Oh, Luke.'

When she didn't speak he continued to look at her anxiously, but she was smiling so radiantly, he knew it wasn't a refusal he was facing.

'I couldn't speak for a moment, I felt such joy welling up in me. Oh, Luke, I can't think of anything I'd like better, only if you don't stand up I won't be able to kiss you properly and I'm quite desperate to seal this with a kiss.'

When that was done, the door was flung open and they turned round to see Gabby and Dee, with all the guests standing in the hall behind them.

'I put a microphone in your office because I wanted to hear whether you did propose tonight,' Dee said. 'I thought you were going to, you were fussing with something.'

'Only I was helping and I turned up the sound too much,' Gabby said, 'and it came out all loudly so everyone at the party heard it.'

The two girls waited with anxious expressions, clearly expecting him to be angry, but suddenly a bubble of laughter filled him and when he turned to Claire, he could see that she too was having difficulty holding back her amusement.

'I don't think we'll have an uneventful life together with these two around, do you?' he asked her.

'Definitely not. And who'd want it?'

He turned to the girls and the smiling guests waiting behind them in the hall. 'I haven't quite finished so you might as well hear the rest.'

He took a little box out of his pocket and opened it, holding it out to Claire. 'This was my grandmother's ring. I'm hoping you'll love it as much as I do and wear it for me.'

She took the beautiful ring with its deep blue sapphire surrounded by tiny diamonds. 'It's gorgeous.'

'I've never offered it to anyone else,' he added in a whisper, then said more loudly, 'If it doesn't fit, we'll have it altered.'

He slipped it on her finger and stood admiring it. 'It fits perfectly. And you're perfect for me.'

Dee and Gabby came closer to examine the ring, then Gabby could stay still no longer. She danced up and down on the spot, but that wasn't enough so she did two cartwheels across the room and two more to bring her back, bouncing to her feet and slapping a kiss on Dee's cheek.

'Isn't this the best Christmas that ever was, Dee! The very best. And you're going to be my real sister now.'

'It definitely is the best.'

Tom put his arm round Hilary as this scene played out but she was coping with the party better than he'd expected.

They didn't stay late, but as they went to get their coats, someone tugged at his arm and he smiled down at Gabby. 'Well, young lady. We have further to go than the others, so we're going to take our leave now.'

'I'm so glad you could come tonight, Gramps. Did you like the little cakes? I iced them all myself.'

'They were pretty as well as delicious.'

She turned to Hilary. 'I still want to learn how to crochet, you know. Mum can't do it. Will you teach me next time you come to visit us?'

'I'd love to. Would you give me another hug?' Hilary asked suddenly.

'Yes.' Gabby suited the action to the words and stepped back, beaming up at Hilary. 'Me and Mum hug a lot and now I've got Dee and Luke to hug as well as you two. Isn't it wonderful?'

'Yes, it is.'

Tom put his arm round his wife and led her out to the car, but Claire and Luke followed them with Gabby still hovering nearby.

'Next time you come to visit we won't have a house full of people,' Luke said. 'And you'll always be welcome.'

'Thank you.' Hilary blinked hard and got into the car.

Tom said quietly, 'She's getting better each day. We're both so grateful that you haven't kept us from the child.'

'We'd never do that. She regards you as her grandparents and I doubt that'll ever change. I think that child is going to collect people to love all her life long.'

'She's adorable, a miracle in our lives.'

There were a few other miracles taking place lately, Claire thought.

Gabby ran back into the house and Claire took hold of Luke's hand. 'My daughter can make anyone feel better. Thank you for letting those two into the family.'

'They're nice people. As for Gabby, I fell for her charm from that very first night you fell into my life and so did Dee.'

'I suppose we'll have to go in and mingle with the guests. I'd rather stay here with you.'

'Well, it's too cold to linger outside. But can I make a

date with you for an hour or so after everyone's left or gone to bed? I want to make wedding plans – but without an audience. And I'll need a few more kisses to keep me going.'

'I shall look forward to it.' She chuckled. 'It was funny, though, wasn't it, everyone hearing your proposal?'

'I'll never live it down.'

'Trust Gabby to do something like that.'

Hand in hand they went back into the house. It felt as if everything there was sparkling with a reflection of their own happiness.

'This is going to be the happiest Christmas of my life,' she said softly.

ANNA JACOBS is the author of over eighty novels and is addicted to storytelling. She grew up in Lancashire, emigrated to Australia in the 1970s and writes stories set in both countries. She loves to return to England regularly to visit her family and soak up the history. She has two grown-up daughters and a grandson, and lives with her husband in a spacious home near the Swan Valley, the earliest wine-growing area in Western Australia. Her house is crammed with thousands of books.

annajacobs.com